Paige Turned

ERYNN MANGUM

Paige Turned

A PAIGE ALDER NOVEL / Book 3

TH1NK

TH1NK, an
Imprint of
NavPress

NAVPRESS

Discipleship Inside Out®

NavPress is the publishing ministry of The Navigators, an international Christian organization and leader in personal spiritual development. NavPress is committed to helping people grow spiritually and enjoy lives of meaning and hope through personal and group resources that are biblically rooted, culturally relevant, and highly practical.

For a free catalog go to www.NavPress.com.

OTHER NOVELS BY ERYNN MANGUM

PAIGE ALDER SERIES:

Paige Torn

Paige Rewritten

LAUREN HOLBROOK SERIES:

Miss Match

ReMatch

Match Point

MAYA DAVIS SERIES:

Cool Beans

Latte Daze

Double Shot

For my mom – "Thank you" doesn't cover everything you do for me. I only hope that someday I can be the kind of mother, wife, and friend you are. I love you.

Acknowledgments

To my Jon — I love you. Let's keep laughing together. ☺

To my sweet Nathan — thank you for dropping your one and only nap during the writing of this novel. It stretched my creativity even more. I love you so much, dear boy.

To my miracle baby, Parker — You have been so prayed for, little one. You and your brother are the best, most precious things in our lives. I love you so much!

To my family — Dad, Mom, Bryant, Nicole, Caleb, Nicole, Cayce and Nama — Y'all are great and I like being around you.

To my friends — Shannon, Leigh Ann, Eryn, Melanie, Thalia, Jamie, Jen, and Kaitlin. Love you guys. You make life fun.

To my NavPress Awesome Squad — thanks for taking the jumble of words I give you and making it sound like a novel. You guys are fantastic.

And finally, to you, my dear friend — may we learn together how deeply God loves us, how gently He cares for us, and how perfectly He prepares for us the road ahead.

Chapter

1

Here's the thing about roller coasters: I like them. Most of the time. I like them when they are completely enclosed in a building, and I generally prefer them to be in the dark so I can't see what's coming next.

One of my biggest fears is that I will be on an outdoor roller coaster and get hit in the face by a bird.

It could happen.

So the fact that I've now talked my new boss and the youth pastor of our church, Rick, out of going to Six Flags three times in the last three months is something of a personal feat for me.

"I think it would be great fun and so we shall do it," he says now, slamming his hands on his desk.

This action would have sent me into a nervous twitch only a few short weeks ago, but I'm getting used to Rick and his ways.

That's almost a scarier thought than being hit in the face by a flying bird on a roller coaster.

"What will be great fun?" I ask, distracted by my new

planner that is stuffed with names, dates, and times. I had no idea there were so many girls in the youth group until I took this job. Now it's all I can do not to double book myself. Last week, I scheduled for three different girls to meet me at three different Starbucks at the very same time.

I went that same day and bought the planner.

Considering my past abuse of planners, I have conveniently forgotten to inform a lot of the people in my life of this fact.

"Six Flags," Rick says. "We're going next weekend. Sort of a 'Good-Bye Summer, Hello Fall' trip. I'll make up the postcard and you address them."

Rick is very good at delegating tasks to me. Too good. I look up at him briefly. He's wearing loose jeans and a polo shirt, and he's drumming out a little tune on his desk. Rick is a huge, barrel-chested man and is completely bald. Supposedly by choice. Either way, he's a scary person to run into when you happen to be by yourself at the church after dark.

I take pride in the excellent bladder control I had on that night.

"I thought we were thinking about doing a park barbecue sing-along thing as our 'Good-Bye Summer' event." I look back down and scribble in my planner while studying the text I'd received. MOLLY, 3 PM, JAMBA JUICE BY THE GALLERIA.

"Oh yeah . . ." Rick says slowly, twisting his lips and staring out the window. "I do like the idea of a sing-along."

"Of course you do. It's a great idea. And Six Flags has totally been done." I am casual but still convincing.

"True." Rick nods. "All right then. Forget Six Flags. We're sticking with the original plan. I'll draw up the postcard."

I smile to myself and nod to Rick. "Sounds good."

I have a meeting with another girl in twenty minutes, so I stand from my tiny desk and stretch. "I'm out of here. I'm meeting with Bethany and then I'm going home. I have four weeks of laundry I have to do."

Rick makes a face. "Sounds like a great night."

"Oh yes." I shoulder my purse and walk out of the church, waving at Geraldine, our church secretary.

I've been on the payroll at this church for two months this week, and while it feels like a lot longer in some respects, the summer has gone by fast.

I climb into my car and look at my planner to see what Starbucks I'm meeting her at. I have three I try to cycle through so I'm not going to the same one twice a day. And I also try to throw in the occasional Jamba Juice or semi-healthy place because there have been a few days I have been so shaky at the end of the day from all the caffeine, I can barely sit down.

My phone buzzes as I'm driving out of the parking lot, and I click the button before mashing it against my ear. "Hey, Layla."

Layla is my best friend, and she is getting married in a little over two months. I can't even believe it. Especially since I've been so busy with this new job I've hardly had a chance to hang out with her all summer. Since all the kids are out of school, I've had back-to-back-to-back meetings for weeks. Rick keeps swearing the whole year will not be like this.

Exhaustion is pulling at my brain, but I shake it away so I can appear happy and peppy for Bethany in fifteen minutes.

"Hey." Layla sounds tired.

"You okay?"

"No. I miss you. I haven't even seen you in like nine years and I'm tired of people asking me questions, tired of caterers calling to tell me about there being no spinach because of a mad cow disease scare, tired of realizing that hey, we forgot to order napkins, and tired of being engaged."

I immediately feel bad. "I'm so sorry, Layla. I am an awful maid of honor."

"You aren't an awful maid of honor. You're just really busy and it just makes me wonder if you aren't sliding back into the can't-say-no Paige we all knew and didn't love very much."

"Ouch."

"Anyway. I'm coming over for dinner tonight and I'm bringing Panda. So I don't care what you have written in that planner you're trying to sneak around. Cancel it. Call in sick or say you caught the mad cow disease."

"How did the spinach get the mad cow disease anyway?"

"I don't know. Maybe it was from the fertilizer or they grew it on the same farm as the cows or something. Or maybe it was salmonella."

"Well, I was just planning on doing laundry tonight, so as long as you're okay with that, come on over." I am already looking forward to the orange chicken.

Layla cannot come over without bringing Panda Express. It's a tradition now.

"You weren't going to see Tyler?"

I bite back a sigh at the name.

Tyler, for all intents and purposes, is my boyfriend. But if you look at the eight times I've seen him all summer, he's more like a casual acquaintance than anything else. I've been working like crazy, his sister had a baby, and they had a family reunion so he was gone for a week. He has had some big projects come up at work and all manner of excuses.

It all started after Tyler happened to see Luke, my ex-boyfriend, giving me a hug and kiss at our end-of-the-school-year youth party at the beginning of the summer. I didn't intend on either of those things happening, and I explained everything to Tyler at coffee the next day, but he's been a little standoffish since then.

I don't know what to do about it. Tyler is a slow mover anyway. It took him about six months to ever officially ask me to be his girlfriend in the first place.

I've always wondered about it. And now I'm wondering whether the girlfriend thing is still even on.

"No," I tell Layla. "He's got a big project due this week."

"He always has a big project due."

"I know. Hey, I'm at Starbucks to meet a girl so I need to go."

"You're always meeting with a girl. Except never this one."

"I know, Layla." I sigh. "I'll see you tonight."

"Okay."

We hang up and I try to leave the guilt in my car. So I'm a terrible maid of honor. So I'm an awful girlfriend. So I can barely keep track of who I'm meeting with next. I swallow the big lump in my throat and blink back the tears—whether from the sense of failure or from exhaustion, I'm not sure.

I paste a big smile on my face and wave at Bethany across the fragrant store. "Hey there!"

Apparently this is what I quit my secretarial job at the adoption agency to be.

Fake.

* * * * *

I get home at six o'clock and just lean back against my door after walking in. My apartment is immaculate, but that's because I've hardly been home in the past eight weeks of summer. I've spent my days waking up, showering, getting dressed, and running out the door to either a staff meeting or meeting with a girl over breakfast or meeting with Rick to convince him not to go to Six Flags this summer.

The man is nothing if not stubborn to an idea.

Layla will be here in fifteen minutes, so I change into yoga pants and an oversized baseball-style T-shirt that was my dad's. I yank my hair into a long braid down my back, then I check my pantry and decide to make some chocolate-chip cookie dough.

It's doubtful it will become cookies with both Layla and me in the apartment tonight. Cookie dough is like our kryptonite.

I'm just finishing adding the chocolate chips when Layla comes walking into the apartment. Layla is not one for knocking. There have been a couple of times when I've accidentally left the door locked and she's about fallen down my stairs from bouncing off the door so hard.

"So, I have good news and bad news," she announces, carrying in a paper take-out bag from Panda.

"Bad news first." I lick some cookie dough off my hand.

"I'm going to start with the good news first." Layla shakes her head and sets the bag on the kitchen table.

"Okay."

"The good news is that the people at Panda seem to have been extra generous with the orange chicken tonight."

"That's not good news for my waistline," I tell her.

"The bad news is that our girls' night is about to get crashed so it's good that we got extra food."

I look at her questioningly, but I don't have time to ask because right then there's a soft knock on the door. I go open it and Tyler stands there, rubbing his hand over the blond five-o'clock shadow on his jaw.

My stomach twists, but it's not in the butterfly-style that used to be even a few months ago. Now, if anything, I'm just dreading the day he officially ends it. He looks terrible. My breath sticks like I swallowed too much gum as a child.

"I'm sorry, Paige," he says before even telling me hello. "I didn't realize tonight was girls' night."

Already digging a spoon into the cookie dough, Layla moves her hand from her left to her right in one of those weird waves at Tyler from the kitchen.

"I'm sorry," Tyler says again.

I shrug. "It's fine." He's here and I've barely seen him all summer so I feel bad just asking him to leave. But Layla obviously needs some best-friend time.

And honestly, if he leaves, he can't tell me it's over.

I look at Tyler and nod to the porch. "Let's just go out here for a minute." I push him out the door and close it behind me. I pull at my shirt, not necessarily appreciating the fact that I've hardly seen him recently and he shows up when I'm in my yoga pants and have my hair in a braid that is quickly loosening, letting pieces of hair fall around my face. He couldn't happen to come by when I'm dressed cute and have my makeup still intact.

Nope.

Tyler smiles at me, but it's not like one of the old Tyler smiles. This one seems forced. Sad. "So, I haven't seen you in a while." He rakes a hand through his blond curls.

"I know." And most of the times we have seen each other have been around youth events. Not necessarily the best place to have a date.

Or a real conversation. Or a real apology about what happened with Luke.

The awkwardness buzzes between us, and if I could just wish us back to that wonderful day at the beginning of the summer where he asked me to be his girlfriend at the Dallas Arboretum, I would do it in a heartbeat.

He smiles another sad smile. "Well. I won't keep you from your time with Layla. Maybe we can get dinner? Tomorrow night?"

I think through my schedule, and I can't remember what tomorrow holds. It's Friday, which has been filled up with events for the youth group, but since we've got the backyard barbecue thing next weekend, Rick mercifully let us leave this weekend free.

"I can probably do that." I nod.

"Really?" A mix of shock and enthusiasm crosses his face, and I'm sad to see how many times I've obviously said I was busy.

Maybe most of this weirdness and awkwardness is my fault.

Whatever it is, I miss the old Tyler. The one who called me out on all my crap and was constantly bugging me with his happy-go-lucky self. I just don't know how to tell him that.

And now is obviously not the right time.

Tyler nods like we just decided on a business lunch. "All right then. So, I'll pick you up at six tomorrow night. Does that sound good?"

I nod because I don't know what else to do. "See you then."

He looks at me for half a second and then just nods again and starts back down the stairs. No hug, no kiss on the cheek. No physical contact at all.

I rub my arms, blink back tears, and watch him disappear around the corner before going back inside to face Layla, who is already halfway through her orange chicken.

"Sorry," she says after she swallows. "Lukewarm Panda does not a good meal make. So . . . how's the Tyler man?"

"Weird." I pull the bag over and get my two-entrée dinner out. It is pointless to even bother attempting to pay Layla back for tonight. I'll just buy next time we eat out.

"Well. He's always been a little on the odd side. No offense."

"Not like that." I stab my chicken so hard, my plastic fork breaks.

Layla watches me, frowning. "What's wrong with you?"

"Nothing. It's just . . ." I sigh, go get a real fork and knife from my kitchen drawer, and then use them to cut the chicken open so I can dig out the plastic fork tines. "Things are just . . . weird." I haven't told Layla about the thing that happened with Luke at the beginning of the summer. First because Luke is her brother and second because I've just barely seen her.

She shrugs. "With what?"

"Me and Tyler."

Layla purses her lips. "What did you do?"

"Why do you automatically assume it was my fault?"

"Because Tyler is a saint. And he's obviously head over heels for you, so anything that happened is consequently going to be on your hands."

"Well. It's not so obvious anymore."

"That it's your fault?"

"No, that he's head over heels for me." I think to the zero affection even two minutes ago and bite the inside of my cheek, half debating just telling her about the whole thing with Luke.

Then I look over at her. She's wearing sweatpants. Her brown curly hair is in a sloppy knot on the top of her head, and she looks exhausted.

No good can come from adding one more thing to Layla's plate.

So I stay quiet. I'm getting used to the wad hardening in my stomach. "Let's talk about the wedding."

"Let's not. I'm wishing we had just eloped now. I cannot understand how there is so much divorce in this country because it seems like the engagement process would be enough of a struggle for people, the weak ones would be voted out of contention."

I did not follow that at all. The more tired Layla gets, the less she makes sense. And she doesn't start out making a lot of sense to begin with.

"What?"

"I have seriously cried nine days this week."

I'm going to assume Layla knows there are only seven days in a week and she's just making a point.

"About what?" I again feel like a terrible friend. I should have been there. Instead I was comforting other crying girls, attempting to answer questions about obscure Old Testament references, and trying not to get killed in a game of dodgeball.

She shrugs miserably. "You name it. Whether or not we

ordered enough hors d'oeuvres. Whether or not I even still like my wedding dress. Whether or not I like the bridesmaids' dresses anymore. I mean, is rose even an in color nowadays?" She rubs her forehead, then cups her face in her hands, looking down at the table.

"Layla—" I start but she cuts me off.

"And Peter and I have been fighting like nonstop lately. I mean nonstop. And when we aren't fighting with each other, which is rare, we are fighting in other ways because the temptation is so stinking ridiculously hard, Paige."

I just watch her, not sure of what to say. She's treading in uncharted waters for me. I mean, my boyfriend hasn't even held my hand in eight weeks. The closest I've ever come to having to avoid that particular temptation was when I was dating Luke and he thought he was going to just spend the night.

I was so shocked that it wasn't a big deal to send him right back out the door.

This is much different.

Layla is rubbing her temples, looking for all the world like an exhausted little kid, and I'm overcome with compassion for my best friend.

I don't say anything, but I pull my chair around next to hers and wrap my arms around her shoulders. She lays her head on my shoulder and just sighs. "Tell me we should elope."

I rub her arm. "You don't want to elope, Layla."

"I know." She's quiet for a minute. "Tell me I need to get a new dress."

"You love your dress. It's perfect for you."

"I know. And the bridesmaids' dresses?"

"Also perfect. And rose is definitely an in color. And I don't know what to say about you and Peter, but you could bring it up in premarital counseling."

Rick is marrying Peter and Layla, so he's been meeting with them. They had to take a big break over the summer just because everything with the youth group got so busy, but they are back to meeting again.

"Don't you ever struggle with this kind of stuff with Tyler?"

I take a breath. "Not really." You have to be around someone in order to struggle with sexual temptation, I would think.

"Oh." She sighs and straightens, smiling over at me. "I'm glad we are having dinner together."

I nod. "Me too."

Chapter
2

Friday dawns hot and sticky. I swipe at my forehead while I'm waiting to meet a girl for lunch at Panera, and my foundation comes off on my finger.

I don't know why I bother putting on makeup in the Dallas humidity sometimes.

Today is technically the last day of summer work hours for me, so I packed the girls in. I've already met with two, and I've got two more after this. According to Rick, my job during the school year will be much more manageable.

"Maybe one kid a day," he told me. "Actually, I'd even go so far as to say I'd like you to meet with five girls a week, so divvy that up however you want. I don't care."

Rick, for all his obnoxiousness, is really a very good boss. I do my job and he does his. I hand him the receipts and get my reloadable Visa card reloaded, and he gasps at the number of Frappuccinos I've consumed with the girls but continues to pay for them.

Danika walks in then, and I wave at her from the booth I'd saved, since Panera on Friday at lunchtime can be comparable to hell, except I was sitting inside so we didn't have the heat.

Still had the gnashing of teeth, though. I have been watching a woman decide what kind of bread she wants for the last ten minutes. "I don't know," she keeps mouthing over and over.

She is likely speaking aloud, but my booth is too far away to hear her.

I grab my wallet but leave my purse to save the booth. My father would have a heart attack if he ever saw me do that. But I figure, we're at Panera. Most people aren't paying attention to my purse sitting there anyway, and if someone tries to steal it and make a break for it without my wallet in it, all they'll wind up with is a half-gone pack of gum and a cosmetic bag filled with tampons.

Danika orders a bowl of soup and I order a small salad. After the two coffee drinks I've ordered today, I need something semi-healthy.

We go back to the booth and my purse is still there, like I knew it would be. "So, are you ready to go back to school?" I ask her as we sit down. I've only met with Danika twice or so this summer. She's a hard one to get ahold of. Apparently her family spends most of the summer visiting all of their obscure relatives across the country.

Our food comes, I pray for the meal, we chat about random things while we eat, I share a quick verse I've been thinking about this week, and then I give her a quick hug as we leave.

Danika is an easy one. She comes from a great family and has been in the church her whole life.

Others are not so easy.

Like my next appointment. I climb in my car and start the air-conditioning. I have half an hour to kill before I need to be ten minutes away. So I reach for the phone and call my mother.

"Hey, Paige," she answers, crunching into the phone.

"Lunchtime?"

"Mm. My doctor told me the only way to lose the peri-menopausal weight I've gained is to start eating six small meals a day."

"So you are supposed to eat more to lose more?"

"Didn't make sense to me either, but I'm sitting here eating celery and peanut butter because what do I know? I didn't go to medical school."

I grin. I love my mom.

"So, have you talked to Preslee recently?" Mom asks, apparently eating another celery stick. The crunching is a little obnoxious.

"No." My used-to-be-but-no-longer-estranged sister moved back to Texas about four months ago. She's engaged to a man who is, for all I can tell, a giant, real-life Ken doll. He's blond, he's beautiful, and all he does is just stare at my sister like she's the most incredible thing he's ever beheld.

It was cute the first time I was around him. Now it's just kind of weird.

I'd hate to be there the first time she has the flu in his presence.

"Well, I just talked to her and she was going to call you and find a time for you to come try on dresses."

Preslee's wedding is exactly one month after Layla's. I will be the maid of honor in both of them.

In other words, I will be holding up a lot of big, white dresses while the women pee.

Joy and gladness.

"Okay," I tell Mom. "I guess I'll wait for her call." Not a lot else I can do.

"And she's thinking about going with a mint color scheme."

"Mint. Like peppermint?" I think immediately of a barber shop pole–inspired dress, and I'm suddenly very nervous about what exactly I will be wearing.

"No, I think like that weird color between green and white and blue. Not that you need to inform her that I just called it weird."

I smirk.

"Anyway. How is your day going?"

"Fine." I look at the clock and shift into reverse. "I'm on my way to my fourth meeting of the day."

"How do you have anything left to talk about?"

"Mm." I shrug because I have no idea. Normally on a day like today, I would go home and crash in front of some brainless TV. But I'm going out to dinner tonight with Tyler who I really do want to talk to, but I'm afraid I will be all talked out by then.

My stomach cramps up again.

It will be an exhausting day.

"Well. I'll let you go," Mom says, still crunching. "Enjoy your meeting! Let me know when you and Preslee decide to go dress shopping because I want to come too."

"Sure thing, Mom. Have fun with the celery."

"Oh yes. Old age stinks."

I hang up smiling and drive to Starbucks. My third Starbucks visit today. By the end of the day, I'm going to smell like I work here.

Tori is already here and we spend the next hour talking

about her non-Christian parents, her older brother who is running straight down the path leading to jail, and her little brother, Jake, who is starting to follow in her big brother's ways. "I don't know what to do," she mumbles, trying to hide her tears by furiously chugging her vanilla-bean Frappuccino. "Jake was coming with me to church and everything. And now, I can't even get him to look at me."

These are the meetings where I end up praying through the whole thing. God blessed me so much. I had parents who loved me, who raised me in the church, and who taught me about Jesus. I have no idea what Tori's life is like.

I know a little about sibling issues, though.

I pull my mini Bible out of my purse, just praying like crazy. "Tori. I'm not going to sit here and pretend that I know what your life is like."

She nods, swiping at her eyes with a napkin.

"But I know what the Bible says." I flip over to the same verse I shared with Danika, and I read Psalm 27:8 after clearing my throat. "'When You said, "Seek My face," my heart said to You, "Your face, O Lord, I shall seek."'"

She looks at me confusedly. "How is that going to help Jake? He's not seeking the Lord. He could care less. I've tried talking to him, yelling at him, bribing him . . ."

My parents did the same thing with Preslee. I look at Tori. She's fifteen. She shouldn't be the parent in the family. Tears are spilling down her cheeks and she's trying to be nonchalant about them, though I can tell she's one wrong word away from full-fledged sobbing. She's holding her Frappuccino in front of her face.

I have met with Tori many times and she hates to cry in public. An overwhelming sense of a million different emotions flood my chest. I reach for her hand. "I love you, Tori. And Jesus loves you too. And as much as we want to save those around us, we can't forget that it's only Jesus who saves. We can only tell them about Him."

Tori is nodding repeatedly like a bobblehead doll, and I can see that we need to end this meeting so she can feel like she has some shred of dignity left. "Praying for you, my sweet girl." I pull her into a hug as we walk out of the door.

She latches on to me on the sidewalk like I'm part of a mining team headed to some asteroid in space. Then she pulls away and doesn't say a word, but she manages a shaky smile and a quick wave before half jogging to her car.

I watch her leave and my heart hurts.

This is the worst part of my job.

I started working at the church to change girls' lives, but sometimes I feel like all I'm doing is poking at festering wounds.

* * * * *

It's six thirty and somehow I have found the time to run home and change out of my coffee scent–soaked clothes and reapply some foundation. I run the curling iron back through my hair and frown at myself in the mirror.

My hair has no definite color. It's red, it's brown, it's blonde. It's also the longest it's ever been at just past my bra strap, and since it has been so humid, it's very frizzy. I try to tame the frizziness into actual curls, but it usually only lasts until I get to the bottom of my apartment's staircase.

I am wearing a skirt with a fitted T-shirt and flip-flops, and I am starting to second-guess my outfit. I don't know the proper T-shirt length to skirt ratio here and it's worrying me. What if the shirt is too long? What if the skirt is too short?

A knock sounds on my door and I have to just hope for the best. I find my purse and force a smile as I open the door and see Tyler in all his curly blond-hair cuteness. He's wearing plaid shorts and a polo shirt with leather sandals and a slightly awkward smile.

The awkwardness is what kills me. So I muster my courage and stick my right hand out to him. "I'm Paige Alder. It's nice to meet you."

He grins a full smile then and bypasses my hand to pull me into a hug. "I've missed you, Paige."

We stand there like that for a couple of minutes in my doorway. His arms around my shoulders, my arms around his waist, my purse dangling from my hand behind him. My head comes to just below his collarbone, and he rests his head on mine while we let all of my cold, very expensive conditioned air fly right past us out the door.

And I don't even care right then. My heart is settling into a less-frenzied beat, and I take a few deep breaths.

Finally we break apart, and he pulls my door closed while I fish for my keys in my purse to lock it behind us. "Where are we going tonight?" I click the dead bolt.

"Well, that's kind of up to you. I was thinking we could go to the Cheesecake Factory."

"Sounds great to me."

He opens the passenger door of his blue truck for me. I slide in and watch him walk around to the driver's door. There's still this twinge of awkwardness between us, but surely that's because it's just been so long since we saw each other.

Surely.

Surely not because he's planning on ending it tonight or something.

My stomach is back to gnawing on itself.

We start driving toward Frisco. My apartment is in Richardson, which is a northern suburb of Dallas, so it's a short drive. Tyler tells me about some of the projects he's working on.

"I swear the second I think we are in the clear and we're going to finally have a slow season, three more clients sign on," he says.

Tyler is a software engineer and I have never for the life of me been able to picture him at work. Tyler is totally an outdoorsy type. The idea of him sitting at a desk, wearing a suit and tie and staring at a computer all day is just weird.

"I guess that's a good thing." I look over at him. "Right?"

"It's good for the company, sure. And I just got another raise, which is great. But I'm to the point where I would sacrifice the money just for some time off." He smiles sadly over at me. "I mean, this is ridiculous that we haven't even been able to have a date in eight weeks."

I agree.

We park in the always crowded parking lot and then walk through the thick, hot air into the cool restaurant. There's already a thirty-minute wait, so we find a little bench to sit on by the glass window showcasing all the different cheesecakes they offer.

I am already drooling.

Tyler looks over at me. "So. How's the intern thing going?"

"Good." I tell him about the girls and then how Rick told me that the hours were soon going to be much better. "Apparently the craziness is just a summer thing."

"I hope so."

Our buzzer starts going off and we get seated at a booth in the far back of the loud restaurant. In a way, it's good because as I'm scouring the menu, I'm also scouring my tired brain for topic ideas to discuss with Tyler.

I hate that I now have to create a conversational list in order to talk to him.

I peek over my menu and Tyler is studying the book closely. In the old days, he would be pestering me about the time I spend at work, asking me how my time with the Lord is, and working me for details about my relationship with my sister.

Not tonight, apparently.

Maybe he is just tired from work.

That must be it.

The waiter comes by for our drink order and then quickly leaves us to our silent perusal of the menus. I decided what I wanted before we even walked in, so I'm quietly reading through the appetizers again, waiting for Tyler to decide what he wants. There's a couple at a table semi-close to us who are holding hands across the table, staring lovingly into each other's eyes while they talk quietly.

My gaze flickers back to Tyler, and I gnaw on the inside of my cheek, worrying. What if he's stopped thinking of me like that? What if all this work stuff we've both had going on has just made him question whether we should even be dating?

He looks up at me. "Decided what you'd like?"

"Yes." I'm just worried I decided too late.

The waiter brings our food after a very uncomfortable amount of time. Tyler prays without reaching for my hands as customary, and I just reach for my fork, anticipating a dinner that will likely not result in cheesecake because my stomach is hurting so badly from all the tension that I don't want to attempt it. There's not much worse than having to find a new favorite dessert because you spent the whole night upchucking your used-to-be favorite.

"Paige," Tyler says two bites in, and something in his tone makes me set my fork down. "We need to talk."

I nod. Well, here it comes. I am fighting the sting of tears in the back of my eyes. For all the weirdness this summer has been, I really like Tyler. I really loved the time we spent together.

There was a big part of me that thought this was finally *it*.

"We need to talk about Luke."

I nod, even though I really don't like to talk about Luke any more than I like to talk with my great-uncle Sam about his digestive issues. I keep nodding, though, because yes, we probably do. Not that we haven't before. I tried to explain everything.

Maybe now that the memory of me wrapped in Luke Prestwick's arms isn't so fresh, Tyler will be more open to hearing the truth.

"Look. I know there is a . . ." He pauses, waving his fork. "Past," he settles on finally. "I know there is a past between you two and I'm . . . I'm okay with that."

He says it like he's just agreed to eat an entire jar of pickled beets. I'm having trouble believing him.

"Look, Tyler, the 'past' you're talking about isn't some fantastical thing. We dated. We broke up. He moved far away, and honestly I wish he'd stayed there." No offense to Luke. My life was just a lot less complicated before he came back.

Luke Prestwick is like a taller, darker Zac Efron. He's beautiful to look at, and he's as charming as a free gallon of ice cream and about as sweet.

He's just not Tyler.

I'm struggling to find the words to tell Tyler this without sounding like I need to immediately be transported to the nearest Disney Channel stage from all the sugariness.

"I know what it looked like," I tell him quietly, not wanting to share my entire relationship history with the whole Cheesecake Factory. "But like I said before, I don't like Luke anymore. I haven't for a long time. I finally have been able to forgive him for things and move on, and whether or not he has is not my problem anymore."

Right at the beginning of the summer, Luke came over to my apartment and confessed his undying love for me over a box of Krispy Kreme doughnuts. The setting was good but the timing was very bad.

Part of me has wondered, though, what would have happened if he'd said all those things back when I wanted him to while we were dating.

Then I realize that my life right now would be completely different. I probably wouldn't be working at the church with the girls I love. I probably wouldn't have reconnected with Preslee, and I certainly would not be having dinner with the cute guy across the table from me.

I like my life. Without Luke in it.

Or at least without him as a major player in it.

Tyler nods. "I believe you." He looks down and continues to pick at his food.

No. I don't think he does.

The rest of dinner is almost tedious. We both start and

stop conversational topics about eight times, and in the end we just eat our food in relative silence. Tyler pays the bill and then looks at me. "Ready to go?"

I have morphed into one big tension ball, but I manage to nod. "Sure." I know he's going to end it as soon as we get to the car. He's nice enough that he won't break up with me in my favorite restaurant. Maybe he picked here to symbolize the Last Supper sort of a thing.

Then he takes me home, says good night, and leaves with a squeeze of my hand that seems more like a placating little nudge than anything else. No "it's over, Paige" or "I think we should take a break" or "it's not you, it's me."

This stinks.

I toss my purse on the couch and go find the salted caramel truffle ice cream I'd stashed in the back of my freezer for emergencies only. As a general rule, I'm a cookie kind of a girl. Baked or unbaked, I'll take chocolate-chip cookies any day.

But for particularly bad days, I always turn to ice cream.

My mother told me that was a genetic trait. "One day your father and I had the worst fight of our entire married life. I slammed the door right in his face, walked into the kitchen and ate an entire half gallon of Blue Bell ice cream." She even rubbed her stomach while telling me the story, making a terrible face. "An *entire* half gallon of The Great Divide. Seemed fitting at the time." She shrugged, looking somewhere far into her past. "Anyway, the ice cream worked, I went and apologized to your dad, we made up and nine months later, you were born."

It was a little too much information about my birth story, and I suddenly had a terrible sense of camaraderie with those poor kids born on that Discovery Channel show.

Someone knocks on my door as I've got a spoon full of frozen caramel cream deliciousness lodged in my mouth. I remove the spoon with a frown, walk over to the door, and open it, half hoping it's Tyler and he'll drop me back in one of those amazing movie kisses, and we won't even have to say the words. We'll just know everything will be all right.

Layla is standing there, so all hopes of romantic kisses disappear. She looks terrible. She's wearing yoga pants, a tank top, and even though it's ridiculously hot out, she's got on her fuzzy gray jacket, which means she's either had such a bad day that she has taken off her bra in utter defeat, or she's just sad and needs to have some snuggly warmth around her.

I look at her for a second, turn around, walk into my kitchen, pull another spoon out of the drawer, and hand it to her as we both collapse on the couch with the tub of ice cream between us.

She's had about three spoonfuls before she starts talking. "I'm going to quit my job."

"I already did that." Part of me misses the office environment. No emotional high school drama, no crazy work hours, no shaky hands from all the trips to Sonic.

I also didn't have any fun and felt like I was making zero difference in the world, but that's beside the point right now.

Layla sighs at my TV. "I'm going to call off my wedding."

"I think Tyler is going to break up with me."

"And it didn't even work to take off my bra tonight."

"I haven't gotten that far yet."

We sit there, both staring at my blank TV, dipping our spoons in the ice cream and eating in total silence.

Finally I break it. "You aren't going to call off your wedding."

36   ERYNN MANGUM

"I might. I can't even stand it anymore, Paige. The man makes me insane. Did you know he keeps a jar of his left pinky toenail clippings?"

I make a face. "Ew."

"Exactly. I mean, who does that? How did that even get started? I'm all for a greener earth, but some things just shouldn't be saved, you know?"

She does not have to talk me into that one. "What does he even keep them for?"

"I don't know. Fish bait? A potential source of calcium if the earth ends? A way to weed out prospective wives?"

"Surely if that were the case, he would have shown you the jar earlier." I drag my spoon through the ice cream, aiming for some of the truffle goodness.

"I don't even know." Layla rubs her head and leans back against the couch. "I just want it to be winter already. So the wedding can be over and I can be married and deal with these things as a married couple who has no way out."

"Now that's the romantic spirit."

"Why is Tyler going to break up with you?"

I pause, spoon in mouth. Do I tell Layla what happened even though Luke is her brother? Or do I nose around the issue so she'll drop it and we can move on through our topical conversation list?

Now I know why some of my girls cower when I come to the door. There's nothing fun about getting a scab picked at.

"I don't know." I feel like we have both said this eighteen times tonight. Probably why there's a tub of ice cream between us. "He's lost that loving feeling." I paraphrase from one of my dad's favorite songs by The Righteous Brothers.

I hated that song growing up. Anytime Dad thought we

were sleeping too late on a Saturday when Preslee and I should be up "being productive," which basically meant helping my Dad with the yard work, he would blast that song so loud through the house that no amount of hiding under the pillow could mute it.

I pulled many a weed with that song stuck in my head. It was fated that I would hate it.

"Like what do you mean?" Layla licks her spoon. "Like he won't hold your hand anymore, or he has stopped with the flattering compliments? Because the last one is just part of the circle, you know."

"What circle?"

"The circle. You start off all whatever around each other and everything is all cool. Then you start to think he's cute and he thinks you're cute and he says all these cute, funny things and you think he's so brilliant and dreamy and then all of sudden he doesn't say it as much but holds your hand more and you see him all not showered and he's becoming more gross and less cute, then you start being all comfortable around him again." She shrugs. "It's the circle of life, baby."

"You are making that up."

"It's the cirrrrclllllleee . . ." she sings like on *The Lion King*.

I do love this girl. And what I love almost more than her right now is the distraction from her own train of thoughts she just provided for us.

Chapter 3

onday morning and it's the last week before all the kids go back to school. And for whatever reason, I am standing in the middle of Target, trying not to be mowed down by some crazed mother with kids hanging off her back. The whole store is just filled with this sense of urgency like *150 No. 2 pencils will never be enough*!

There are days when I have to move "Done with School" up a few notches on my list of blessings.

I steady my little basket over my arm and try my best to mash through the crowd to the makeup aisle. I wouldn't even be here but I ran out of my foundation yesterday, and after my Friday night ice cream binge, my face is still recuperating.

I grab the foundation, find the two other things on my list, and go stand in the mile-long line to the registers. I look at the people's carts in front of me and just frown. I never remember buying that much crap when I started school.

Then again, my mother was more the type who was like, "This is what is on the list from your teacher and that is *all* we are getting. I don't care how cool the Lisa Frank folders are."

I blame Mom for my uncool status in elementary school.

I finally pay for my couple of things and then drive to the church for my weekly Monday morning staff meeting with Rick. Natalie and baby Claire sometimes join us with muffins, and I smile as I see their car in the parking lot.

I can hear Claire the moment I open the church door, much less the office door. Geraldine is sitting at her desk, wincing at the shrill chatter coming from the back office.

"She's a loud one, isn't she?" Geraldine says.

"She's Rick's daughter. I guess I didn't expect any less." Geraldine shrugs. "That's the truth."

Natalie starts waving Claire's hand at me as soon as I walk in the door. "Hi, Auntie Paige!"

"Hi, Clairey girl," I say all baby-talk like, bending down to nuzzle the little peach-fuzzed cheek.

Claire lets loose another shrill squeal that makes my right ear immediately start ringing.

"Yep," Natalie says, noticing my wince. "That would be why I'm already looking into whether or not our health insurance covers hearing aids."

"And?" I straighten to dump my purse on my desk.

"And it's not looking good for my ears." Natalie nods to the basket on the floor. "Doughnut muffins this morning. Dig in."

Rick is silent up until now because he has been stuffing his face with muffins, and a sugary sprinkle covers his whole desk. "These, baby, are the reason I am going to stay with you through our old age."

"You old romantic, you." I roll my eyes at Rick and reach for a muffin.

Natalie has brought these before and they are delicious,

but they really go better with coffee. I find the little mini coffeemaker I unearthed here during the Great Cleaning of Late Spring while Rick protested that *yes*, he was going to throw away the pizza box with the moldy pizza in it, *eventually*.

Eventually is my least favorite word ever. I'm with the people at Nike on this one. Just do it, for Pete's sake.

Anyway, I found the coffeepot and Rick swore he'd never seen it, which probably means it belonged to whoever owned the office before Rick.

Disgusting.

I spent about three hours cleaning it and now it works perfectly. I brought in a pound of coffee, especially for days when it's just me and Rick here all day, and the little maker has been chugging along ever since.

I find I can handle Rick a lot better when I'm properly caffeinated.

Natalie is talking while I get the coffee going. Sometimes I think she misses being around more adults because anytime she's here, she hardly ever stops her monologue long enough to catch a breath.

"So then we went to the grocery store because we were all out of milk and I was standing there by the milk and I was looking at all the different kinds and I just started thinking about how many millions and millions of cows there have to be to produce this much milk for every grocery store in every town and city and state and it just totally overwhelmed me with this sense of compassion for these cows because I feel like Claire wants to eat like every twelve minutes and I get really overwhelmed thinking about how much milk I have to produce to keep her alive so I cannot imagine what those cows must be thinking when the weight of the whole world is on their shoulders."

Rick is nodding and eating his doughnut muffins through her entire speech. I'm just watching her as she talks. She barely even notices what she's doing with Claire, she's so focused on telling Rick her story. But she bounces Claire on her lap, yanks a piece of fuzz out of Claire's mouth, checks her watch, and then lifts her shirt and starts nursing all while telling us her story.

"Personally, I worry about goats," Rick says.

"What do you mean?"

"Well, hon. Cows are like created for milk. I never really think of goats that way. And obviously neither does America because you never see people buying a gallon of goat's milk for their kid. But now all of a sudden, everyone's all into goat cheese–stuffed dates and goat cheese pizza, and whatever those little pastry dealie things are with goat cheese, and I'm just feeling bad for those poor goats. They didn't even see it coming."

Natalie is nodding with this extra thoughtful look on her face. "I hadn't ever considered that. Poor goats."

Then they both just sit there in this sympathetic silence for the goats.

Sometimes, despite the eardrum-splitting squeals, I really feel for Claire.

* * * * *

The week passes by in a blur. I meet with twenty-six girls and by Saturday, I'm so excited for the regular school year, I can taste it. Forty hours a week is a great number to be working.

Seventy-six is not.

"It will get better" has become Rick's mantra. "This is only for a season, Paige. It will get better. In fact, why don't you take the first week of the school year off. Don't meet with anyone. Don't even come to the office. Just sit at home and wash your hair or paint your nails or do whatever you single, nonmotherly girls do."

"I wash my hair every day, Rick."

"Oh. Well, all I know is Natalie is always talking about how she never has any time to wash her hair anymore and she's going to turn into a big blob of grease."

I washed my hair extra well that next morning.

Saturday is a beautiful fall day and miracle of all miracles, it's even a little bit overcast, which just makes it the most-perfect temperature for an outdoor karaoke picnic. I've never heard of a karaoke picnic, but Rick threw the idea out there during one of our leader meetings, and everyone kind of got attached to the idea of seeing our little puberty-stricken junior high boys singing "Call Me Maybe" in their squeaky voices.

I am definitely videoing most of tonight on my cell phone.

I get to the park a little after four. I'm carrying a box with eighty bags of chips. I'm wearing my cutoff denim shorts and a looser dark gray knit T-shirt and flip-flops. I've got my hair in a sloppy bun at the top of my head and I'm wearing sunglasses.

I never dress up for youth events. I learned that lesson after playing Ultimate Frisbee in my favorite white capris during my first year volunteering with the youth group. I had to throw the capris away because I couldn't get the grass stains out.

It still sort of makes my stomach hurt to think about it.

And speaking of stomachs twisting . . .

Tyler climbs out of his truck and gives me an awkward wave as he crosses the field over to where I am.

"Hey." He takes the box from me.

"Thanks." We keep walking to where Rick is busy setting up long white tables. He and I spent all of yesterday at Costco shopping for today. We've got chips, deli meats, cheeses, rolls, lettuce, and tomatoes, all kinds of dips for the chips, and every flavor of soda imaginable.

"So, um, how's your weekend so far?" I ask Tyler, rubbing my now-empty arms and wishing I had something else to carry so I don't feel so weird.

"Good. Fine. I had to go back into the office today to work on that project some more." Tyler's curly blond hair is in top form today, probably because the overcast skies have also made it extra humid. He's wearing cargo shorts and a white polo over a T-shirt. I sort of want to warn him about the potential grass stains, but I don't want to sound like his mother so I keep my mouth shut.

Tyler glances over at me and forces a smile. "How are you?"

"Good. Rick gave me the next week off." I don't even know what I will do with myself. I'm going to start by cleaning my apartment but after that, I have a feeling I will get very bored.

"Cool. Maybe we can hang out." He doesn't look at me as he says it, though, so he's only saying it because he doesn't know what else to do.

I hate this.

We either need to just have it out or end it. This teetering halfway between relationship and strangers is about to kill me.

"Well, if it isn't my favorite karaoke singer!" Rick booms, wrapping an arm around Tyler's shoulders. "I've already got 'Single Ladies' queued up for you, man. No need to thank me. You can just dedicate the song to me."

Tyler shakes his head. "You have definitely got the wrong guy. I don't sing."

I've sat next to Tyler in church and I can kind of vouch for him on this one. It's not that he has a bad voice. I just wouldn't send him to try out for *American Idol* or anything.

Not to be mean.

"Well, we will just see. 'Single Ladies,' friend. 'Single Ladies,'" Rick takes the box of chips and sets them on the one table he set up. I start popping the legs out on the other tables and before we know it, a million kids are at the park, tossing footballs back and forth, bringing more food, chattering in huge groups about what they're wearing for the first day of school, and someone brought a volleyball net.

Rick halts the construction of the net. "Nope, peeps, this is not your normal park picnic," he announces in a loud voice.

"What are you talking about?"

"No one reads my postcards!" Rick points to where he has built a makeshift stage out of two-by-fours and plywood. The man is really taking this karaoke thing seriously.

"You want us to dance?" one kid yells from the football-tossing area.

"I want you to *sing*!" Rick yodels the last word and everyone groans.

Natalie shows up right then, Claire dangling from the weird fabric-wrap thing Natalie always carries her in. "Oh, perfect timing!" She grins and sets a plate of celery sticks swathed in peanut butter on the table.

"Dieting?" I ask her.

"No." She is horribly offended. "We are clean eating. I just spent the entire day throwing out every artificial food in our home."

Fabulous. Anytime Natalie goes on a diet, Rick becomes the worst person on the face of the earth. He's grouchy, he's mean, and he tends to make me do tasks I think are purely for his twisted sense of enjoyment on those days. "Natural sugar" does not a happy Rick make.

This is not the first time the clean-eating bug has bitten Natalie.

"Pinterest?" I ask her.

"What?"

"Never mind."

Rick is professional tonight. He has a projection screen he set up right beside the stage and a Bluetooth microphone and speakers he's using alongside his laptop.

He starts blasting "All By Myself" and the crowd groans.

"Seriously?" "Get with the right century, Rick." "Can't we hear something peppy?"

I pat his shoulder. "Tough crowd tonight."

"Not for long." *NSYNC starts blasting through the park and I just laugh. One of our not-shy-at-all boys reaches for the microphone and sings the song, complete with botched motions.

The crowd is loving it. I watch all the kids' faces. Some are eating; some are just sitting on the grass watching. Most are hollering and cheering and giving Zach a hard time.

After that, the night takes off. There are song requests, groups of people go up to perform, and people eat their weight in sugar cookies made by the mom of one of my girls.

This was a great idea.

I look over during the commotion and Tyler is watching me. I smile. The corners of his mouth lift and he walks over, holding a plate with a couple of the cookies on it. He hands me one without saying anything, and we watch one of his freshmen boys and one of the freshmen girls sing one of the songs from *High School Musical* to the joy of the crowd.

"She's actually pretty good," Tyler says.

I finish off the cookie. "Wish I could say the same about him."

"Cruel, Alder. Just cruel."

He grins at me, though, and there's this flash of normalcy after a summer of strained conversations and awkward pauses, and I just want to soak in that moment. But then it's over because Rick is smashing a microphone into my shoulder.

"You're up, Paigey."

I blink at the microphone. "I don't think so, Ricky."

Music starts playing and it's "Ain't No Mountain High Enough," and I am immediately shaking my head.

"Nope. No way. There is no way I'm going up there and fulfilling some sick goal you have of watching me sing the same song they sing in *Remember the Titans*."

Rick is grinning all crazy and looks at the group of kids. "Paige! Paige! Paige!" He gets them all chanting and I cover my face with my hands.

Here's the thing. I am not a public performer. When I was in school and had to give a report in front of the class, I could barely eat that morning, I would be so nervous.

Tyler reaches for my elbow and grins at me. "Come on, Paige. I'll do it with you."

There's a mischievous gleam in his blue eyes and I love seeing it again. How can I say no to that?

Knowing I'll regret it, I yank the microphone away from Rick and shake my head as I climb onto the teetering stage as the kids go crazy. "That's right, Paige!"

"Yay, Paige!"

I hate working with the youth. I miss my desk.

Tyler grabs the extra mic and leans into it, dipping his head down to look at me as he starts singing, "Ain't no mountain high, ain't no valley low . . ."

He is loose and funny, exaggerating his dance steps and the vocals. I stand with both hands on the mic, straight as a board, and sing exactly the lines I am supposed to sing while Tyler fills in with ooos and ahhhs.

This is the longest song ever in the history of the whole world.

Tyler turns to look at me during the echoing chorus as it ends, reaches over, grabs my hand, and twirls me around, dipping me down into a grand-finale finish. I'm laughing by this point and his face is an inch from mine. He winks at me and then stands me back up.

A few of the youth-group girls get all giggly and twittery, and I just shake my head. Nothing like a little romance between the leaders to get the rumor mills going.

Rick is cracking up by the computer as the song finishes. "Encore!" he yells.

"Rick's turn!" I announce into the microphone and the kids go nuts.

He starts waving his hands. "Uh-uh. I'm the guy in charge. Public humiliation is for all you commoners."

"Give it up for Rick!" I yell into the microphone. The

kids are chanting his name, whistling, yelling. Natalie is bouncing Claire in the back, grinning big time.

"Yeah, baby!" she yells as a glaring Rick snatches the mic from me and stands on the stage.

"Any requests?" I ask him, my voice all syrupy. I'm scrolling through the incredible collection of songs on the laptop.

"Yes," Rick says into the microphone. "Song number sixty-seven."

I laugh as I click it and the music starts. Rick grins at Natalie. "This one is for you, babe."

The music starts and everyone is dying by the time Rick starts singing Taylor Swift's "I Knew You Were Trouble." Rick is ridiculous. He was born for karaoke.

I watch as the kids laugh and cheer and yell catcalls at Rick, and a warm, little knot starts in my chest.

These kids love Rick. For all his weirdness, he really is a good man with a good heart that always points back to Jesus.

The song ends. Rick blows a kiss to his laughing wife and hands the mic over to one of the kids.

He joins me back by the computer and grins at me. "Not a bad way to spend a Saturday night, is it?"

I watch the kids, catch Tyler's sidelong gentle smile, and nod at Rick.

Not a bad way at all.

Chapter
4

onday morning and I am officially off of work duty. I am free as a little jaybird.

And I'm about as bored as one. I watch a tiny sparrow hopping around on my porch railing and think about birds. No wonder they fly south for the winter. It's incredibly boring to do nothing all day long.

And it's only three o'clock. I've barely even begun my break.

Months of working around the clock, and you'd think I'd be dying for the rest, but I am just not used to sitting still.

I've already been to the grocery store and the car wash and Target, and I've called my mother three times today.

When we hung up the last time, she said, "Have you considered maybe asking if Rick would reconsider your break?"

Apparently all those guilt trips in the past about how she wished I would call her more were just to fill conversational space.

I pull out crafting stuff and turn on HGTV when I get home, but it only holds my attention for an hour before I'm ready to do something else. I love crafting and I love HGTV, but until I get my own home, there's only so much I can do. My apartment manager has been kind so far by letting me paint one of the walls in the living room and by allowing me to hang up pictures and wreaths, but I doubt he would look kindly on me ripping up the carpeting and putting down hardwood floors or refinishing the kitchen cabinets.

I find my sneakers and head down to the gym that's part of my apartment rent. I used to go there several times a week. Then work at the adoption agency got busy, then I started dating Tyler, then I quit the agency and started working seventy-six hours a week.

It's kind of nice to be back. And it's only four o'clock, so I have my pick of all of the equipment. I get on the elliptical, turn the TV to HGTV since I'm the only one here, and start the machine.

I glance over at the treadmill once, considering, but treadmills have a way of making me feel like a hamster with all the running and not getting anywhere, so I stick to the elliptical.

I am not going to be able to move tomorrow.

My phone rings as I walk back home. It's Layla. "Hey," I answer it.

"Hi. So listen I've been doing all kinds of research and I think that my problem is centered on the fact that I don't have any creative outlets for my frustration about the wedding."

Anytime Layla starts talking about creative outlets, it goes downhill and fast. One time she got so obsessed with even the idea of creative outlets that she took her outlet covers off at her apartment, spray painted them all bright pink, and put them back on. Her apartment manager came in later that month to spray for bugs, and he fined her fifty dollars.

It's best if Layla just steers away from creativity.

"Well, I'm officially scared."

"You haven't even heard what I'm going to do." Layla is giddy. "I kept reading and people kept suggesting this over and over and so I'm just going to do it."

I'm nearly audibly praying that she's going to say something along the lines of read more books or plant those little rock gardens in barrels on her patio or learn how to bake.

Actually, scratch the last one. Last time Layla decided she would become the next Pioneer Woman, she made scalloped potatoes with gelatin. The whole dish looked like it was breathing.

Books. That's where she needs to feed her energy. Not that Layla would ever sit still long enough to read.

"What?" I ask when she waits for me to answer.

"I'm getting . . . a *dog*," she says it with flourish, and I am shaking my head before the word is completely out of her mouth.

"Oh no, no, Layla, that is a terrible idea."

"Says the girl who hates dogs."

"I don't *hate* dogs." I don't like dogs, but goodness knows that the hate category is already filled up with snakes, lizards, mice, rodents, and turtles.

It's the turtles' feet that landed them in that category. I can't stand the look of them, all wrinkly and weirdly colored and poking out crookedly from their shells. Ick.

"You do too. You have ever since the sixth grade when Logan O'Neil's boxer slimed your favorite pair of Doc Martens."

Now there was a throwback reference.

"Those shoes were expensive," I protest.

"And now completely out of style. See? The dog was just saving you from yourself. He knew that if he didn't destroy them, you would wear them forever."

"Layla, you live in an apartment."

"Yes. An apartment that allows dogs."

"Is that fair to the dog, though? To make it just sit in an apartment all day while you're at work? Don't they want to be out, you know, running through an open field or something? Or chasing cows? Or mailmen?"

"You know nothing about dogs, do you?"

I didn't know much. I didn't grow up with a dog. Dad liked having a nice backyard and Mom liked not having to clean up fur. Up until the point where Preslee went off the deep end, we had a calm childhood. None of those weird the-dog-dug-up-the-yard-and-found-the-skeleton-of-the-man-who-used-to-own-the-house stories.

I watch too much TV.

"Have you talked it over with Peter?" Surely he will have some sense. You can't count on the man for a laugh or even a conversation, but maybe all the stoic silence is covering up a brain full of intuition.

"Yep. He's all for it. Says it will give me someone else to talk to."

Peter. Well, he is a fan of silence. Maybe he figures that if Layla is talking to the dog, then she won't be talking to him.

"Anyway, I'm going to look at the pound tonight. Want to come with me?"

"I still think you need to rethink the whole keeping a dog cooped up in an apartment." It's my only argument that she hasn't had a comeback for.

"As opposed to them being killed in the pound?"

Welp. It was a good try.

I climb my stairs and rest my forehead against my front door. "Fine," I mumble, eyes closed. "What time?"

"I'll pick you up in fifteen."

That did not leave me a lot of time to shower. I hang up with Layla, run for my bathroom, take a very fast shower while I moan as I reach for the bottom of my aching feet with the sponge, hop out, and towel dry my hair. I have ten minutes. My hair is going to just have to air dry.

Now is when I usually start wishing for Katherine Heigl's hair in *27 Dresses*. The woman was caught in a rainstorm and still looked beautiful afterward.

I don't have that kind of luck. My hair is half wavy, half straight, and then there are like twelve strands that are completely crazy curly. Between that and the four different colors on my head, it's like I was born with eight different people's hair.

I slap on some mascara and a little bit of eye shadow, pull on a red T-shirt and a pair of jeans, slide into my shoes, and I'm picking up my purse off the couch when Layla comes into my apartment. I gave her a key a long time ago after we watched an episode of *NCIS* or *Bones* or one of those crime shows where a girl lived alone and was murdered in her kitchen and no one even knew about it until she was completely decomposed.

That freaked us both out, so we exchanged keys the next day. And I made my mother promise that if she ever tried calling me three times over two hours and I didn't answer to send 911 out to my apartment.

I really do watch too much TV. There's only so much you

can do when you live by yourself, I guess.

"Ready?" Layla is ecstatic. She can't even stand still, she's so excited. She's bouncing back and forth from foot to foot, grinning like a creepy cartoon character. I just shake my head and follow her out the door.

"Last chance to heed my warning." I lock the door behind us.

"Save it, Dog Hater. I love animals. I am going to rescue a little dog from the shelter and she will be so overjoyed that she will never do anything wrong."

"Uh-huh. Okay." We go to my car. I never ride in the car when Layla drives. The woman is the most-distracted driver on the planet. I've lost years of my life from being in the car with her.

I drive to the closest shelter and park outside. "You can still change your mind," I singsong and pull the key out of the ignition. I know as soon as Layla walks in to see the dogs, she is never going to walk out of there with empty arms.

"No more, Paige. I've made my decision and I'm sticking with it."

Oh the awful memories that one sentence brings back. I tag along behind Layla as she marches into the building that smells very strongly like ammonia. Maybe that's how they get people to take the dogs. They weaken their senses with the overpowering, poisonous smell.

"Hey, girls."

Luke is standing there, leaning back against a wall, arms crossed over his chest. He's wearing jeans and a plaid shirt, but unlike Tyler who wears that style all the time and looks like a lumberjack, Luke somehow makes it look all cool and hipsterish.

Maybe it's the knitted cap on his head or the dark hair poking out the front and the back.

"What are you doing here?" I gape at him. Of all the dogs I knew were at the pound, Luke was not one I thought would be here.

Yes, that was definitely meant to be an insult.

Luke gives his sister a hug and shrugs at me. "Layla texted and said she was going to get a dog. I thought I'd come help pick it out."

Layla is even more excited now. "I'm so glad you're here!" She grins, all giddy. "This is going to be *so much* fun!"

Oh yes. So much.

A man with a nose ring points the way to the kennels, and we all walk down a creepy, tiled hallway. The barking that starts off muted becomes louder and louder until we reach a heavy blue steel door.

Luke pulls it open for us and the barking is deafening. Surely this, beyond any of my arguments, will make Layla see the stupidity of this decision.

But she's totally in the moment. Hands clasped to her chest, eyes big and sad, mouth in a continual *aww*. "Aww, look at this one!" "Oh my goodness, did you read this dog's story?" She flits from cage to cage, sticking her fingers through the fence, reading the dogs' fake names, cooing and wiping tears at the idea that these dogs are stuck in the wire cages.

I, meanwhile, am staying directly in the center of the path so I don't get too close to the dogs. A couple of mean-looking shepherds are glaring at me, and one is snarling in a vicious, toothy, ready-to-attack mode.

Luke is suddenly beside me. "So. I haven't seen you in a while," he yells over the noise, hands in his pockets.

"I've been really busy." I nod.

"Busy or just avoiding me?"

"Both." If he's going to be direct, I can be too.

He looks away at a beagle mix, nodding. "I'm sorry."

"For what?"

"For whatever I did that is making you avoid me. I really do want to be friends, Paige."

"No you don't." It's hard having this conversation above eighteen dogs sounding off at us. Layla is totally oblivious to us, though. She's found a litter of puppies in the last cage, and she's talking with one of the guys who works here while the puppies lick her fingers through the chain link.

Luke looks at me, takes my elbow, and leads me back out the door we came in. "I can't handle the barking." He rubs the bridge of his nose.

"Me either. Layla is making a really bad decision."

We both stand there for a minute in the creepy hallway. Luke leans back against the wall, tucking his first two fingers into his pockets. "So . . ."

"So." I mimic his tone and his posture, leaning back against the other wall, and shove my hands in my pockets. We just stare each other down for what feels like half an hour but is probably closer to barely a minute.

"What did you mean when you said I didn't want to be friends?"

"Luke. That night . . . at the end-of-the-year party?"

He nods. "What about it?"

I shake my head. Of course he wouldn't think twice about it. I'd forgiven him for everything he'd done in the past, but then he reached out and pulled me into what looked like a very intimate embrace. Which was when Tyler saw us.

Of course.

"You said you forgave me. I thought that meant we could be friends."

I close my eyes and pinch the bridge of my nose. "It does. No, it doesn't. It . . . look I don't know, Luke, okay? I'm frustrated and annoyed. I really think I might have something with Tyler and you keep messing it up."

He looks at me all innocently, eyes big. "Me?"

I sort of want to hit him. But considering we just talked about me forgiving him, it doesn't seem like the best example of my supposed new feelings.

The door opens and Layla comes skipping out followed by a man leading about the ugliest-looking dog I've ever seen in my life. Luke and I both just stare at the dog while Layla starts chattering excitedly as she continues down the hall. "I found a dog! I'm going to meet her in one of their little get-to-know-you places and we are going to get to know each other! Oh I am so so so so so happy!"

Her voice trails off as she gets farther away. Neither Luke nor I have moved positions. He finally clears his throat, looks at me, and bites his lip. "So . . . that was . . . interesting." Then he makes this little face, and before I know it, I'm dying laughing.

I can't breathe. That poor dog. "Bless her heart, it's even a *girl* dog," I manage between giggles.

"She was definitely a looker." Luke is grinning, shaking his head and laughing. "Okay. Let's go see how Layla and that beautiful dog are getting to know each other."

We walk down the hall and find a little area outside. There are about eight cinder-block cubicles scattered around, and we finally find Layla and the dog in one of the far ones.

The dog, bless her heart, is even uglier than I remember. She doesn't even have a color. She's white, she's gray, she's black and brown. One of her eyes is brown and the other is this weird teal color. One ear sticks up, one ear lies down. Her fur looks wirier than anything and she's short and long, like a dachshund, but bigger and curlier like a terrier.

And she's yippy. Oh my, is she yippy.

If Layla gets this dog, the people who live in the apartment next to her are just going to love her forever.

"Isn't she a doll?" Layla giggles, attempting to pet the ugly dog while it runs in circles around her, yipping away.

"Yeah . . ." Luke leans his arms on the cinder blocks and looks down at them. "She's something, all right." He grins at me.

I do the best thing I can do right then and keep my mouth shut.

Chapter
5

Tuesday, Wednesday, and Thursday are the slowest days on the planet. I watch endless amounts of TV, I make a big batch of chocolate-chip cookies and tell myself it's an incentive to go to the gym, and I get about 834 texts from Layla filled with pictures of the ugly dog she named Belle because it means "beautiful one."

I think I lost weight over the tears I cried while laughing after I found that out.

Anyway, my phone is now full of pictures of this dog. Belle at her first vet appointment. Belle at the park. Belle going down the slide. Belle snuggled up on the couch sleeping. Belle in an apron helping Layla make dinner.

It made me frightful for the days when Layla and Peter have a baby. I will know that child's face better than my own. I'm already trying to figure out how to hijack her Facebook account so she can't post two hundred pictures a day of the future child.

I'm sitting there like a blob Thursday late afternoon,

finishing off the cookies and debating whether to make more when someone taps on my door.

I immediately look down at my outfit of choice. The only place I went today was the gym, and I came home, showered, and put on the same sweatpants and oversized T-shirt I've been wearing all week.

I peek out the peephole and it's a girl selling Girl Scout cookies. Well. That's convenient. Now I don't have to make more.

I buy a couple of boxes from the vested girl and her tired-looking mom and sit back down on the couch and open the box of Thin Mints.

Then I stop and look down at myself again. Cookie crumbs are stuck to my shirt. I haven't styled my hair in days, and if I go any longer, I might forget how to put on my makeup.

This is bad.

I reach for the phone and dial the first person I think of who has a flexible job and isn't my mother.

"Hello?" Preslee is eating something.

"It's not polite to answer the phone while chewing." It's still weird to me that I can just pick up the phone and call my sister. After years of estrangement, it's a welcome change.

"It's also impolite to call during lunch, but you don't hear me getting all up in your face about it."

"Can you technically get in someone's face on the phone?"

"I guess that *technically*, you already are, considering where most people hold the phone."

"Against their ear?"

"What are we talking about?" she asks.

I grin. "What are you doing tomorrow? I've had the week off work, and if I go one more day without being in public,

I'm going to turn into one of those Discovery Health channel specials."

"Ick. Have you seen the one where the lady had to walk backward on every city bus or she thought it would blow up like in *Speed*?"

"Well, to give her the benefit of the doubt, I bet the bus never did blow up when she walked backward."

"Don't ever go into psychotherapy, Paige. Now about your question. It just so happens that I have the ability to take tomorrow off."

"Yay!"

"What do you want to do?"

Preslee lives in Waco and honestly, there is not a lot to do in Waco. "Want to come here?" I ask her. "We can shop and get lunch and maybe catch a movie or something."

"Oh! Could we go to the Dallas Arboretum? I have *always* wanted to go there, and I've heard it's beautiful in the fall."

That would not be on the top of my list. Last spring, that's where Tyler asked me to be his girlfriend.

It was such a happy day. I purse my lips thinking about Tyler. I haven't talked to him all week. I sent him a text on Monday and told him I had the week off, and he only sent back a quick, HEY, THAT'S GREAT, PAIGE. Nothing like let's get together or let's hang out or let's cut all this ridiculousness and just talk for Pete's sake.

It's like the sweet moments at the karaoke party never even happened.

I don't know what to do about him.

"Paige?" Preslee cuts into my thoughts.

"Oh. Sorry. Yeah, we can maybe do the arboretum."

With any luck, we will find incredible sales and just not have time to go there tomorrow.

"Yay! Perfect. I'm glad you called! I'll try to leave here around eight tomorrow morning so I can get there around . . . what, like nine thirty?"

"Assuming traffic is good, that sounds about right." I sigh. Tomorrow is already looking better.

* * * * *

I climb in bed that night, not tired but needing to sleep for tomorrow's activities, and pull my Bible over. I've not been doing very good at reading through a book. I've just been grabbing for a quick verse before turning the light off. The summer was exhausting.

This week, though, I've been trying to get back on track. So I started reading Ecclesiastes. It has been making for some depressing reading on a few nights when I've already started out kind of depressed. I guess Solomon and I had that in common.

I start reading in chapter 2. *"Thus I hated all the fruit of my labor for which I had labored under the sun, for I must leave it to the man who will come after me. And who knows whether he will be a wise man or a fool? Yet he will have control over all the fruit of my labor for which I have labored by acting wisely under the sun. This too is vanity."*

There's a tiny italicized letter under the word *vanity* and according to the footnote, the word could also be translated *futility.*

Lots of talk about labor in there.

I start thinking about my work, or lack thereof, this week. I had the week off and what did I do? Nothing. Sat here and watched mindless hours of HGTV and *Friends*. I was no use to anyone. No help. I could have done so much, but I just sat around eating cookies.

I didn't even spend that much time reading my Bible or praying or doing anything worthwhile.

The old me, the one who used to run herself ragged trying to serve every place it was needed, pipes up. *Yes, but remember: I had to learn how to rest!*

Resting and vegging are two very different things, I think.

I turn off the light and my chest feels a little like there are three rubber bands wrapped around it, squeezing.

* * * * *

Preslee knocks on my door at exactly nine forty-five, right as I am sliding on my shoes. It's September and still hot and humid, but the idea of walking around in flip-flops all day doesn't sound that good for my feet, so I opt for ballet flats today.

I open the door and she grins at me. "Hi, sis!"

I smile. This is so weird in such a good way. Preslee looks beautiful. I still can't get over how much she has grown up over the years. Her dark hair is long, long, long and curly today. She's wearing a black shirt and white shorts and red ballet flats.

We apparently think alike.

She's got a little bird tattoo on her ankle, and I've always meant to ask her about it but have always forgotten. She's got another tattoo on her shoulder blade. That one was traced there during the awful years and was more of a way to tick off Mom and Dad than anything, I think.

Every time I see her, she's wearing black and white. This is good to know that my sister's clothing tastes aren't too complicated.

"Let me grab my purse," I say, letting her in.

"Can we stop by Starbucks? I made coffee before I left, but I forgot to grab my Thermos." She makes a sad face.

I nod. "You drove all the way here with no caffeine?"

"Shocking I made it here alive, huh?"

"Kind of." I find my purse, throw my cell phone in there, follow Preslee out of the apartment, and lock the door behind me. Preslee drives a little silver sedan that is so tame considering what she used to drive and how she used to act.

We go to Starbucks first and I get my customary caramel macchiato. Preslee orders a cinnamon dolce latte with extra shots, and we are good to go.

"Mm. Much better." Preslee massages her head after a few sips. "Where to, Paige?" She's driving and I'm busy licking the caramel off the green little stopper sitting in the top of the lid.

We decide on Stonebriar Mall and spend the rest of the morning discovering that we had apparently just missed all the good back-to-school sales.

"Well, this stinks," Preslee says at eleven thirty, hanging up yet another very cute but very full-price shirt back on the rack. "Too bad you didn't have the week off two weeks ago."

"True." I found a pair of boots but considering it is hot, hot, hot outside, I'm just not sure I'm in the mood to buy a pair of boots I won't wear except for two months out of the year.

"Lunch?" Preslee asks and I nod and put the boots back.

"You aren't going to get those?"

"I'll think on them." That's my code for no. Wearability is too important to me. If I don't think I'll wear it more than thirty times in a year, I don't buy it.

A holdover from my poorer days. When I first moved here, I was completely broke. I didn't shop for new things. I didn't even shop for fairly new things like at those "barely worn" boutiques.

Goodwill and I were friends way before it became cool to shop there.

"Paradise Bakery?" Preslee suggests and I nod. It's cheaper than my first choice of the Cheesecake Factory, and it's got chocolate-chip cookies to die for.

Maybe that's where the *Paradise* part came in.

All these theological questions before lunch.

We get in line, I order a turkey sandwich, and Preslee decides on a salad. "So I found a bridal gown," she says offhandedly as we sit with our trays at a table in the echoing food court.

I just look over at her. I never even considered she would be going wedding-dress shopping.

I am officially the worst maid of honor ever.

"By yourself?" I ask, worried.

She looks up at me, sees my expression, and starts waving her hands. "Oh no, not in a store. I just found one I really liked in one of those wedding magazines. I haven't tried it on or anything."

"Oh." Whew. I was about to feel very guilty.

"I am planning on going some weekend with you and Mom soon, if you can make it."

"You probably should go very soon. Your wedding is November 25th, right? You haven't moved it back or anything, have you?"

She shakes her head. "Let's pray so we can eat, and then I'll talk about the wedding."

She ducks her head and holds out her hands. I hold her fingers and she prays. "Lord, thank You for this precious time with my sister and bless our delicious-looking lunch. Amen." She looks back up, spearing a thick piece of lettuce with her fork. "I really need to get moving on it. It's just that with the house stuff and the work stuff and everything else, I haven't had a lot of free time. And the free time I've had, I haven't wanted to deal with things that just make me depressed. Do you know how much a wedding costs these days?"

"Aren't Mom and Dad paying for it?" I guess I didn't know. I just assumed.

She nods. "They're giving us a lump sum and anything we don't use on the wedding, we can just keep. So, obviously, we really want to keep wedding costs down so we can use the rest to work on our house."

Wes and Preslee had bought a fixer-upper in Waco during the summer. The only thing I really remember about the house is the bright orange shag carpets.

Flooring is expensive.

"Honestly." Preslee drops her voice into a conspiratorial tone. "And you can't breathe a word of this to Mom, but Wes and I have even considered maybe just doing like a family only thing in someone's backyard. I don't have a lot of friends I care to invite, and Wes's parents will want to make it *huge* since his dad is a pastor and all." She winces. "I'm worried Mom will freak, though."

She has good cause to worry. When we were little girls, Mom would always talk about the day when we would get married. "I promise, sweethearts, I will give you the prettiest wedding we can afford," she'd always say. I think at one point she told me that on the day they found out we were both girls, they started saving for our wedding days.

Mom was nothing if not a hopeless romantic.

"I don't think you should mention the word *backyard*," I say after chewing a bite of my amazing sandwich. "That might send her over the edge. At least you're looking for dresses. That might placate her a little bit."

"Well." Preslee shrugged. "My first stop was going to be one of those used bridal stores."

I swallow another bite. "Please make sure I am not there when you tell Mom that."

She laughs.

* * * * *

After we get a quick dinner at In-N-Out, Preslee leaves at seven to drive back to Waco. It's way early and I try to talk her into staying and watching a movie or something with me before she leaves.

"I have to get home and go to bed at a decent time," she says. "Wes wants to work on the house tomorrow morning."

"Like what time?"

Preslee sighs and rubs her forehead. "When Wes says morning, he means he's going to be there at five."

"A.M.?" I gasp. There have been precious few moments in my life when I've seen that number on the clock in the middle of the night. I believe the last time was during a bad bout of food poisoning over the summer.

I will not be eating at a certain deli here ever again.

Preslee nods. "He's a morning person." She says it in the same tone as saying that he has a collection of belly button lint.

I grin.

"Bye, Preslee."

"See you Sunday afternoon, Paige."

We decided over dinner that it would probably be best if she went to look for a wedding dress this weekend. We called Mom and she is going to pick up Preslee on her way up from Austin, and we'll go shopping here.

I think all of the customers at In-N-Out could hear the joy in Mom's voice when Preslee called her.

She grins and waves, then slides her glasses on her face and walks down my apartment steps.

I close the door, still smiling. Today was good for us. We have not done that enough.

I sit on my sofa and yawn, then consider turning on the TV for a few minutes before heading to an early bedtime. I want to read more in Ecclesiastes but at the moment, I kind of want cookies.

Maybe I could do both. I mean, if everything really is meaningless, what's a few extra calories?

Probably would be good if I didn't always use that logic. Oh, the examples of taking verses out of context.

I pull my mixing bowl out of the cabinet, and my phone buzzes on the counter in a text.

It's from Tyler.

HEY. HOPE YOU HAD A GOOD WEEK OFF.

It's like overflowing with sentiment. I just look at the text for about five minutes, conjuring up a MISSED YOU THIS WEEK or a THOUGHT ABOUT YOU OFTEN or even an exclamation point for goodness' sake, but nothing.

I finally write him back, pausing after typing every word.

THANKS. IT WAS A QUIET WEEK. HOPE YOU HAD A GOOD ONE AS WELL.

It's like we are business associates or something for the lack of affection in our communication.

Now I really need cookies.

I start dumping the ingredients in the bowl and plug in my beaters. I'm scraping the bowl, gnawing on my lip, and praying.

Seriously, Lord. What is really going on here? Tyler has never been like this before.

A big part of me is pretty convinced that it doesn't have anything to do with the hug from Luke at the beginning of the summer.

Something is wrong.

Chapter
6

Sunday morning and I am back at church. After being away for the entire week, it feels good to be back. Especially when I walk into the youth room and find a harried Rick trying to organize the band, type up the words to the songs for the projector, and greet the kids as they come in.

"Thank God you're back." Rick grabs my shoulders. "You can never have another week off again. You're a faster typist than I am. Can you get these songs in the computer? Brandon decided to use all new songs this week." He sends our lead guitarist the evil eye and Brandon grins and waves.

"Hey, Paige. Glad a civilized person has finally arrived."

I smile. There's something good about being needed.

I take the papers from Rick and start copying the lyrics into the computer. Our computer is old, old but instead of purchasing a new one or saving for a new one, Rick decided that the youth room needed an espresso machine.

I couldn't argue with his logic. Especially since the lady who used to make the good coffee in the church's welcome station moved.

Army wives. You should never get used to their amazing coffee. Unless you're married to one, I guess.

One of the high school girls already has the espresso machine whirring and hands Rick a latte in a girly mug.

He glares at her but drinks it anyway. "This would be a ten out of ten if you'd put it in a manly cup next time, Brittany."

Brittany grins. I smile. The kids love to pick on Rick.

Kids trickle in over the next fifteen minutes, and once the band starts playing the first worship song, the youth room is nearly at full capacity. I love seeing it like this, but I know the elder board at the church has concerns, especially since we just built a new youth room. We don't have the money to keep expanding the space.

"What we need," Rick told me one time, "is some of those old church pews."

"Why?" I made a face. Even the word *pew* just didn't sit right with me.

"So we could squish those kids in there. Have you seen how much space is left in the chair with some of these kids? I don't know what it is about this generation, maybe it's the skinny jeans, but I definitely filled out the chair better when I was in high school."

I just looked at my huge, barrel-chested, bald-headed boss and didn't comment for fear of losing my job.

Rick dims the lights now and the band really picks up the song while I flick through the lyrics slideshow. Doing this used to scare the daylights out of me, but now I could do it in my sleep. Or while drinking a delicious cinnamon latte, compliments of Brittany.

If that girl ever needs a reference for a job at Starbucks, she won't have to look far. Every other kid here is drinking her coffee, bobbing their heads, lifting their free hands, and singing along with Brandon and the keyboard player, Ashley.

After music, Rick teaches for about thirty minutes. Rick is a very dynamic speaker and the kids always eat it up. I love seeing the way they all seem like they really want to be here and not like they are being forced to come.

Jesus is working in this room and you can just feel it.

After Rick finishes, the band plays two more songs, and then we dismiss the kids. Most weeks, I go over to the main service, but today is dress-shopping day with Preslee and my mom and they will be here in less than an hour.

Apparently, someone was very excited for this day to finally be here. Mom texted me at six telling me she was already driving the hour to Preslee's house.

I am going to go out on a limb and guess that Preslee was probably less than thrilled that Mom showed up there at seven.

"Well, that's a wrap," Rick says, walking over, stretching his hands out in front of him, and cracking his knuckles loudly.

"Really? Really?" I ask because he knows that I absolutely cannot stand it when someone cracks his knuckles. It's the most awful sound in the whole history of audible noises.

Well. Maybe not the *whole* history. I once babysat this kid who dragged a plastic Lego giraffe's feet down a glass door.

Even the memory makes my back tense up.

"Aren't you glad to be back? Admit it. You missed me."

"Mm."

He nods. "Yep. She missed me. She missed me, ladies and gentlemen!" he announces to the room. Most of the kids are still here talking, laughing, drinking more lattes. There's a line forming in front of the espresso machine.

Poor Brittany needs a raise.

"Staff meeting, nine o'clock tomorrow morning," Rick says to me. "Be there or be in trouble."

"Yes sir."

"I have big news I want to run by you."

I stand there, waiting for him to run the news by me, but he just looks at me.

"Well?" I finally say.

"Well what?"

"You just said that you had big news to run by me. So. Run it."

He shrugs. "But it's one of my subpoints for the staff meeting. If I tell you now, I won't be able to cross it off during the meeting."

"Subpoints. Please, Rick. I've worked with you for the whole summer. You have never actually prepared for a staff meeting. And that's another thing. It's just you and me meeting. Why do you call them staff meetings?"

He shrugs. "Because we're staff?"

I hate talking to him. I rub my forehead. Brittany comes over and hands me a to-go cup that smells like cinnamon espresso heaven. "You look like you need this."

"Just because she rubbed her head? I rub my head all the time and you never bring me coffee," Rick protests.

"No, because she's talking to you. And you only rub your head to try to get the hair to grow back." Brittany grins as she walks back to the ever-popular espresso machine.

"Hey! This is by choice!" Rick yells after her, pointing to his shiny head.

I look at him while I sip my coffee.

"Choice," he says again, nodding to me.

"Sure, Rick. Whatever you say."

* * * * *

I end up meeting Mom and Preslee at a little breakfast place in town right about ten thirty. Preslee is apparently starving to death because Mom didn't let her eat breakfast.

"I gave you plenty of notice that I was on my way!" I could hear Mom in the background of Preslee's phone call. "You could have chosen to get up and taken your shower then instead of sleeping the day away!"

It brought back the olden days, listening to the two of them fight.

But even Mom couldn't say no to the draw of freshly brewed coffee and a cinnamon roll.

"I'm getting the farmer's omelet," Preslee announces after we've been there for a few minutes, then snaps her menu shut.

I smile at her. Preslee is the only person I know who would stuff herself with a gigantic omelet right before spending the day trying on wedding dresses. When it's my turn, I can guarantee I will be starving myself the entire morning so the dresses look smaller in the waist.

All these years of eating straight cookie dough are going to catch up to me eventually.

The thought of trying on wedding dresses myself someday just brings up thoughts about Tyler, and I try to wash them away with yet more coffee.

I will be buzzing this afternoon.

Mom decides on a cinnamon roll and a cup of fruit and sips her decaf, looking at both of her girls at the table and smiling to herself.

"What?" I ask, knowing what she's thinking but wanting to hear it.

"I just love this." She sighs. "I've missed this. The three musketeers."

I grin.

Preslee folds her napkin in her lap. "See? This wonderful, sappy moment would never have occurred if I hadn't just rolled over and gone back to sleep when you called this morning."

Mom rolls her eyes. "Preslee—" she starts but I cut her off.

"How about we talk about where we are going to be looking for dresses today?" I suggest, trying to start the day on a happy foot.

Mom grins. "Oh! I made a list!" She digs in her purse and pulls out a piece of notebook paper, then slides her bifocals on her nose.

"Well, I mean, *of course* we have to go to Walter Mayfield's boutique," she says.

"Who is Walter Mayfield?" Preslee and I both ask the question at the same time.

Mom just stares at us over her glasses. "You have to be kidding me. Walter Mayfield? The world-famous designer? He's up there with Vera Wang and he built a boutique right here in Dallas! Why do you think I wanted to drive all the way up here so badly?"

"I thought it was to see me," I say.

"Well, of course, precious, you were also part of the reason," Mom says dismissively.

"Mm-hmm."

"He makes wedding dresses for all kinds of celebrities. I saw a special about him on that Style network or whatever it's called."

Preslee opens her mouth and just the way she does it brings up all kinds of sisterly intuition, and I kick her ankle under the table and I talk instead. "Sounds great, Mom! Let's go there first."

"Yay!" Mom excuses herself to go to the restroom and Preslee just looks at me.

"Well, thanks for that."

"You know what, you should be thanking me," I say.

"Shabby chic. That's what I'm going for, if we have to do this wedding. Isn't like the definition of shabby a preowned dress?"

Well, she has me there.

Mom returns right as our food is put on the table and I dig into my French toast. French toast is always so perfect at this restaurant. I have tried to duplicate it a million times at home, and it always tastes terrible.

Kind of like baseball-park nacho cheese, I guess.

Mom smiles at me from across the table. "So I have some fun news for you girls. Guess who is going to be meeting us for dinner tonight?"

I try to think through everyone my parents know in Dallas. Layla's family used to live in Austin and moved up here, so Mom knows her parents. And a few random friends of mine from the years I've lived here.

"Who?" Preslee asks, digging into her enormous omelet.

"The men in our lives!" Mom is absolutely giddy.

I just look at her. "What men?"

"*The* men, Paige." Mom shakes her head. "Honestly, honey. Dad, Wes, Tyler? Remember all of them?"

Oh, this is not good.

So not only are things awkward between Tyler and me, now it gets to be awkward in front of my entire family, including my soon-to-be brother-in-law?

Lovely.

"Wait, why didn't Dad just drive up with us? And Wes, for that matter?" Preslee asks, ever the practical one.

"Dad has a meeting up here tomorrow morning, so I suggested that he just fly up tonight instead, and we can spend the night in a hotel. I'll just stay here and drive back down with him tomorrow night. So Wes is going to drive up and then drive you back home tonight because I know you guys have work tomorrow." She grins, obviously proud of her plan. "And I called Rick and got Tyler's number from him, and he's going to meet us at dinner tonight."

Swell.

I manage a smile I hope comes across as delighted and focus on my toast and bacon.

Meanwhile, though, there's this big wad in my stomach that is just hardening, like I accidentally swallowed a ball of Silly Putty.

Tyler. I mean, we've barely exchanged a sentence all week. I didn't even see him this morning because I left before second service and he never makes it there until ten minutes after the service starts.

Tonight is going to be interesting.

* * * * *

"Nope. No, too low cut," Mom says about fifty hours later about the six hundredth dress Preslee tried on.

Preslee lost interest long ago and sighs and slumps back into the closet of a dressing room to change into the next dress Mom picked out for her. Mom and I are sitting on the most uncomfortable couches on the earth in front of a three-way mirror that keeps informing me that my nose is not necessarily the length I would like it to be.

Like a quarter of an inch shorter. That's what I would prefer.

"Don't worry, Paige. We'll find the perfect one," Mom says, more to herself than to me, patting my leg.

"Mm," I say, trying not to yawn. It's already four o'clock. Preslee hasn't found a single dress she likes, and we are at our third bridal store.

In Preslee's defense, though, Mom has picked out every single one of her dresses. And while Mom's style sense is pretty good, Preslee tends to be a little more eclectic. Not so much sweetheart and a lot more punk.

I get up and start flipping through the dresses on one of the racks around the store. This whole place is surrounded by racks and racks of wedding gowns in garment bags. It's like the walls are made of plastic-wrapped marshmallows.

I stop at one and study it.

It's long but doesn't have a train. It's strapless and it has lace on the corseted top, but then it almost looks like the bottom of the dress is made out of feathers or something. It's about the opposite of a wedding dress that I would pick out for me, which probably means it's exactly the one Preslee would like.

I carry it over and knock on the dressing room door. "What about this one?" I ask the saleslady who is helping Preslee in and out of dresses.

The poor woman looks haggard from the search and nods. "Why not?"

Preslee emerges a minute later with the biggest smile I have seen on her face so far.

"Mom," she says, and in that one word is everything I know my mother ever hoped to hear her daughter say while trying on a wedding dress.

Mom is immediately crying, and I'm trying not to tear up as well.

The dress, which looked odd on the hanger, looks amazing on Preslee. The corset top hugs her tiny waist and spills into this huge skirt that has millions of tiny ruffles on it so the whole thing swirls and flutters and looks like a dress made of birds.

It's weird and it's unusual, but then, so is my sister.

They are a perfect match.

The lady who works here can clearly see she has just sold a dress, so she goes and finds a veil, and all three of us immediately start gagging the second it touches Preslee's head.

"Nope, oh no, definitely no," I repeat over and over again.

Mom is shaking her head slowly. I know she's seeing her dream of lifting her daughter's veil to kiss her cheek flying away like the proverbial birds who created Preslee's dress, but even she can tell the veil does not work.

And Preslee is adamant. "No veil," she declares and that's that.

We buy the dress, pick up a few different wedding magazines at the grocery store, and go directly to Starbucks to discuss all the options for a wedding hairstyle that does not include a veil.

"How about one of those French-twist things?" Mom suggests, flipping through a magazine while she drinks her tall decaf Americano.

All we need is some Italian ice, and Mom's got the makings of that country song.

Mom's officially on a new diet since Preslee's wedding is in only two months.

"Do you know how much the camera adds?" she griped on the phone the other day. "No more carbs for me. Or dairy. Or fats or sugar or cinnamon rolls."

I love how cinnamon rolls are their own food group for my mother.

When I was a little kid, Mom would bake homemade cinnamon rolls every Saturday morning. I would wake up to the smell of them and seriously, there is no better way to wake up.

"I don't think my nose is good for French twists," Preslee says, and Mom and I both immediately look at her nose.

She wrinkles it self-consciously. "It's big."

"It's not big. You're weird," I tell her.

"It's bigger than yours."

I just shake my head. "There's no way. Your nose is fine."

"Well. I don't really like French twists." And there is the real reason coming out, forget anything she said about her nose.

"What about a chignon?" I love saying that word because I feel all fancy-like. I sip my caramel macchiato and point to a picture of a rather depressed-looking bride in the magazine with the hairstyle. I don't understand why photographers always take pictures of these girls looking mad. Isn't it supposed to be the happiest day of your life?

Maybe that part isn't really true.

I look up at Mom. "Was your wedding day a good day?"

She frowns at me. "Of course. Should it have not been?"

"No, I just mean, all these girls look mad. Just wanted to make sure Preslee isn't walking into some kind of trap."

Mom starts laughing. "Oh, Paige. Yes. It was a wonderful day." Her eyes get all soft and faraway as she stares behind Preslee out the window. I've seen the pictures of my parents' wedding. It was classic eighties. Big, permed hair. Puffy sleeves on the wedding gown. My dad was rail thin back then and sported a black mustache.

"It was supposed to rain, you know," Mom says.

"On your wedding day?"

Mom nods at Preslee. "It was supposed to. I wanted an outdoor wedding so bad. They were not so common back then. My mother tried and tried to talk me out of it, but that's what I wanted so we planned one. She and I fought miserably over it. I found this beautiful gazebo and rented the space and had everything all lined up when the weather forecast changed to rain."

I don't remember seeing rain-soaked people in the wedding album, so I'm assuming they got the forecast wrong. "But it didn't," I say when Mom gets quiet again, lost in memories.

"It was the most beautiful sunny day," Mom says, all dreamy. For a romantic like my mother, her wedding day had to be like the pinnacle of her life.

Except for maybe planning Preslee's wedding now.

Preslee smiles at me. "Well. We have even tossed around the idea of doing the wedding in one of Wes's family friend's backyard. It's a big backyard but it will only hold so many people, which is fine by us. Honestly, we don't want a big wedding."

I watch to see how Mom takes this. She thinks about it, opens her mouth, and then closes it and nods, maybe remembering what she just said about her and my grandmother fighting over Mom's wedding.

Preslee grins triumphantly, and I just have to give props to my sister for her impeccable timing for once in her life.

Chapter
7

Monday morning and I'm right on time for our staff
meeting.

And Rick is nowhere to be found.

This is typical.

I walk into the empty youth office, flick on the lights,
and turn on the computer at Rick's desk, noticing a few new
pictures tacked to the corkboard in the office.

When Rick first took over as youth pastor, the first thing
he did was install this floor-to-ceiling corkboard that ran the
entire length of the wall. And he's been adding to it ever
since. There are pictures of kids when they were in junior
high who are now off at college, fun youth events that
happened over the years, graduation announcements, Bible
verses, postcards people have sent, cartoons kids have drawn,
everything. Rick even tacked the very first cup of coffee from
the new espresso machine on there.

I took it down right afterward, though. Goodness only
knows what would live in this office if it weren't for my

presence here. He's put up a few pictures from some of the recent events, but really only one stands out to me.

It's a picture of Tyler and me at the karaoke picnic. Tyler has me dipped down in our finale and his face is an inch away from mine, and we are both grinning into each other's eyes.

It was a happy moment in the midst of a bad summer.

I just stare at the picture, biting my lip. What can I do to fix what went wrong between us? I honestly don't think it has anything to do with Luke.

Tyler canceled on dinner last night. Said he was working on a deadline that was due this morning, and he still had a long time to go.

Mom spent dinner sighing over Preslee's beautiful wedding dress, so I don't think she minded too much.

I pull out my phone to text Tyler and Rick walks in right then. "Sorry I am late," he says, balancing a Thermos, a lunchbox, his keys, and a water bottle on top of a yellow legal pad. He slides everything onto his desk and holds up the pad to me. "Fully prepared, just like I said I'd be."

"I'm impressed." I roll my eyes and sit on the couch. I kick my flip-flops off and tuck my feet underneath me, crisscross style. I look at my phone.

I'll have to text him later.

"Okay." Rick sits in his desk chair and rolls over so he's across from me. "First up. How many girls are you meeting with this week?"

I dig my planner out of my purse on the couch beside me and flip to this week. "Eight," I tell him, counting up all the names. "With another four as potentials."

He nods. "Great. I'll reload your Visa card today. Okay.

We need to talk about the new curriculum for the youth nights. I just finished writing it, and I'd like you to read it before I print off the leader copies."

"I can do that. What is this one on again?"

"Sanctification," Rick says in a deep, booming voice.

I just look at him.

"No, really, Paige. It's about sanctification. I'm basically going through the fruits of the Spirit and how God uses them in the process of sanctification."

I have a love-hate relationship with how much I learn while teaching the girls. Sometimes I feel like Rick writes the lessons just for me.

"Sounds like a good series." I look at him. "What's the big news you mentioned on Sunday?"

"The curriculum."

"But I already knew you were writing new curriculum."

"Well, it obviously wasn't as big of news as I thought it was going to be," Rick says.

"What's the big news?" Natalie asks from the door, a drooling Claire on one hip. Natalie's holding a basket with muffins that are quickly filling the room with the smell of cinnamon and sugar.

"Hope I'm not interrupting." She grins and sets Claire on the couch next to me.

"We always welcome muffins and cute little dimples." I kiss Claire's chubby cheeks.

"Just not the carrier of said muffins and dimples?" Natalie rolls her eyes at me and nods to Rick's legal pad.

"How'd she take the new, organized Rick?" she asks him.

"Pretty good. I think she was a little surprised, but overall I think she is handling it well."

"Um, hello? I am sitting right here."

"What did I miss?" Natalie picks up Claire and sits where she was, plopping the baby in her lap. Claire coos at her mama and grabs two fistfuls of Natalie's hair.

"We are just starting," Rick tells her. Natalie comes to most of our staff meetings. She taught the senior girls' small group until she had Claire. I think she misses it.

She told me that when she's not nursing anymore, she's hoping to find a babysitter for Claire on youth nights and come back to join us.

As it is, I love Natalie like an older sister so any time I get to hang out with her is always welcome.

We spend the next hour talking about the kids, about specific prayer requests they have, and family issues that have come up with some of them. Then we spend time praying.

I love this part of my job.

"So. Let's look ahead here." Rick uncaps a pen with his teeth and pulls over a giant wall calendar he got for free from his dentist. It has all these pictures of fake-looking waterfalls with inspirational messages scrolling across the bottom of the pages.

It's never too late to fulfill your dreams.

I have to argue with that one. It is way too late for me to fulfill my childhood dream of being on the United States gymnastics team. For several reasons, but the first being that I am no longer fourteen years old, and the second being that if I was any less flexible, I wouldn't be able to climb into a car.

"Okay. We're in the first week of September. Our first Wednesday night youth group is this week," Rick says.

"There will be a leaders' meeting fifteen minutes before the kids get there."

"Y'all need a name." Natalie hands Claire a slice of apple in a little net thing with a plastic handle. It looks like something my sister used to use to fish her dead guppies out of her fish tank. Natalie notices my look and grins. "Isn't this the coolest thing? Claire can chew on the apple, which soothes her gums, without getting any seeds or big pieces she can't swallow yet."

Claire is going at it like the thing will eat her back if she doesn't get it first, so I keep my mouth shut about the guppies.

"A name for what?" Rick asks.

"For youth group. I mean, *youth group*. Does anyone still call it that? It's so nineties, hon."

Rick frowns at her. "Adolescent collection?"

She rolls her eyes. "No, like a name. Like Wildfire or Fishermen or something that has some meaning to it but is all cool and hip. Pretty much whatever sounds the least like you."

Rick is offended. "Hey! I am cool and hip."

"Sweetheart. You're not."

There are times when our meetings start to get a little uncomfortable for me. This is one of those times.

Rick looks at me. "Do you think I'm cool and hip?"

I look at Natalie, who is shaking her head at me, then back to Rick, who looks all fake wounded. "Uh . . ."

"Babe," Natalie cuts in. "If you have to ask, you probably aren't."

"Well, that's sad. Guess we can't count on Nike calling me and asking me to be their new model anymore then." He sighs at Claire and chucks her cheek. "No college for you, honey love."

Natalie just rolls her eyes.

* * * * *

I spend the afternoon meeting three girls and I get home about eight. I took the last girl to dinner at In-N-Out.

I really need to find healthier options for meeting with people.

I change into workout pants and an old T-shirt that says *Be Safe. Always Watch for Falling Anvils.* It has a picture of the ill-fated coyote on it with an anvil seconds away from connecting with his head. Dad gave it to me in high school.

Which really should just illustrate my need to clean out my closet at some point.

I grab a water bottle, fill it up, and open my front door to head down to the apartment gym.

Tyler is standing on my porch, hand ready to knock on my now-open door.

"Oh, were you going somewhere?" He looks flustered. "Oh, that's fine. We'll just try to get together some other time."

He turns and starts racing down my steps.

"Wait, Tyler!" I follow him. He stops at the bottom of my stairs and I stand on the last one, crossing my arms over my chest. "I don't have to go right now. I don't have to go at all. I was just going to use the elliptical. I had three Frappuccinos and In-N-Out today. I felt a need."

He smiles, but it isn't really a smile.

"What's going on?" I ask him quietly.

He looks at me and opens his mouth but closes it again and shakes his head. He squints into the sun. He's obviously come right from work. He's wearing khakis and a button-down shirt and his curly hair is revolting against the combing that obviously occurred this morning. "Another time." He finally looks at me, the blue sky and his blue shirt making his eyes even bluer than they really are. "Have a good workout."

He turns and heads back to his truck, waving once as he slides into the driver's seat.

At least I now have fuel to work out, I guess.

I walk down to the gym, getting more and more depressed the farther away from my apartment I get. What is going on? This isn't like Tyler. Tyler is funny. He's direct. He doesn't mince words. He doesn't stop short of saying something just because it might be uncomfortable to hear.

This is really weird.

I climb on the empty elliptical and look around. There's a man I used to see in here a lot on the treadmill, and some-one else is using the weight machine. No one appears to be watching the TV, which is tuned to some talk show with some obnoxious women fighting over who had the best hair at the Emmys this year.

"Would you mind if I changed the channel?" I ask them. The man using the weights has headphones in and doesn't respond, but the man on the treadmill pulls an earbud out and says, "For the love of all things sane, *please*."

All righty then.

I flip it to HGTV and *Kitchen Cousins* is on. I glance at the treadmill man and he nods his approval.

I watch the two attractive men demolish an awful, outdated kitchen and rebuild in its place a beautiful one that's all white and stainless steel and shiny for a single mom who just lost her job.

The Kitchen Cousins are attractive and nice. No wonder they are a hit show.

I head back to my apartment about nine o'clock, take a shower, and climb into bed. I look at my Bible lying on the nightstand next to me.

Tonight is a good "everything is meaningless" night.

Maybe Ecclesiastes is not the best book to read right now.

I sigh and open my Bible to Solomon's depressing tale and find where I left off. *"There is nothing better for a man than to eat and drink and tell himself that his labor is good. This also I have seen that it is from the hand of God. For who can eat and who can have enjoyment without Him?"*

I stare at the passage for a long time. What did that even mean? That our labor wasn't really good? That we should just eat, drink, and be merry like the Pirates of the Caribbean?

And the part about not enjoying anything outside of God . . . I think about all the people I knew in high school and college and even now who are definitely not Christians and seem to have such amazing lives. I just saw on Facebook that one of the girls I knew in high school just got married, and she has about the cutest two-year-old I've ever seen. She did things backward and totally without God, and she still seems to be completely happy.

I close my Bible and purse my lips. "Well, Lord, that was not very helpful for tonight. I need to know what to do about Tyler. I need to know how to act forgiving toward Luke without acting like I like him, and I need to know how to be a good maid of honor in two weddings, which granted, is going to include eating and drinking, but hopefully no labor since I will be wearing high heels. So. What should I read next?"

I listen, but there's no voice telling me anything back. I flip through the pages of my Bible, but nothing jumps out at me. I rub my fingers over the front of it and bite back a sigh.

* * * * *

It's Wednesday night and I just got back to the church after ducking out to grab a quick sandwich and cookie at Paradise Bakery for dinner. Our leaders' meeting starts in ten minutes, and I'm gathering all the copies of the new curriculum for the leaders. I spent most of yesterday reading through it.

It's good. I'm not looking forward to teaching it because it was also convicting. The whole thing was about how the fruit of the Spirit can't be learned like a math equation. It has to be given from the Lord. Our job is to focus on our relationship with Him and the fruits will come.

Rick needs to start publishing this stuff.

I walk into the youth room and a few of the leaders are already here. All the volunteer leaders have come back from last year, which is great and pretty unheard of in youth ministry.

Trisha leads the junior girls, and she pulled in the senior girls last year when Natalie got close to her due date to make it just one big class.

Sam is the leader of the junior and senior guys along with Rick. Sam is about thirty-five and has twin girls. He says he does this to get his testosterone fix.

Julie and Trevor are married and they have the sopho-
more guys and girls. They're going on like six years of
marriage, but they are the most nauseating couple to be
around as far as physical affection goes. Particularly if you
are having issues with your current relationship.

And speaking of Tyler, he teaches the freshmen guys.
And I lead the freshmen girls. And that's the staff.

Trisha, who is always notoriously early, is already in the
youth room. She's a legal assistant for some big lawyer in
town, and she always comes straight from work so she always
looks all dressed up. I used to dress up for work.

Now I feel like I'm doing well if I manage something
beyond jeans and a T-shirt. It's hard to dress nice when:
(a) I know whatever girl I'm meeting at In-N-Out will be
wearing shorts and a tank top, and (b) it's In-N-Out for
goodness' sake.

"Hey, Paige." Trisha smiles at me. "How's it going?"

"Fine." I lie like I always do when someone who isn't
Layla or Natalie asks me that question.

"Good!"

I hand her a copy of the curriculum. "I think we'll be
starting next week."

She nods and starts reading through it while the rest of
the leaders trickle in. Rick and I set up a little circle of chairs
and everyone sits down. Tyler comes running in at ten
minutes past when we started.

Typical.

He does not look good. Normally Rick rides him about
being late, but one look at his face and Rick keeps his mouth
shut. "So, guys, tonight is all about welcoming the kids back
to Bible study. Spend time hearing how their summers went,

how everyone is doing, and I'd like y'all to spend a fair amount of time praying in your small groups."

Rick looks around the circle. "Paige handed out the new curriculum, so if you guys could just prepare the first lesson for next week, I think we'll be good. I'll be teaching through the intro tonight during the big group time."

Everyone is nodding like bobblehead dolls. I pass a curriculum to Julie and she hands it to Trevor who passes it to Tyler.

I try not to look at Tyler, but I can't help it. I sneak a peek while Rick is talking and he's staring at me.

Tyler looks like he hasn't slept in days. His curly hair is all messed up, like he's been raking his hands through it all day. His eyes are bloodshot, and instead of his usual clean-shaven face, a fine coating of blond bristles covers his chin.

He manages a sad tilt to his mouth at me.

"And I think that's it," Rick says, and I break eye contact with Tyler to pay attention to what Rick is saying. "Let's pray and go mingle."

Rick prays a short prayer, and we all stack our chairs and head for the door to visit with the kids congregating in the hallway.

"Tyler? Hang back for a sec," Rick says as we all leave. I glance back at them, and Rick nods for me to close the door behind me.

I bite my lip.

Something is bothering Tyler. And I don't know what to do about it. I really like the guy. I care about him. So does that mean I press him for information about what's going on? Or do I hang back like I've been doing, waiting for him to come to me?

I hate seeing him like this.

"Paige!" A few of my girls who are now in Julie's class come running over, hugging me and chattering excitedly about their summers. I try the best I can to push thoughts of Tyler to the background so I can be happy and cheerful for the girls.

My job is hard sometimes.

* * * * *

I have the new freshmen girls, so I spend most of my small-group time getting to know them. I've already taken a few out for coffee. I've got about six more to go before I've met at least once with the whole group, though.

After I dismiss everyone to go back to the youth room for snacks, I pull a couple of them aside and line up dates for next week.

One girl in particular, Emmy, who is about the smallest ninth-grader I've ever met, seems surprised. "What are we going to do at Starbucks?" she asks me, warily.

"Just talk. Hang out. I want to get to know you better," I tell her, trying to suppress a smile.

"Um. Well, I'll have to talk with my mom about it."

I nod. "Please talk with your mom about it. I can even talk with your mom if you'd like."

"That would probably be good."

We join the rest of the girls in the big room. Over the next few minutes, the other small groups let out, and the youth room gets louder and louder as kids stuff their faces with Oreos and Nutter Butters and laugh about what they did this summer.

Tyler's acne-stricken guys are in the room, but Tyler is nowhere to be seen. I'm trying to subtly look for him when someone stops behind my right shoulder.

"I sent him home early," Rick says.

"What? Who?"

He rolls his eyes at me. "Sure."

I bite my lip, feeling a sinking deep in my stomach. "Rick . . . is he . . . okay?" I try not to overstep into the bounds of pastor-parishioner or pastor-volunteer confidentiality.

If there even is such a thing.

Rick looks at me for a minute and then nods. "He'll be okay."

"Is it me?" The dreaded question. I can barely get it out it's so awful to even think about, and now I'm afraid that Rick didn't even hear it because I asked it so quietly and not in his direction. I'm mashing the corners of my eyes with my thumbs so the tears don't start.

Rick, who is never gentle, puts a kind hand on my shoulder and smiles in a way I would imagine an older, wiser brother would to a silly question I asked.

"Normally I would say that I can't divulge any information to you," Rick says quietly. "But he told me I could reassure you because I made sure he knew that you were worried about him. And no, Paige. It's not you."

That makes me feel better and worse. Rick moves on to talk to some of the new ninth graders, and I pick up a tasteless Nutter Butter and start chewing it, just for something to do.

I'm glad it's not me and what happened with Luke.

I think.

That, at least, is a problem I could fix.

Chapter
8

"Well, someone has to tell him!"

I am rubbing both of my temples as I watch Layla pace my living room Thursday night. She is mad and I'm pretty sure everyone in my apartment complex knows it.

It's always interesting to see Layla mad because her cuteness level doesn't change. Layla is one of those favored people who can get so steaming mad and still look adorable. Her wavy brown hair is bouncing as she charges back and forth across my floor, her skirt flying.

I still am not completely sure what happened. I was sitting here, having a perfectly quiet dinner of mac and cheese I picked up at Panera when I met one of the girls there today for tea and scones. I thought ahead and remembered I had no groceries at home. I am still a little proud of myself for that.

Normally, I will meet with a girl for an hour right when she gets out of school, meet another girl the hour after that, and then go home and suddenly remember I have nothing edible in the house since I haven't been to the grocery store in a month.

Not from lack of opportunity but from lack of motivation. The older I get, the more I hate buying food.

And since it's just me here, I've decided that half the time, it's cheaper for me to just get something to go. Or I take someone to lunch and bring back half of it for dinner.

Layla glares at me as she paces. "I don't see how you can just sit there and eat after hearing what happened!"

And there's my opening. "What exactly happened again?" I ask timidly, afraid of the giant alien that has taken over Layla's body suit.

"What happened? What *happened*? I'll tell you what happened! Peter went and bought a KONG for Belle! And then he put peanut butter in it and left it there for her and I just found it when I got home from work along with a barely breathing dog and a carpet of ants that covers my entire floor!"

Ah, Belle. The world's ugliest dog. "Why wasn't she breathing?"

"Because, Paige," Layla says in a *duh* voice, "she is allergic to peanuts. She nearly died. I just spent nine hundred dollars getting the vet to bring her back to life, and Peter just asked me why I paid that much."

Based on her tone of voice, I can see that question did not turn out well for Peter.

Poor guy. He didn't have a chance. You don't mess with a woman planning a wedding for 250 people.

"In his defense—" I start, but I am immediately cut off.

"*Defense!*"

"In his defense," I say again, louder. "Peter most likely did not know that Belle was allergic to peanut butter. He was probably trying to be nice to the dog."

That stops her pacing. She freezes halfway in the middle of my living room. "You think he didn't know?" she asks in a small voice.

"If he did know, why would he give it to her? Unless he doesn't like Belle, but even then, there are quicker ways to get rid of a dog."

When I was a little kid, we lived next to these people who had this mastiff who would bark at the top of its very large lungs every single morning at five thirty. Every morning. Without fail.

Until one day. And then the next and the next. Dad saw our neighbor getting his mail a week later and asked about the dog, and our neighbor told him that his wife had gone all postal because the dog kept waking up their toddler every morning. He came home from work one day, and the lady had given him away at the grocery store.

Yep. The grocery store.

Needless to say, there was much toasting with our milk that night in our neighbor's wife's honor in my house.

Layla's face is slowly crumpling and I know what's coming. My mac and cheese is apparently going to need to be reheated a second time. I stand up right as she collapses in tears on my couch.

"I am the most awful fiancée on the history of the whole earth!"

I don't correct her bad grammar. I just walk over, sit next to her, and sigh, rubbing her arm. "You aren't the most awful. You're better than that lady in McKinney who killed her fiancé last month and left him in their apartment swimming pool."

Layla covers her face with a pillow. "Ack, Paige! Why do

you tell me these things? I'm never swimming in a public pool again."

I smile. "Look, have you eaten dinner?"

She shakes her head, mascara tracing black lines down her face.

"Okay, good. *Leave*. Redo your makeup. Go to Peter's apartment. Ask him to go get Chinese and you can apologize. The dog is fine. You're five weeks away from your wedding. Go and be romantic again. Like the olden days."

Layla nods through my whole speech, snorting and snuffling like an elephant in need of some Claritin.

If this is any indication of what engagement is like, I am in no hurry to experience it.

She hugs me. "Okay." She stands. "I love you, Paige. I don't know where I would be without you."

"Probably trying to drag Peter's body down to your apartment swimming pool."

She throws the couch pillow at my head.

* * * * *

I'm just leaving the church after spending the entire day doing the absolute worst part of my job.

Designing and mailing postcards for youth events.

Rick came in this morning, handed me a chicken-scratched paper with all of the dates and names of future events on it, and asked me to please go ahead and make up postcards for the next eight events so we don't have the mad rush two weeks before like we usually do.

"And what do you think of gasoline?" he asked.

"I'm a fan of it in my car. Probably wouldn't be as big of

a fan of it dousing my apartment," I told him.

He rolled his eyes. "No. Like, welcome to Gasoline Ministries!"

I tried to think of the nicest way to say it. "It sounds like you're starting a ministry to those poor guys who were hosing off with gasoline in *Zoolander*."

Rick just looked at me for a minute. "I cannot believe," he said slowly, "that you not only have watched that movie, but that you just referenced it to me. Your stock in youth ministry just went up significantly." He bowed from the waist, eyes closed and arms outstretched.

I'm feeling like that wasn't a big compliment.

My girl I was supposed to meet this afternoon, Brittany of the espresso machine fame, just came down with the stomach flu this morning, so we have officially canceled our meeting at Starbucks. I never found another girl to meet after Brittany, so I'm officially free for the evening.

I am twenty-three, I have a boyfriend, and I am still free on a Friday night.

It does not get more pathetic than that, ladies and gentlemen.

I drive to the grocery store and spend thirty minutes gathering all the things that show I am definitely single and not wanting to cook for just one person. I'm passing women with kids clawing at them, pushing carts filled with bags of frozen chicken breasts, heads of lettuce, and blocks of cheese. And meanwhile, I've got three Lunchables, two boxes of Cinnamon Toast Crunch, and a couple bags of prepacked salad mixes.

Single life equals gourmet eating.

I check out, load my groceries in the back of my Camry, and drive to my apartment. I do my usual trick of sliding all of the bags over my arms so I only have to make one trip up my stairs.

And that's when I see him.

He's sitting on the bottom step of my stairs. His hair is curly extra today and he's wearing straight-cut jeans and a polo shirt. He's squinting into the sun and apparently hasn't seen me yet.

He looks so sad.

My heart drops into my toes, and I'm suddenly wishing I didn't just wear my usual jeans and a T-shirt today. If you're going to be dumped, you should at least make the guy pause long enough to wonder if he'll regret it. My thoughts, anyway.

I take a deep breath and say the fastest prayer of my whole life. *Lord, please help.*

Then I muster whatever courage I can get from the depths of my intestines and keep walking.

He finally sees me when I get about two yards away. He hops off the step. "Oh! Hi, Paige."

"Hey, Tyler." I clear my throat. "Have you . . . uh, been waiting long?"

"No, no, no, no, no." Tyler shakes his head. "Just a few minutes, actually. Here, um, let me help you." He takes all of the grocery bags and lets me walk up the stairs empty-handed.

"Thanks." I unlock my door and let him in.

He sets all the bags on the kitchen counter and then scoots quickly around me, standing awkwardly by the high counter that splits the living room and the kitchen. He's quiet while I start unloading the groceries into the fridge and pantry.

"So," I say, mentally thumbing through every possible topic we could talk about. "How is work?"

Well. That was a lame one to end up on.

He lets this little tiny breath out like he knows this is terribly awkward, and I'm just waiting for his "Sorry, Paige, but obviously this hasn't been working for a while and I think it's best if we just go back to being friends" speech.

Like that ever happens.

I have never personally known anyone who has dated someone and then remained friends after they broke up.

"It's fine," Tyler says in response to my question. "It's finally slowing down. I just finished the last of my big proposals that were due this afternoon, actually."

"Oh good."

And there is our conversation. This is like talking to Peter.

No, strike that. At least when I'm attempting a conversation with Layla's fiancé, I'm not fighting off tears or feeling like I might throw up the huge knot in my stomach.

Tyler watches as I put away the groceries. I shove the carton of milk in the fridge and shut it, and that's when he pipes up.

"Want to go for a walk?"

Yep, I should just go ahead and change into my post-breakup sweats and start mixing the cookie dough. We have never gone for a walk before. Maybe if this was a normal thing, I wouldn't worry, but let's face it. We aren't Anne of Green Gables and Gilbert. People don't just take walks nowadays.

Unless they want to break up with someone, not in that person's apartment.

I swallow. I might as well get this over with. I've been waiting for it all summer.

"Sure," I say in the tiniest voice possible, but it's the best I can manage.

"We can walk around Stonebriar."

I just look at him. "The mall?" I double-check because this is Tyler I'm talking to. The man avoids malls like I avoid jack-in-the-boxes.

Those things will give me a heart attack someday.

"It's hot," he offers.

He is right. When I got home, the temperature gauge on my car dashboard said ninety degrees, and the weatherman mentioned last night that it was likely going to be upper nineties humidity today.

It's not the best day to be outside. Walking.

But in outside's favor, at least Tyler wouldn't necessarily be able to tell whether I was crying or sweating when he breaks up with me.

I nod, grab my purse, and follow him out the door, down the steps, and over to his truck. I kind of want to offer to drive myself so at least we don't have the courtesy ride back home that will be awkward after he says his piece, but I bite my lip and climb into the passenger seat.

We drive to the mall in total silence.

Almost total silence. I guess he did ask me if I minded if he turned up the music.

We get to the mall, walk inside, and the relief from the humidity is immediate. Stonebriar, for a Friday night, is fairly empty. We walk through a pet shop and look at all the puppies for sale that will not be coming home with me, then we glance in the windows through the rest of the stores.

All in silence.

I'm racking my brain, trying to come up with something to say because he obviously is putting off the inevitable. I kind of want him to just say it so I can leave this place, go home, and watch HGTV while I cry into a bowl of cookie dough.

"So." I finally come up with something to talk about. "Tell me about Stefanie's baby." Stefanie is Tyler's younger sister who just had her first child. A little boy, if I remember right.

"He's really, *really* cute." Tyler manages the smallest of smiles. "I mean, I figured he would be because Stef and Mason are both pretty attractive, but seriously, he's definitely the cutest baby I've ever seen."

"How many babies have you seen?"

He pauses, eyebrows knitting together as he thinks. "Unimportant," he finally says.

I wish I felt like laughing.

We are passing a little area squared off with a love seat and two chairs. It's an advertisement for some furniture store near the mall, but I imagine it's usually populated with poor men dragged here by their wives and girlfriends. Tyler stops suddenly and nods to the love seat. "Do you mind?"

I follow him over to the white leather love seat and sit down, fighting the urge to just keep walking and leave. The couch is comfy, but not as comfy as the couches I already own. And my couches were free.

Well, for me. Not for my grandmother forty years ago.

Maybe I should be in the market for some new furniture.

I'm trying to distract myself and it's not working. Tyler looks awful. He's sitting there, hands clasped tightly together between his knees, biting his lip. His eyes are raw.

"Thinking of buying a couch?" I ask Tyler because he still isn't saying anything. I've only been to his apartment once, and it's about as opposite of mine as you can get. While I tried to go for a homey feeling—adding pictures, staging the furniture, setting out a welcome mat and a wreath—Tyler's house is basically bare. He's got one very old black couch, and it's plopped right in the middle of the room in front of the TV, which is sitting on an upside-down neon-orange eighteen-gallon plastic tub. And that's it for living room furniture. No coffee table, no end tables, no bookshelves. Nothing.

It's no wonder he enjoys being at my apartment more.

He looks over at me. "Why would I be looking for furniture? I'm good."

"Oh."

"You think I need new furniture?"

"New implies that you started with some old stuff," I tell him.

"I have a couch."

"Right. And?"

"And a TV."

I nod. "Okay. And?"

"And what else do I need?"

Men. I give up and lean back against the couch, crossing my arms over my chest so my hands won't shake so badly when he tells me the news.

Just say it, Tyler.

"I wonder what happens to couches after they are display pieces?"

I try to think about that, watching a couple walk by pushing a very new baby in a stroller.

Paige Turned   111

I remember my mom telling me that the only place she went for weeks after I was born was to the mall to push me around in the stroller. "It was that or sit at home and sob," Mom always said.

My birth was apparently not a happy occasion.

"We need to talk," Tyler suddenly says.

I look at him and his expression makes everything in my chest go very still. Here we go. I can't even answer him. I just try to force my head to nod.

He leans his elbows on his knees and looks at his hands. "Paige." He glances over at me. "I'm . . . well, there's something I've never told you about myself."

A million thoughts go through my head at once as I watch him nervously pick at a hangnail, his expression sad and serious: He doesn't really like me after all. He's got a prison record. He's not really a computer-software engineer. He's an operative for the CIA and he's fallen in love with Sydney Bristow. He's a recovering addict. He was formerly a female.

I look at him again and give my head a slight shake, scratching that last one. I've seen all the extreme makeover shows on TV, and they don't ever make people look quite as good as Tyler does.

He clears his throat. "I didn't become a Christian until college." He talks so quietly I have trouble hearing what he's saying with the loud ambient noise in the mall, so I lean a little closer to him.

"I didn't . . . I wasn't raised to . . ." He sighs and rakes a hand through his curly blond hair. "I made mistakes." He finally looks me in the eyes. His blue eyes are big, tortured. "Big ones. Particularly in the area of relationships." He drops his gaze to his hands again.

He looks so broken that my heart immediately aches for him. I want to reach out for his hand, but I don't know if I should. So I sit quietly beside him and weave my hands together between my knees.

He finally continues after what feels like hours but is likely closer to minutes. "I just . . . I've felt like I've been living a lie with you. Always encouraging you to be honest and do the right thing, meanwhile I haven't told you about my past. That's probably partly why this" — he waves his hand between us — "has been so stiff lately. And I'm sorry." He doesn't look at me. "I'm sure you've wondered why I've taken things so slow, and honestly, Paige, it's because you're the first girl I've dated since I became a Christian."

Tyler is twenty-five years old. He hasn't dated anyone in five years?

He rubs the back of his neck. "I've been so worried about screwing up, losing control again. And I could never . . ." He looks up, straight into my eyes. "I could never forgive myself if it happened with you."

He drops his head back down, staring at his hands again, apparently done talking.

I sit there quietly. I look at him. I look at the people casually walking past. I watch the overly pierced vendor selling hats shaped like animals and then look back to Tyler. I think. And I pray.

He didn't break up with me. Or at least, he hasn't yet. I hold my hands together tightly.

Oh Lord, what do I say? This isn't a small deal.

I'm thinking through the particulars, trying to formulate a response that doesn't sound trite and doesn't start with,

"Why have you dragged this on all summer?" because obviously this is hard for him.

And I pray some more.

Tyler is working the inside of his cheek in between his molars, and I worry about nerve damage there for him.

What do I say, God?

Nothing falls out of the sky with a message. No one taps me on the shoulder and tells me what I should say. The pierced vendor never flashes a reference made out of studs to me.

But the verse I shared with Tori several weeks ago comes back to my mind.

"When You said, 'Seek my face,' my heart said to You, 'Your face, O Lord, I shall seek.'"

Perhaps there was my answer.

I reach for his hand and he latches on to mine, looking up at me, his expression tormented.

"Thank you for telling me," I say quietly. "And for the most part, I have appreciated you taking this slowly. I haven't really been a fan of these last eight weeks . . ."

He huffs a half laugh, half exhale.

"But Tyler, as far as your concerns about making the same mistake with me, I think you're forgetting something very important."

His blue eyes are studying mine and I squeeze his rough hand. "You're in Christ now," I tell him. Quietly but firmly.

He blinks and all of a sudden, this strong, big-shouldered man who has always made me laugh and forced me to think has tears swimming in his eyes.

Chapter
9

I t doesn't look like I will be getting a restful night of sleep tonight.

I start like I always do when I fall asleep — lying on my left side, hands under the pillow. Then I switch to my right side. Then I try my stomach. Then I roll to my back and squinch my eyes shut, trying to tell my brain that it's time to turn off and go to sleep.

I keep replaying Tyler's speech. Keep seeing the tears that made his eyes seem even bluer. Keep feeling the way he held my hand like he was worried I was going to change my mind and leave.

Ironic when you consider the way I thought the conversation was going to go.

When he walked me to my door tonight, there wasn't any weirdness left on his part. I gave him a hug. He kissed my cheek and then left, promising to come by tomorrow since I pretty much had the weekend off, except for Sunday school with the youth.

Now, though, the doubts are poking at my brain until

I finally throw the covers off and grasp around in the dark for my robe.

I stumble out to the kitchen, put some water in my teakettle, and light the stove under it. Then I go sit at the table and wait for the water to boil.

On the one hand, a part of my brain always kind of guessed this about Tyler. After all, he didn't come to Christ until college, and someone who is that cute was most likely not lacking in female attention growing up.

Maybe there's just a difference between guessing and knowing.

The teakettle starts whistling and I pour the water over a decaf Earl Grey tea bag, watching the amber liquid seep out of the bag and into my cup. I look up at the clock on my microwave. It's nearly one in the morning.

Preslee was always kind of a night owl. She might still be up. And if she's not, hopefully her phone is on silent.

I find my phone and press the Call button before I can change my mind.

A minute later, she answers. "Hi, sis."

For whatever reason, I just need to talk to my sister right now. I settle in the upholstered rocking chair in my living room, tucking my feet up underneath me, cradling the tea on my knee.

"Hey, Pres." Sometimes it still amazes me that I can actually pick up the phone and call her.

Preslee has had a long past for being only twenty-one years old.

"It's late," she says. "Aren't you usually asleep by ten?"

"Eleven."

"Oh yes. Very late." I can hear the smile in her voice.

"Did I wake you up?" I ask her.

"Nope. I was just sitting here working on the wedding budget while watching *My Fair Wedding*."

"Getting ideas?"

"Gosh no. If I had the wedding budget he has, I would elope and use the money to gut the kitchen in my house. What's up? I'm sure you didn't just call to see what I was up to at one in the morning."

I bite my lip, wanting to ask her a question but not wanting to share Tyler's confession without his permission. I rephrase the question eight times before I finally ask it. "So, when you and Wes were dating . . ." I start and then I stop again.

I should just forget about it and hang up.

"Yeah?"

"Never mind. I don't know what I was about to ask."

"Something about me and Wes dating? Did you want to know how long? The ratio of dates to nights of the week? When was the first time we went clothes shopping together for him?"

I laugh. "No. I just was wondering when you finally told him . . . everything." My voice falls flat on the last word, and I know that Preslee knows my real question.

Preslee did not become a Christian until she was nineteen years old. And considering the moral, Christian home we were raised in, Preslee went about as far opposite of that as she could go.

"Ah. You mean like the substance abuse and the sexual sin?"

Preslee is not one to mince words or beat around bushes.

"Um. Yeah," I mumble. Meanwhile, I'm all for mincing and foliage.

"Well, remember that Wes was in the room when I shared my testimony with the youth group at the church I was going to," Preslee said. "And I didn't really leave anything out. I mean, I didn't go into graphic details, but I also didn't portray it as all rosy and pretty. So he knew a lot before he even asked me out. Then I just shared details as we got closer. Some I have never shared with him just because, and Wes agrees with this. There are some things that just don't benefit him to know. I truly believe I am a new creation. The old is gone. And Wes is completely in agreement with that too. That's not to say he doesn't struggle with it sometimes, but in premarital counseling, we've been learning that he has to forgive me just like I have to forgive myself. Jesus is bigger than my sins."

I'm nodding in the dark through this whole speech, even though I'm on the phone and she can't see me.

"Paige," Preslee says, her voice gentling. "What is this about?"

"Oh, nothing. I was just thinking about it."

She's quiet for a long moment. "It's good talking to you like this."

"Yeah."

"How are things? Are you still crazy with work?"

"It's starting to slow down."

"Good," Preslee says. "You are too busy. When can I see you again?"

"What are you doing on Sunday?"

"Nothing after church. I'm volunteering in the nursery, though, so if we do something I will likely smell like spit-up."

"That's okay." I used to smell like two-year-olds on Sunday, but when I took the intern job I had to quit so I could be in the youth room every Sunday.

There are days where the differences between the two classes are very, very few.

"Great. Want to meet at that Dairy Queen again?" I ask her. One of the first few times we met at the beginning of the summer when we were finally getting our relationship back on track, we met at a Dairy Queen about halfway between Dallas and Waco. We ended up sitting there for two hours talking on the most uncomfortable bench I have ever sat on. By the time we left, my butt was completely numb.

"Not really," she says. "I have like a once-every-three-years policy when it comes to Dairy Queen."

"Well, our options aren't very good unless you want to drive all the way here again or I can drive there." I don't really want to drive all the way to Waco, but I could. Plus then I could see all the improvements Wes has been making to the money pit of a house they bought at the beginning of the summer.

I am a new house kind of a person. I don't buy into any of this character crap. To me, a house exists to provide shelter and conveniences with zero to little upkeep.

"I can come back there. I think I'm going to register in Dallas since y'all actually have a Crate & Barrel. If I drive up right after church, I could be there by lunch. Want to have lunch with me and then help me register?"

"Register what?"

"Stuff. For the wedding? Dishes? Appliances? Stuff like that?"

"Oh. Right." It was too late for me to still be awake. "I need to go to bed."

"Yes, you do. I'll text when I'm leaving on Sunday. Have a good night, Paige!"

"Night, Preslee."

I hang up, set my empty cup in the sink, trudge to the bedroom, and I'm out within seconds.

* * * * *

I wake up at eight o'clock to my phone buzzing with a text.

MY MOTHER RAISED ME TO BE COURTEOUS. YOU WILL BE HAVING COMPANY IN 30 MINUTES, SO CONSIDER THIS YOUR WARNING. ☺

It's from Tyler.

I roll off the bed and stumble to the bathroom, gripping the countertop as I squint blearily at the mirror. I'm hoping it is just the sleep in my eyes making me look that bad. Otherwise, Tyler should have given me way more than thirty minutes to get myself presentable. My head pounds and I immediately blame my less than eight hours of sleep. I cannot function on little sleep. I've never been able to. Preslee stole all those genes from me.

I will be a terrible mother of a newborn.

I start by brushing my teeth while I turn on the water for the shower to warm up, then try to lather up as quickly as humanly possible while still giving myself some time to wake up.

Forget courtesy. "A rushed shower equals a crappy day." That's what my mother taught me. And she's right.

I hop out, dry off, run for some clothes, and end up picking skinny jeans, a button-down red camp shirt, and gray flats.

I'm blow-drying my hair when I start to worry about the outfit, per my usual ways. Do gray and red even go together?

If I switch to my red flats, is that too much red? Are camp shirts and skinny jeans even in style still?

All of the sad issues that come with living alone and having no one to ask these mysteries.

I brush on my makeup and the worrying turns to bigger things. Tyler's confession. What if he acts all weird today? What if I act all weird today?

I grip my eye-shadow brush with both hands and stare into the mirror. What if I can't get past it?

Wow, that sounds self-righteous.

I take a deep breath.

Lord, really, I am really going to need some help today.

Short, frequent prayers are becoming the new thing for me, apparently.

Tyler shows up exactly forty-five minutes later, which is typical Tyler. If I ever have to be somewhere on time with him, I always tell him it starts fifteen minutes earlier than it actually does.

I like being on time. I really like being early, but Mom informed me once that not only does no one enjoy an early guest, she's had homicidal thoughts when they show up fifteen minutes early and she isn't even dressed.

My mom tends to operate more on Tyler's time, though.

I open the door and he's standing there in khaki cargo shorts and a polo shirt, slinging his keys around his finger. His hair is a mess of crazy blond curls; his blue eyes are sparkling. "Hey," he says, and something about the way he says that one word makes the whole morning better, mood and all.

This. This is the Tyler I know and really, *really* like. All worries are melting away like a jar of coconut oil in my grandmother's un-air-conditioned home. Gran didn't even know that coconut oil was usually in a solid state.

I smile all brightly at Tyler like I just woke up all sunshiny and pretty like this, instead of telling him how it took several days' worth of makeup and a fairly loud pep talk, which may have included one of the more inspirational passages from Ecclesiastes to get into a decent mood.

There is a time to laugh!

"Want to join me for some breakfast?" he asks.

"Probably."

He grins.

We drive to a little hole-in-the-wall place that specializes in pancakes and omelets. I order the short stack with a side of bacon. Tyler gets the meat-lover's omelet with extra bacon and hash browns on the side.

The man is a cardiac arrest waiting to happen.

He grins across the table at me as the waiter leaves, and it's like the entire summer didn't happen and we are back in that first couple of days after he asked me to be his girlfriend. He's reaching for my hand and talking about how today is going to be such a good day, and he is completely back to normal.

I, on the other hand, am not.

I force a smile on to my face and half listen to his chatter about how glad he is that his projects at work are lightening up and my work load is getting a little more manageable and watch him fiddle with my fingers. Meanwhile, I can't stop thinking.

About Preslee and Wes, about forgiveness and the orange shag carpet that used to cover every floor except in the kitchen at Preslee's new house. I think about my ex-boyfriend Luke and how he walked in and declared me to be a prude way back in college, and then I start to worry that maybe worse than that, maybe I'm one of those Pharisee Christians who can't see their own sin and can't accept sin in others either.

The waiter brings our food and the fragrance of freshly cooked pancakes is wafting up into my nose. Tyler holds his other hand out and then grasps my hands tightly on the table. "Lord, thank You for this beautiful girl and for this breakfast feast You have given us. May we focus on You today. Amen."

Tyler's prayer brings me back to the present and I reach for my fork, pushing my snowballing thoughts away for now.

"So how's Layla? Not too much longer for her and Peter," Tyler says after he swallows a bite of omelet.

"Five weeks." I nod. "She's stressing out."

Tyler shrugs. "Eh. People get married every day. She'll be fine."

"Don't ever talk to her while she's in labor."

Tyler laughs right as his phone chimes in a text. He pulls it out of his pocket and then looks up at me. "It's a dinner invite from Rick and Natalie for us."

"For when?" I feel bad shoveling my pancakes in my mouth like I'm Keira Knightley's character on *Pirates of the Caribbean* going after that turkey leg, or whatever it was Barbosa offered her, but I am hungry and pancakes are not nearly as good cold. I usually eat my breakfast pretty quick after waking up. It's been almost an hour and a half now since my alarm buzzed this morning.

"Today at five," Tyler answers me. "Wanna go? We could go try to catch a movie before then. Or go do something else."

I nod. It looks like I'll be spending the day with Tyler.

I've had worse Saturdays.

We finish our breakfast, Tyler pays the waiter, and then we drive to a little fishing pond a little ways away. There are dads with their sons, teaching them how to fish; couples with their dogs, tossing Frisbees and tennis balls; a group of teens laughing over an early picnic lunch, backhanding footballs over the blanket.

It's a beautiful morning. The humidity is low and it's starting to actually feel like fall.

Tyler chatters without stopping. It's like he's trying to fit eight weeks of conversation into this morning. He tells me about his sister, Stef, and his new nephew. "Kamden Mitchell," he says, lightly shaking his head.

"What's wrong with his name?" I'm watching a couple with a black Lab puppy whose head is bigger than the rest of its body, except for its feet. The dog is completely awkward and the girl is just laughing at him, which makes the guy laugh as well and kiss the girl's forehead.

Ah, love over a dog. How poetic.

"Kamden? No offense to Stef, but Kamden just isn't a name that strikes me as a football player."

"So? Maybe Kamden wants to become something other than a football player." I nod pointedly to Tyler. "Maybe a software engineer."

He thinks about that and then shakes his head. "He won't be allowed."

"Stef have something against engineers?"

"She is antitechnology."

I did not know this about his sister. I frown and look at him. "Like how much is she antitechnology? Like she doesn't like video games or she doesn't have electricity?"

He grins. "She has electricity. Are you kidding? Stef can barely go twelve hours before she feels like she needs to take a shower."

"Huh." If I showered more than once a day, my skin would crack and fall off my body in ways that only the scientists on *Bones* could figure out. And I live in a state that is like a rain forest when it comes to the water-to-oxygen ratio.

I will never be able to move from Texas.

"She doesn't like computers and she's definitely against video games. Sometimes she'll watch TV, but mostly she just likes to read. Or cook."

I nod. Stef's husband, Mason, probably appreciates the cooking. "What does Mason do?"

"He's a pharmaceutical rep."

"Travels a lot?"

"Mm. Kind of. More just around the San Antonio area, so he gets to be home every night unless there's some kind of conference he has to go to. He hasn't had to travel since Kamden was born, so that's good, I guess. It's good according to Stef, anyway."

I stayed with Natalie for two nights when Rick was out of town right after their daughter was born. Claire was nocturnal, basically, and after being around her for two nights, I was fairly convinced that it would take an act of God for me to even want kids anymore.

Every so often, I see a baby or a picture or a toddler who is just so cute that it makes me all soft and squishy for what might be someday.

More often, though, I see kids throwing tantrums in the grocery store, boys with their fingers up their noses, or babies sobbing as loud as humanly possible, faces all red from the effort. And then I remember why I am very content to be single and waking up at whatever time I want to in the mornings.

Around noon, Tyler asks if I want to go get something light to eat, and we find a little smoothie shop for lunch before heading over to the theater. There's a romantic comedy showing and Tyler shrugs his okay.

He begins shaking his head the second the movie starts and still has not stopped by the time we are walking back to his truck.

"Seriously? You have to have the worst headache in the world now." I look at him as he holds the door open for me.

"That . . ." he mutters, as his hand cradles my elbow as I climb in, and a tiny part of me tingles at the touch.

"That," I start for him when he stops, "was adorable?"

He is back to shaking his head.

I grin.

He closes my door, walks around the truck, and climbs into his seat, then turns on the ignition. "How . . . ?"

"Wonderful?"

"I mean . . ."

"It was the best movie you've ever seen?"

He starts laughing. "Oh, Paige." Then he grins at me, reaches across the console, and laces his fingers through mine. "I have missed you so much, beautiful."

It's the first time he has ever called me anything other than my name. My whole chest warms and I smile back at him.

"Me too." I nod.

He starts driving toward Rick and Natalie's house, and he doesn't let go of my hand. We talk about random things. Preslee's wedding. Layla's ugly dog. Peter unintentionally putting the dog into anaphylactic shock.

Tyler thought that one was hilarious.

We get to Rick and Natalie's right at five, which just gives me this sense of pride because I got Tyler to actually be somewhere on time.

It's a miracle, folks.

Natalie opens the door all suspiciously, squinting at us. "You can't possibly be Tyler Jennings."

Tyler rubs his smooth chin. "I finally shaved."

"No, I mean, it's five o'clock. *Exactly*. I can't even remember the last time you got anywhere on time. I haven't even put the chicken in yet because five o'clock is five fifteen to you."

Tyler rolls his eyes. "You guys exaggerate." He lets me go inside first.

Natalie just looks at me and I shrug. "You are often late," I tell him.

"We can't all be perfect."

We walk into the kitchen. Rick is sitting at the table, reading possibly the thickest book I've ever seen in my life while drinking a cup of coffee and using his foot to bounce Claire in a little bouncy seat.

He doesn't say anything, but he looks up at me and Tyler together and just smirks in this knowing look.

"So, I am making chicken," Natalie says, sliding a Pyrex baking dish into the oven. "It's a new recipe so if it's awful, don't blame me, blame Pinterest."

I grin. "If that isn't the sound of confidence, I don't know what is."

"Oh it gets better." Rick sips his coffee and closes his book. I peek at the title. *Systematic Theology*. I'm immediately thankful that reading books like that are not part of my job description.

"The chicken or the confidence?" Tyler reaches over and unbuckles Claire out of the baby seat. He picks her up easily and settles her into the crook of his arm like he's come over and done this a million times.

I just watch him and then look at Rick and Natalie for their reactions, and they don't have any.

How often is Tyler over here? Apparently more often than I thought.

Claire's pacifier bobs in her mouth as she looks expressionlessly up at Tyler.

"We're clean eating," Natalie declares.

"Were you eating off of dirty plates before?" Tyler asks.

I'm impressed. That means she's stuck with this for over two weeks. "Wow," I say, trying not to seem too shocked.

If there were a land of people who went through fads like chewing gum, Natalie would be their queen.

The first time I met Natalie, she was super into natural cleaning products. She tossed every commercial product out the window and made all of her own stuff. Her own laundry detergent, her own dishwasher detergent, even her own Windex.

Then she got tired of mixing up the batches of ingredients every time she wanted to clean her windows, so she went back to the stuff from the store.

She's done gluten free, Paleo, and CrossFit. At one point at the beginning of the summer, she was really into decorating cake pops. There was always a big arrangement of cake pops every day when I went into the office.

That was not a bad phase for her.

"No." Natalie rolls her eyes at Tyler. "It's all about eating things that are free of artificially produced ingredients. So no sugar, no white flour, nothing refined."

"Two weeks strong, huh?" I ask her.

She grins, all proud of herself.

"Wait, I've been here in the last two weeks for dinner. What did you feed me those times?" Tyler asks.

"Clean food."

"Is that why y'all have been eating so many salads lately?" Rick sighs. I laugh.

Dinner is strange but we are at Rick and Natalie's house, so I kind of expected it. The chicken is actually delicious, but the cookies Natalie "whipped up" left a lot to be desired.

"Aren't these amazing?" Natalie raved. "It's whole-wheat flour, honey, and smashed bananas. I think these are just wonderful."

"Yeah," I manage between chewing. It's amazing I could say anything at all, seeing as how the cookie sucked all of the saliva out of my mouth.

"Mm-hmm," Tyler hums enthusiastically, but I notice he only takes one cookie.

Rick just looks defeated and depressed.

Poor man. I decide right then that I will bring Krispy Kreme doughnuts to our staff meeting on Monday.

Hopefully Natalie won't make that one.

We end up leaving about nine, which has become kind of normal for Rick and Natalie's house. Before they had Claire, I would stay over until after midnight some nights, watching movies, playing games, or just talking about the most random things in the world. Now that Natalie is up a couple times a night with Claire, though, she starts to fade quickly.

And Natalie has never been shy about kicking people out of her house. One time there were a bunch of us over, and she looked at us and said, "I wish I was at your house so I could go home and go to bed."

We all took the hint.

Tyler opens the passenger door for me and I climb into his truck. He goes around and slides into the driver's seat, puts the key in the ignition, and then just sits there, hands on the wheel, frowning.

"What's wrong?"

"So. That cookie."

I grin.

"Was it just me, or did it taste like what I imagine the slop they feed the monkeys at the zoo tastes like?"

"Well, I've never tried the slop at the zoo," I say, making a face. "So I couldn't really say for sure."

"Seriously, though. I mean, I know I'm not the world's healthiest guy—"

I interrupt him with my laugh. "Oh come now." I roll my eyes. "Surely the most carnivorous plate and a cobbler at Cracker Barrel make you into the picture of health."

He brightens and looks at the clock on the dashboard. "Cracker Barrel? We could go get cobbler!"

I shake my head. Tyler is like an eighty-year-old living in a twenty-five-year-old's body the way he loves that restaurant. I shrug. "Why not?"

He drives there chatting the whole time about how much he loves their cobbler. Like he has to remind me.

I smile at him, but my thoughts are someplace else.

I watch the way the red lights glint off the windshield and glow on his face. I think about what he said to me at the mall and start chewing on my bottom lip, worrying that he'll look over and notice my not paying attention to what he's saying.

It's so hard for me to imagine Tyler before he became a Christian. Maybe that's a good thing. I look at him now, and it's just difficult to picture him any other way. His blond hair is curling like crazy right now—which is probably a good indication that the rain the forecasters were predicting for later tonight and all day tomorrow is a good possibility. His blue eyes are shining as he smiles at me while he talks, head relaxed against the headrest, one hand lazily gripping the steering wheel while his right hand reaches for mine.

He looks innocent. And incredibly cute.

Luke's voice echoes in my brain. *"So you're still a prude, huh?"*

I'm back to chewing on my lip and praying silently. *Please, Lord, just take that memory away!*

"What do you think?" he asks me and I realize I didn't hear the question.

"Sorry, what did you say?" I blink away the thoughts racing through my head.

"Have you ever ridden on a motorcycle?"

I just look at him.

And maybe innocent was the wrong word.

"No . . ." I say, drawing the word out. "Have you?"

"I actually used to ride one back in high school and college," Tyler confesses, turning into the Cracker Barrel parking lot.

I am really having a hard time marrying the guy who used to ride a motorcycle and do all kinds of other things with the guy who leaves a youth pastor's house at nine and then hits up the local Cracker Barrel for cobbler.

He looks over after he shifts the truck into Park and grins at my expression. "And you're officially shocked." He lets go of my hand so he can release his seat belt.

"Not shocked," I say, though I'm not sure I ever got away from shocked after his last confession to me. "What else do I not know about you, Tyler Jennings?"

He squints out the windshield, thoughtful creases between his eyebrows, flipping his keys over and over his index finger. "I once owned a box turtle I named Wally. I fed him every single day for two months before I realized he had probably died when I first put him in the cardboard box." He looks at me sadly. "There was like a two-month supply of leaves and mulched-up dandelions in there that never got eaten."

"The smell didn't clue you in?" I ask, gagging. My second-grade teacher had a box turtle that died over one of our three-day weekends. We all came back to the class and the stench was so bad, our teacher made us sit in the hallway for the next three days while she alternated holding her nose and throwing up into a trash can.

We found out a little later, though, that she was pregnant at the time—my teacher, not the turtle—so that probably had something to do with the hall sessions.

Poor lady.

"A nine-year-old boy's room stinks regardless of whether or not there is a dead turtle in there," Tyler says.

I gag.

Chapter 10

"Earth to Paige!"

I blink and look up at Layla holding up a single yellow long-stemmed rose and waving it in front of my face.

"Yes?" I ask.

"Yellow roses. Iconic or traditional for a Texas wedding?"

I frown. "Is there a difference?"

"There's a huge difference! Iconic is one thing but traditional is *so* not me, Paige." She paces the floor and her gauzy, Easter egg–colored short skirt floats and tangles as she walks.

No. Layla has never been traditional about much. The wedding is about as traditional as I've ever seen her.

"I say iconic," I tell her. Mostly because I'm tired of having this conversation. Her wedding is four weeks away. She already ordered the flowers months ago, she's just now in the stage where everything is done, ordered and paid for and now she's second-guessing everything.

"I really worry that I should have gone with a round cake," she says, flouncing on my couch next to me.

I look over at her and bite back a yawn.

I have not slept well the last few nights. It's Tuesday and I have a packed-full day of girls tomorrow on top of teaching the small-group lesson on peace.

Which I should be studying for instead of listening to Layla change her mind about everything wedding related. But part of me feels bad. Between the job change, finally spending more time with Tyler, and seeing Preslee on some weekends, I haven't spent a lot of time with Layla lately.

And as I imagine how much a sympathetic audience Peter is, no wonder she needs some girl time.

I cup the hot mug of chai tea in my hands and look over at my best friend. Her brown hair is yanked into a sloppy ponytail and she's not wearing any makeup.

Which, for Layla, is usually a sign that the end of the world is near. If her life were a movie, Will Smith would be suiting up for his role by now.

"Hey." I nudge her with my shoulder.

She looks over at me and sighs, rubbing her cheek. "Paige. I'm so nervous."

I force a smile at her because I know she is and there's nothing I can do to help. "I know," I say quietly. "Why?"

She shrugs, looking at the blank screen of my TV. "It's just such a big change, you know? Married. I'm going to be *married*. What if it's not what I think it's going to be? What if I find out I can't stand Peter or his weird ways, and there's nothing I can do about it then?"

"Layla."

She sighs again and messes with her ponytail. "And then there's you."

I look over at her. "What about me?"

"That's my question. What about you? Are we even

allowed to be friends after we get married?"

"Yes?" I say, but my voice ends on a questioning note. "Why wouldn't we?"

"My mom doesn't do anything with any girlfriends of hers. She just stays home with my dad every night."

"Well maybe your mom doesn't have any close friends." I start to get worried. Maybe I shouldn't have been all supportive of this upcoming wedding. Not if it meant losing Layla.

"Maybe." Layla seems so forlorn I have to say something.

"Look." I set my tea down on the coffee table and lean forward to look at her. "I don't know what it's going to be like after you get married, but I know we are *never* going to stop being friends. Okay?" I stare at her right in her brown eyes. "Never."

She reaches over and gives me a big hug. "Thanks, Paige."

"Sorry I haven't been able to answer any more of your wedding problem questions."

"Eh." She shrugs. "I know I'm flipping out for no reason."

I grin.

"Panda?" she asks, and I realize that neither of us ever ate. Layla came over right when I got home from meeting Tonya at Starbucks and has been questioning every detail of her life since then.

No wonder I'm tired.

I smile at her. "My grandfather would have told you that you're going to turn into a piece of orange chicken someday."

She shrugs at me. "It's my curse."

We do something different and actually go to the restaurant to eat. Usually one of us just picks it up on the way to the other's house.

We order our Americanized Chinese food and sit at one of the uncomfortable plastic booths. Now I remember why we prefer to eat in the comfort of our own apartments and in our jammies.

"So." Layla stabs a piece of orange chicken with her plastic fork. "Tell me about you."

"My name is Paige. I'm twenty-three years old. I live in an upstairs apartment that I — "

"Paige!"

I smile at her. "What about me?"

"Well, okay, not about *you* singular but you plural."

I squint at her while I chew. "The test came back negative for multiple personality disorders, Layla."

"Paige!" she says again, but this time she laughs. "No, you and *Tyler*, weirdo! How is it going? I haven't talked to you about him since y'all started being all cute together again."

I shrug, poking at a square of pineapple on the paper plate, half smiling. "It's fine," I say, because I'm not about to confess Tyler's past to Layla.

Besides. I'm attempting to forget about that. If God can take my sins and remove them as far as the east is from the west, then surely I can do the same for Tyler.

Layla shakes her head. "Nope. Not enough details. How did you guys patch things over? And what ever really happened?"

I still haven't breathed a word to her about the Luke Incident at the beginning of the summer, and I don't plan on ever doing so. It's over, it really didn't have much to do with the awful summer Tyler and I had, so it doesn't make sense to tell her.

Besides, I haven't even seen Luke since the day she bought Belle, the world's ugliest dog who is also apparently allergic to peanuts.

I shrug her question off. "It was just a big misunderstanding." Sort of, anyway. "We got it all sorted out and he's back to acting totally normal." Not quite. He's different, somehow.

Maybe it's just my imagination.

Layla nods, chewing a bite of fried rice. "That's really good to hear. I was worried about you guys for a while."

"I've been worried about you for basically your whole life." I grin across the table at her.

She rolls her eyes. "Says the girl who got in a car crash because she 'might have' seen a 'rabbit' in the parking lot." She sprinkles her speech with air quotes.

"There was no might have. And car *crash* is a little exaggeration." What really happened is I was driving out of the church parking lot when I was fifteen and my cell phone rang. I looked down for half a second and when I looked back up, I saw what I thought was a rabbit running right in front of me. So I did what any fifteen-year-old girl who happened to like animals would do: I slammed on the brakes and swerved and managed to run the little sedan into the curb. I messed up the axle and something else and found out a few minutes later that the rabbit was actually a paper bag.

Layla has never let me forget that. My dad hasn't either, actually.

For the next year plus, every time I would see my dad he would say, "Paige. You're driving down the road and a dog runs out in front of you. Do you stop? Swerve? Or hit the dog?" Or, "Paige. You are driving down the road and a chicken tries to cross in front of you. Do you stop? Swerve? Or run over the chicken?"

Or my favorite, "Paige. You are driving down the road and a giraffe steps out in front of you. Do you stop? Swerve? Or hit the giraffe?"

When he asked me that question, I asked if I could do none of the above and instead take a picture of a random giraffe in the middle of the road.

My dad, ladies and gentlemen.

I twirl a long chow-mein noodle around my fork and look over at Layla. "I think we might have been friends for too long."

She just laughs.

* * * * *

Wednesday night and I am doing what is my new normal for Wednesday nights — running to the copier to make more copies of the stack of papers Rick always has for the leaders that he never remembers he needs copies of until he goes to hand them out.

It's like he gets to the meeting and suddenly remembers that it's not just him doing this youth-leader thing.

I lay the paper on the glass, close the lid, and mash the button, watching the bright neon-blue light wave back and forth as the machine spits out the pages. I pick one up out of the tray and look at it.

How to Achieve Peace.

Sometimes I feel woefully unprepared to lead these girls. Yes, on the one hand, my life has calmed down a little bit. I made amends with my sister; I haven't seen Luke in a while, which always drops the drama level; and Layla, for all her freak-outs, is really doing okay.

And then there's Tyler. Sweet, adorable Tyler who somehow has a crazy past that I just try not to think about.

I've never been a jealous person. Well, I mean, occasionally I struggle with it, but it's always been more along the lines of, "Hey, those people have the money to eat out at Olive Garden every night, and I'm sitting here trying to convince myself that a cheese stick and a saltine cracker are not only gourmet, but filling."

Even in high school, I was completely okay being me 90 percent of the time. Everyone else was going on crash diets and joining clubs and trying to attain popularity, and I was more than content to just sit by myself in the cafeteria and read during lunch.

It's a new thing. This jealousy.

I sigh and close my eyes, rubbing my temples. I've spent the entire day trying to figure out what is wrong. I'm happy, but I'm not. I'm content, but I can hardly sleep lately. I love that Tyler and I are back together, but I can't help this feeling of just . . .

Jealousy. I don't even know why. Or of what.

I finish with the copies and head back down the long, dark hallway to the youth room, shelving the issues in my brain for another day. Everyone except Tyler is already here for the meeting.

Typical.

I hand Rick the stack of papers and sit in one of the chairs.

"Thanks, Paige. Alrighty, guys, there are a few things I wanted to talk about with you before the kids come.

Tonight's lesson is on peace, and I trust that everyone got the chance to prepare for the lesson beforehand."

Nodding occurs around the circle and Tyler walks in right then.

"Hey." He grins all cutely at me.

"Nice of you to join us, Tyler." Rick rolls his eyes. "Have you ever considered just setting your clock like fifteen minutes ahead of time?"

Tyler nods, sitting in the only other empty chair across the circle from me. "My mom actually did that when I was fifteen or so."

"Did it work?" Sam asks.

Tyler shrugs. "Only until I found out about it, then I started adding fifteen minutes to the time everywhere we went. She finally changed the clocks back, and then I was thirty minutes late everywhere for a while." He sighs. "I have tried for years to be on time. I just can't do it."

"Tyler, my grandfather would have hit you over the head with a fork if he heard you say the word *can't*," Rick says. "The man was brutal. He was a former Marine sergeant. Loving most of the time but brutal." Rick shakes his head and then continues his talk about how interesting his study on peace was as one of the fruits of the Spirit.

I try to pay attention. I honestly do. Tyler's gaze is on Rick and he nods occasionally, grinning when Rick cracks one of his customary dry-humor jokes.

It's like the Tyler of the summer never even existed.

He's smiling at Rick, and then he glances across the circle and sees me looking at him. And something in his expression sends warm shivers all the way down into my toes.

Rick leads us in prayer and then offers a couple more

questions to get the small-group conversation going. "And that's it. Go forth and conquer, friends."

All of us stand, fold up the chairs we were sitting on, and stack them back in the corner.

Tyler comes over as everyone else clears out to go talk to the kids already filling the hallway.

"So," he says and then just grins all cheekily at me.

"So." I nod, feeling a little squinch of something in my stomach. Dread? Hunger? An impending sense of doom and destruction?

"I'm going to teach you how to operate a motorcycle."

Yep, it was definitely the latter thing I was feeling. I just stare at him. "Why?" I blurt out finally, frowning.

"Because. What if you are out someday and someone has to go the hospital and the only way to take them is on a motorcycle? You need to know how to ride one."

"Tyler, if I'm out and someone needs to go to the hospital, couldn't I just take the car I came there in?"

"What if your car is dead?" He leans one shoulder against the wall, smiling at me.

"How am I supposed to get the person on a motorcycle anyway? It seems like if the injury was mild enough that they could ride on a motorcycle, they could wait to go to the hospital."

Tyler shrugs. "I chopped off the tip of my pinkie finger when I was twelve in a freak pocketknife accident. I could still hang on to the back of a motorcycle driver, but I definitely needed to go to the hospital."

I grab for his hands and study his pinkies. "You did not."

"Did too. See that scar right there?" He points to his left hand.

I lift his finger three inches from my eye and squint at it. "That's a hangnail, Tyler."

"I've always been a quick healer."

I open my mouth and then stop. "Was that from *The Princess Bride*?"

"You know what I love about you, Paige? You're quick. I like quick."

I try not to read too much into the word he just said. "Quick, but just not on time, right?"

He grins, loops his arm around my neck, and knuckles my head. "Get to class, smart aleck."

"I'm not going to learn how to drive a motorcycle, Tyler," I say as we walk into the hallway.

He grins at me, walking backward down the hallway and spreading his hands. "You know you've always wanted to. Saturday, Paige. *Be prepared*," he sings the last two words like Scar from *The Lion King* as he turns and disappears into the classroom where he meets with his freshmen guys.

"A motorcycle?" Brittany, one of the high school girls, starts twittering. "Oh, Paige, that's *so* romantic!"

I watch her scurry away to tell her friends, who all start twittering and giggling at the idea of Tyler and me on a motorcycle together. I try to breathe through the knot in my stomach like Jillian Michaels always talks about.

Saturday can take it's time getting here.

Chapter
11

"**W**ait, you're doing what?"

I tuck my cell phone between my shoulder and my ear and reach for the bag of popcorn that is steaming hot in the microwave.

"Tyler wants to teach me how to drive a motorcycle tomorrow," I tell Preslee, holding in a yelp as the hot steam hits my fingers when I rip open the bag.

Preslee is dying of laughter and I dump the popcorn into a bowl, frowning. "Why is that funny?"

"Because, Paige, oh my gosh, I would *pay* to watch you learn how to *drive* a *motorcycle!*" There is so much overemphasis in her squealing voice, I am wincing.

I wait for her to finish laughing. Which means I have time to toss the popcorn bag in the trash, pick up the bowl of popcorn and the cheese slices that are making up my dinner, walk over to the couch, settle into the cushion that is quickly conforming to the shape of my butt, and flick on the TV to HGTV, muting the volume. I've eaten three handfuls of popcorn and watched a very cute Australian man talk about backyard décor, if my lip reading is right, before she finally stops laughing long enough to breathe.

"Oh gosh, oh gosh," she says, over and over again, and I can picture her swiping tears away. "Oh, Paige, I haven't laughed like that in *years*."

Now I'm just trying not to get offended. "I don't know what's so funny about it."

"You? Paige Alder, the world's most-perfect Christian on a motorcycle? It would be like watching Mother Teresa get on a Harley."

"It would not," I mumble, staring at a slice of cheese.

"When are you doing it? And where? I'm sure if I got up early enough I could come watch."

"Absolutely not."

"Oh, come on, Paige, why not?"

"Are you kidding me? After the way you just spent twelve minutes laughing your head off?"

She starts giggling again. "I mean, the thought of you sitting there, gripping the handles and oh . . ." She's gone into hysteria again.

Honestly, I don't see what is funny about it at all. I see what's terrifying about it, but not what's funny. I have spent the better part of today praying for God's protection over whatever awful things Tyler has planned for tomorrow.

I may or may not have also prayed for one of us to contract some mild form of measles so we just have to postpone indefinitely.

He sent me a text earlier today while I was meeting with one of the girls. HEY! WE ARE ALL SET FOR TOMORROW — I'M BORROWING MY BUDDY'S BIKE. I'LL COME BY FOR YOU ABOUT TEN IN THE MORNING! THIS WILL BE FUN!

I'm not sure that *fun* is the word I would have picked. And I like how it seemed like he was almost trying to convince me.

Well, that was not going to happen.

I hang up with Preslee, who is still laughing, and turn up the volume on the TV. It was nearly eight o'clock. Fridays are long days now that school is in session. I met with four girls today, one after the other as soon as school let out.

My drama quotient is filled up for the night.

I'm pretty sure if I hear Zach's name one more time today, I'll have an allergic reaction. I'll need to warn Sam since he's in charge of the senior guys. The boy has no idea how popular he is with my girls.

A light knock sounds at my door and I freeze on the couch, one hand in the popcorn bowl.

I am fairly certain I am not expecting anyone. Tyler said he was going to be working late tonight so he didn't have to go in tomorrow, Layla is on a much-needed date with Peter where they apparently aren't allowed to talk about any wedding details, and I can't think of anyone else who would be coming by my apartment.

I sneak over to the door and peer through the peephole.

Luke.

I look up at the ceiling. "The drama quotient, Lord," I whisper. "It's filled, remember?" I tug at my old T-shirt and yoga pants.

Luke has impeccable timing when it comes to finding me looking like the Feed the Birds lady in *Mary Poppins*. I'm nearly afraid to open the door since the odds are good that a few pigeons are going to waddle in as well. If pigeons waddle, anyway.

I open the door and just look at him.

Luke, of course, looks gorgeous, which is typical. The boy is one of those freaks of nature who never looks bad. Ever. I've seen him in braces, on crutches, and while he had the chicken pox.

Beautiful, every time.

There's something to be said for finding a man who is not prettier than you.

"Paige!" he says my name all exuberantly, like we do this every Friday. "I was hoping you'd be home."

"Did you need something?" I ask, because obviously the only reason I could see for him being here is he felt the need to drive ten minutes and past two grocery stores to borrow a cup of sugar from me.

"I saw this today and thought of you." He hands over a small brown-paper sack, and I look at him for a half second before opening it.

It's a DVD. *Monsters Inc.*

I just stare at the movie. A million years ago, our first date was going to see *Monsters Inc.* during one of the summer movie specials one of the theaters by our houses in Austin did.

Luke is smiling at me, and if he thinks this is weird, he's not showing any sign of it. "Remember? Mike Wazowski! And we laughed at the way that huge slug monster walked for like the rest of the night?"

"Luke—" I say, about to start in on the *hey, remember? We are no longer dating. We're not even really friends. And good grief, I just spent* weeks *reminding you of this!*

"It was five bucks by the checkout, Paige." Luke cuts me off, his expression and voice getting serious. "I just thought of you and how much you liked that movie and I didn't remember seeing it in your collection. So you can keep it or you can get rid of it, but I just thought maybe this could be the first step to us really becoming friends."

I look back and forth from the DVD to Luke's sober brown eyes. He appears to be telling the truth, but he's fed me this friends bit before, and it had nothing to do with being friends and everything to do with trying to get back together.

And that ship has sailed.

"Thanks," I say, flatly.

"You're welcome." He looks around me and sees the popcorn and the cheese slices on the couch, the HGTV blaring something about how to safely remove kitchen cabinets without causing mass destruction.

"Alone tonight?"

"Thankfully," I say, hoping he'll get the hint and not think he should stay and keep me company.

He nods. "Well. Have a good night, Paige. Enjoy learning how to remodel your kitchen. Though, and this is just some friendly, unsolicited advice, I wouldn't try anything here." He smiles a small, questioning smile, and I remember what I told him at the beginning of the summer with a sigh.

I forgave him. And really, I have. I've just learned the difference between forgiveness and friendship.

And honestly, it was better for Luke and me both to just go our separate ways.

"Thank you for the movie, Luke," I say, trying to instill some kindness into my tone.

"See you later." He leaves and I close the door, sliding the dead bolt back in place. Most of the time, I love living by myself. But sometimes, I can make myself a little creeped out. It's better if I don't open the door once I am in for the night.

I climb into bed at ten thirty, fully educated on the correct way to reinstall kitchen cabinets after refinishing them.

Too bad the apartment wouldn't look kindly on that. I think the creamy white they used on the show would be beautiful in here.

I pull my Bible over and flip to my place in Ecclesiastes, hoping it says something like, "There is a time to live and a time to stay off of motorcycles."

"He has made everything appropriate in its time. He has also set eternity in their heart, yet so that man will not find out the work which God has done from the beginning even to the end."

I look at the last sentence and think it over. What does that even mean? That we will never find out the whys of our everyday life until we get to heaven and see the whole picture?

I click the lamp and set my Bible back on the nightstand.

Lord, I'm excited for heaven and to find out what my life as a whole looks like. But could we please postpone heaven for a bit? At least past tomorrow — please keep Tyler and me safe as we do this ridiculous thing.

* * * * *

"Ready?" Tyler is giddy.

I mean really, *really* giddy.

I stare at him, still groggy. I barely slept last night. All I kept thinking about was going to heaven, how my parents used to see motorcycles driving down the street and my mom would immediately start tsking and saying things like, "Well, *that guy* is certainly not the brightest!" Or worse, "He's just driving that motorcycle straight to the fiery pit, isn't he?"

Motorcycles were on the same list as tattoos as far as my parents were concerned. And that was the "Thou Shalt Not" list.

Never mind that we knew and were friends with several very dear Christian people who had ink on their bodies and a Harley between their legs.

Tyler is nearly ridiculous with his joy. "Oh, I am so excited to teach you this, Paige!"

"When did you get so into motorcycles?" I rub the bleariness from my eyes and stumble to the kitchen for another refill on the coffee. I was on cup number four.

The end was clearly not in sight, seeing as how I still could only fully open one eye at a time.

"I really liked having my bike in high school."

"I still can't believe your parents let you do that." Tyler and I have nothing in common except an apparent propensity to get hangnails.

Although, excuse me, I'm pretty sure he still thinks his is a scar.

"Yep." He grins, leaning against the high counter, watching me inhale the coffee like it's the last cup I will ever drink.

Oh, Lord, please don't let this be the last cup I ever drink!

To say I'm nervous is a huge understatement.

"Dad helped me pay for one when I was seventeen. Good gas mileage and they never had to worry about me driving home with too many people in the car."

"My parents equated motorcycles with Satanism."

He grins wider. "Sometimes there's a very thin line. Are you finally ready? I have to have the bike back by one."

Three hours. Something else ominous was three hours . . .

My brain fills in the words. *"A three-hour tour . . ."*

Yep. I think all of 1960s America remembers how that little adventure ended. Ninety-eight episodes later, Gilligan finally got off the island and got to go home.

I look at Tyler, who is antsy in his excitement, and drain one more cup of coffee.

"Let's get this over with," I say, groaning. I grab a jacket. I tried to dress as prepared for death as I could. I shaved my legs, I made sure all of my important documents were in the fire safe where I keep them, and I left instructions for Rick on how to collate the copies from the machine properly.

Anytime Rick makes copies, all of the even numbered pages are always upside down.

"This is going to be fun!" Tyler declares, running down my stairs. "Ta-da!" He does a Vanna White impression directing my attention to the parking lot.

There's a shiny silver machine of terror parked right beside my five-star safety rating car. "Yay."

"You're not excited?" Tyler asks me.

I'm trying my best not to show how my hands are shaking. Maybe honesty is the way to go. "I am completely terrified."

He looks at me and the sweetest expression crosses his face. "Are you really?" He walks over and takes my hands, eyes widening. "You *are* terrified!" He pulls me in for a hug. "Look, honey, it's going to be fine, okay? We are going to be completely safe. I'm not even going to really drive on the roads. Deep breath in, okay?"

I take a shuddering breath. "Maybe we could just take my car."

He pushes me back to shoulder length and flicks a hand through my hair, blue eyes staring right into my soul. "Paige, sometimes the best adventures are the ones that scare you the most."

He hands me a helmet and I hold it, looking at him. "Where did you get that?"

"A fortune cookie last week from Panda."

My boyfriend, ladies and gentlemen.

"Okay." Tyler straddles the bike and clicks his chin strap down. "There's a huge empty parking lot about two miles away. I'll drive there and then you can take over."

I just look at him, still holding the helmet.

"Well?" he asks me.

"This goes against everything I was ever raised to believe as a child. Except maybe the 'you can always get more but you can't put it back' advice my dad used to lecture us with after we were too exuberant with the ketchup bottle."

Tyler is laughing. "Will you just climb on, Paige?"

It's a good thing I believe in once saved, always saved. *God forgive me.* This is ridiculous. I'm twenty-three years old. I don't think this qualifies as disobedience.

Tyler pulls his helmet back off his head and looks at me, blond hair glinting gold in the sunlight. "Paige?"

"I'm scared."

"Just hold on." He reaches out a hand to me. "I'm not going to let anything happen. Are you going to trust me or not?"

He says it jokingly, but deep in my heart I hear the question in a different way. Am I going to trust Tyler? Ever since his confession at the mall, I've been holding back in a way, worrying that maybe, just maybe, he will hurt me in the end. That maybe he really hasn't changed like he's said he has.

I bite my bottom lip, take a deep breath, and pull the extremely tight helmet over my head.

His grin is worth it.

I hold on to his shoulder and kick my right leg over the bike. The seat is cushier than I imagined it would be. Tyler turns around to look at me, still smiling. "Okay, so you put your feet on these little foot pegs. Whatever you do, do not take your feet off the foot pegs."

I anchor my legs in place, fear turning my stomach cold. "Why? Could we crash? Will we die?"

Tyler pulls his helmet on. "It just makes it easier for me to balance. Try to keep your weight in the center of the bike, and it's best if you don't anticipate the turns. Just hold on to my back."

It's hard to hear everything he says with the helmet on, so I just latch on to his back like some helmet-wearing leech. He turns on the motorcycle and the engine roars in my ears.

We slowly step back out of the parking space and then Tyler turns slightly. "Ready?" he yells at me.

I take a deep breath. "Okay." I nod.

He starts driving and my stomach is somewhere down in the toes of my shoes. I'm hanging on to him with every stitch of strength I've got, making sure my feet are completely planted on the foot pegs.

We turn out onto the road and Tyler picks up speed. The landscape is flying past — much faster than it looks when I'm in a car. I lock my hands together around his chest and keep praying, squinching my eyes shut.

I peek them open when I feel us slowing down. We are in a huge church parking lot and Tyler comes to a stop, pulling his helmet off and grinning at me.

"All right, Speedy Gonzales, you're up." He sets the

kickstand and then holds a hand back to me. "Go ahead and climb off because I want you to try climbing on by yourself."

It's not like this was a horse and I was learning how to step into a saddle. I take his hand, though, and hoist myself off, standing there and feeling huge-headed and awkward in my helmet.

"Okay." Tyler slides off. "Now, the first thing I want you to do is to just sit on it with the kickstand off, just to get used to the weight you'll be balancing on."

I swing a leg over the motorcycle and Tyler nudges up the kickstand. Immediately I feel off balance and clumsy. I grip the handles tightly.

"Okay, I've got the back, Paige. See? You aren't going anywhere." Tyler holds the back of the bike with both hands.

I feel like when I was seven and my dad was teaching me how to ride a bicycle. "Now, Paige, a bike is a huge responsibility and I expect you to ride it safely. Do you understand?" Dad used to say to me, making sure I knew how to check the spokes and fill up the tires before I ever even sat on it.

My parents were very into safety.

Still are. I'm hoping Preslee doesn't tell them about this little experience I'm currently having.

Tyler spends the next hour showing me where the gas is, where the clutch is, how to use my tiny mirrors, and how to make turns. Finally, when my brain feels like it might pop and I'm wishing I'd consumed even more coffee before we came out here, he pulls his helmet back on and nods to me.

"Well. Let's do it."

"Do what?" I hope he means drive back to the apartment and spend the rest of the day at a nice restaurant known for their desserts.

"Let's go. You're going to chauffeur me around the parking lot."

I just look at him. "You cannot be serious."

"Oh, I'm as serious as they come, sweetheart." He grins. He slides behind me on the bike, then nudges me up a little closer to the handlebars. "Do it just like we talked about. Kickstand up, now shift your weight so you're leaning to the right . . ."

He talks me through it, and what feels like a small eternity later, I slowly press on the gas and the motorcycle shoots forward.

Tyler starts laughing and grabs me around the waist. "See? You've got it!"

I'm losing feeling in my hands with how tightly I'm gripping the handlebars.

"Now, remember what I said. Lean into the turn . . ."

Twenty minutes later and I've circled the parking lot at about the same speed as my neighbor's ancient German shepherd could have done, and the dog was half blind and pretty much lame.

Poor dog.

Tyler has talked nonstop the entire twenty minutes, throwing out words like "engine shut-off switch" and "downshifting."

Because obviously I know what those mean.

"Okay. Try giving it a little more gas," he says when we get back to where we started.

"More gas?"

"Don't worry, Paige. You're doing great. You're a natural on one of these things. Your parents should have named you Harley."

"Thank God they didn't."

He laughs.

I add a touch more gas and suddenly we are going at a good clip. It's easier to balance and I take a deep breath, trying to relax my grip on the handlebars. Tyler's arms are loose around my waist, his head close to mine.

This isn't so bad.

"You're doing great," Tyler says again, and this time I believe him.

I pull to a stop a couple of minutes later and set the kickstand. Tyler slides off and holds his hand out to me, helping me off and then pulling me in for a super awkward helmet-bonking hug.

"That was fun, wasn't it?" He pushes me back and pulls off his helmet. His hair is all sweaty and creased, and it makes me think about what a sight my own hair is likely to be. Lovely.

I try to fight the smile on my face but it wins out. "Okay. It was pretty fun."

"Ha!" Tyler's shout is victorious. "I knew it!"

"Okay, okay. You win. You were right." I take off my helmet, and rake a hand back through it. "I have no idea what I am going to tell my parents."

Tyler laughs. "You are a funny person, Paige." He settles his helmet back on his head. "Come on. I'll take us back to your house."

We drive back and this time I keep my eyes open for the ride. Tyler pulls in beside my car again, and I slide off after he puts the kickstand down.

"Okay." He grins at me behind his helmet. "Go inside, take a shower, and I will be back in time to take you to an early dinner."

"Is a tattoo parlor a stop along the way? I mean, since we're marking off all the things on my 'I Swear I Will Never Attempt' list anyway."

Tyler laughs. "Admit it. You've always wanted an *I Love Mom* on your bicep."

"At one point I considered tattooing a coffee cup to my wrist."

He just stares at me. "Wow. Really?"

"No, Tyler."

He grins.

"Drive safe, please."

He nods and slowly backs out of the space. I wave once and walk up my stairs, exhausted.

Time for confession.

Mom answers on the third ring. "Hello?"

"I just rode on a motorcycle."

"Well, that's fun. Your dad used to ride a Suzuki something or another back when we first got married. He actually proposed to me on the back of it. We took a picnic lunch out to this little random, abandoned road that was covered in wildflowers."

It's a good thing I don't have one of those little robotic vacuums because I'm pretty sure my jaw would have gotten sucked up into it at that comment. "Are you serious?"

"Sure. He was pretty cool back then. Had the long hair and the motorcycle jacket. I thought he was something else."

I sit on the couch, in total shock.

Mom's still talking. "Your dad stopped alongside this little river with all these little poppies blooming and told me that he wanted to be the river to my poppies." She sighs. "It was very romantic."

It was actually pretty cheesy, but I wasn't about to tell that to Mom. "Dad drove a motorcycle?" I ask again, incredulously.

"Up until you were born. Then he decided to get something that would fit a car seat."

I have never known this. Ever. I've never seen pictures or anything of my father on a motorcycle. You'd think that would be something you'd show to your kids, like, look children, your father used to be cool.

"How come y'all never said anything about this?"

Mom pauses. "I'm not sure, really. When you guys were little, it just seemed pointless, and then as you got older, we wanted you guys to live as safely as possible so it seemed better not to mention anything."

I'm thinking about that when she starts talking again. "Well, anyway, honey, I need to go. Preslee really should have some sort of guest favor so I'm off to look for some. Have a good afternoon! Wear a helmet if you go out again."

She hangs up and I pull the phone away from my ear, staring at it before mashing another button.

"Did you know Dad used to drive a motorcycle?" I ask Preslee as soon as I hear the click that she's answered.

"It's a little late in the day for lying," Preslee says.

"What does that mean?"

"I don't know. Didn't Mr. Rogers say that in one of his episodes?"

I open my mouth and then change my mind as far as replying to that comment. "Seriously, though. You can call and ask Mom. Dad drove a motorcycle. He even proposed to Mom on the back of it."

Preslee is quiet for a minute. "So how come . . ." she says slowly, drawing the words out, "when I was fifteen, Dad nearly had a heart attack when I told him I'd gone riding on the back of Cal Risewine's motorcycle?"

"Probably more because it was Cal Risewine, Pres. Didn't he get kicked out of school for distributing marijuana?"

"Well. That could have also played into it, I guess."

"My point, Preslee, is I have spent my entire life believing that motorcycles and tattoos and gauged ears were all the worst things you could ever possibly do, and now I'm finding out that the people who raised me to think those things got engaged on a motorcycle!"

"I have two tattoos. What does that say about me?"

I just sigh.

I can hear the smile in Preslee's voice. "I might be wrong about this, but I'm pretty sure there are only ten commandments."

"What are you saying?"

"I'm saying to relax. If it's not a sin, don't make it one."

I rub my temples and stare at my blank TV, thinking about what she's saying. When did my baby sister become so knowledgeable?

"Well. Listen, I have to go. Mom's trying to talk me into getting favors for all the guests, which I think is ridiculous because we are already feeding them an entire meal and giving them cake and a reason to spend the night dancing. I've never kept one of the favors I've ever received at a wedding, including the beta fish I got at the last one."

"What did you do to the poor fish?"

"I did what anyone does with a fish they don't want."

"You flushed him?"

"No, I took him to the grocery store and left him on the fresh-seafood counter with a sign saying 'Save me!'"

"Seriously?"

"Of course I flushed him, Paige! 'All drains lead to the ocean.' Didn't you learn anything from *Finding Nemo*? Really, I was just setting him free."

I don't bother informing my sister that most city drains lead to the sewage company. "Well. Have fun with Mom."

"Thanks. Less than eight weeks to the wedding and it's like she's not going to live long enough to see it with how stressed out she is. I've been calling Dad to make sure he gives her like melatonin or something at night because she's so wired she can barely sit, much less sleep."

So my parents got engaged on a motorcycle and now Dad's drugging Mom.

Lovely.

"Bye, Preslee." I hang up and stare at my TV for another couple of minutes.

"If it's not a sin, don't make it one."

I think about all of the rules I had growing up. Obey my parents. Stop at all intersections. Don't even think about being late to curfew. Say no to motorcycles, drugs, alcohol, piercings, tattoos, and bleached hair. Buckle up any time in a car. Shorts need to come to your middle finger. No being alone with a boy — sex leads to babies out of wedlock and terrible diseases.

Maybe . . .

Maybe instead of hearing my parents' warnings for what they were — warnings — I took them instead at the same face value as everything else they told me in lecture mode.

I really was the perfect daughter.

But maybe there is such a thing as too perfect.

Chapter
12

I turn to Layla, who is slumped over like a Creamsicle sitting out in the sun too long, and poke her shoulder. "Pastor Louis said we can go," I tell her.

The pandemonium that usually follows our pastor's dismissal is in fine form today. Kids are yelling, parents are yelling back at them, people are laughing and hugging, and it's like there's this uncontainable joy in the room because it's officially fall and not in the nineties outside.

Layla looks over at me and rubs her blotchy red eyes. "Oh. Yeah. Guess we can go now, huh?"

Peter is busy talking to Tyler on the other side of me, which is just a complete shock because Peter doesn't talk to anyone. It's like Layla and Peter have exchanged personalities here in the last three weeks before their wedding.

"You okay?" I ask her quietly.

She nods. "I was up super super late last night. Or early this morning. Or however you would say it."

"What time did you go to bed?"

She pulls her cell phone out of her purse and squints at the numbers. "Well, if all goes well and traffic is good, hopefully in about twenty minutes."

"You didn't sleep all night?" I gasp.

Layla is not like this at all. Layla is the girl who refused to go to summer camp one year because the year before she didn't get her customary ten hours of sleep every night. She's been known to miss parties, graduations, and wedding receptions so she can go to bed.

Her mother always said she was the perfect baby.

"I was working on the programs," she mutters, rubbing her hair.

"Programs."

"For the wedding? You know, the who's who of the ceremony." She sighs. "Apparently it's a big deal."

"A big deal to who?"

"Pinterest."

I close my eyes. "Layla . . ."

She yawns at me.

"Why didn't you call me? I could have come to help."

She shrugs. "I figured you were hanging out with Tyler. And plus, I wasn't even totally sure what I was doing until I finished it."

"Well. Next time, call me. Please. This is ridiculous that you aren't sleeping to get things done for the wedding. Isn't it supposed to be the happiest time of your life?"

Layla waves a hand. "Oh, Rick told us that's all just a made-up thing by Disney to help them keep selling copies of *Cinderella* whenever they let her out of the Disney vault."

Well, that was encouraging.

Natalie walks over then, a drooling Claire on her hip.

She's shoving what looks like a wafer at the baby's mouth, but Claire is having nothing to do with it.

"Come on, kid, you're supposed to love these very expensive disgusting treats," Natalie grouses at her daughter.

"So marriage isn't really a happy time?" I ask Natalie.

"Not when I'm PMSing and he's in one of his fatalist moods. But otherwise it's fine. Why? Who is married and unhappy?"

Layla raises her hand.

Natalie rolls her eyes. "You're *engaged*. Big dif, my friend. Engagement stinks. Best thing to do is just accept that fact and plan a short one." She nods to me. "Words for the future."

My cheeks suddenly share a lot of resemblance with that lobster from *The Little Mermaid* when Tyler looks over right then and winks at me.

My stomach drops.

Layla yawns again like nothing earth-shattering just happened.

"You need a nap," Natalie says. "Not sleeping well? I did the same thing before my wedding day. I kept telling myself that these were the last few nights in a queen-sized bed without the gargantuan Rick, and I was trying to soak in every second of it, so I ended up working too hard to sleep and then couldn't actually rest. Want to come over and use Claire's bouncer? That thing knocks her out flat every time."

"She was up late making programs," I say.

"What kind of programs?" Natalie asks. "Like to a play?"

"Yep. The production called our wedding."

Natalie shrugs. "Unnecessary."

"Not according to every single wedding blog in the entire universe," Layla moans, rubbing her face. "I read like thousands of them. Millions. Every single one said that guests expect a program and apparently most people now expect some sort of a slideshow. So I e-mailed Peter's mother at three in the morning and asked her to send me all of his baby pictures."

Natalie just shakes her head. "That's ridiculous! People expect to see you get *married*. When Rick and I got married, I had a dress and some flowers and we served people some of that pretzel party-mix stuff and cake. I didn't have a program or a five-course dinner or anything. People walked in the church, saw us get married, and then we had a little reception in the courtyard afterward. The whole thing lasted two hours."

"No dancing?" I ask.

"Nope."

"No dinner?" Layla is in shock.

"Nope."

Layla is just staring at Natalie openmouthed like Natalie has suddenly taken on the form of Casper or something.

I, meanwhile, am thinking that Natalie and Rick were on to something. I've been watching Layla and my mother stress out now for the last few months, and it doesn't look fun.

At all.

Someday when, or if, I ever get married, I want a stress-free wedding.

I glance over at Tyler and he sees my look and grins at me.

A dozen or so grasshoppers invite themselves into my stomach and start making up for the dancing that was not at Rick and Natalie's wedding.

Claire chooses that minute to puke all over the front of Natalie's shirt and then grabs both sides of her mother's cheeks and laughs a toothless grin at her like, "Wasn't that amazing? I am so talented, Mom!"

Natalie looks at her daughter and then down at her shirt and sighs. "I'm going to go find an unsoaked burp rag." She nods to Layla. "Just think about it this way. Engagement is hard enough without adding all kinds of unnecessary stress to it." She smiles at Layla and then leaves.

A mother has to deal with the nastiest things on her person.

Layla is still just staring after Natalie and I sort of think she might be in a slight daze. "Layla? Layla!" I snap my fingers in front of her face and she jerks.

"What?" she mumbles.

"Did you drive here?"

"Yeah."

"That was good and unsafe. Peter?"

Peter stops talking to Tyler and looks at me. "Hi, Paige."

"Hi. Could you drive Layla home? She's a danger to the people on the roads right now."

He looks curiously at her and she smiles a very tired smile at him.

"Sure," he says immediately, obviously seeing the way her eyelids aren't creasing in the right spot. "Come on, honey, we can go now."

He picks up her Bible and purse and helps her up, wrapping an arm around her shoulders.

I don't get to see this side of Peter very often. It's sweet.

They leave and I look at Tyler who grins at me. "Well, darn, we got rid of all of the people around us." He reaches for my hand. "So, I was thinking." He pulls me a little closer. "There's this really beautiful girl I know and I'd like to ask her out to lunch, but I'm not sure where she would like to go."

I shrug, trying not to blush so deeply. "Well, I don't know about her, but I've always been a little partial to that little sandwich shop down the road."

"Paige?"

"Yes, Tyler?"

"Would you like to go to the little sandwich shop down the road with me for lunch?" He grins.

"Well. If you insist."

I follow him out to the parking lot, and we take his truck and leave my car at church. The sandwich place is like three minutes down the road, so it takes us no time to get there. I come here a lot when I only have ten minutes to grab a quick dinner before youth group these days.

Their chicken-salad sandwich is to die for and it's one of their Wednesday specials.

"Hi there," the guy working behind the counter says, pulling on a pair of plastic gloves. "How's it going today, Paige?"

I come here too much. When the servers know your name, it's usually a good sign to find a new spot.

"Hey, Randy." Yes, I know his name too.

Tyler grins.

"I'd like the turkey on the whole wheat," I tell Randy, not even looking at the menu. This place bakes their own bread and it always smells like a corner of heaven in here.

"Cheese?"

"Lots. Let's go with hmm . . . how about provolone today?"

"One turkey with provolone. And for you?" He looks at Tyler.

"Meat lovers."

I probably could have guessed that.

Randy tells us the total, Tyler pays, and we go sit with our sweet teas in the corner booth while Randy makes the sandwiches.

"So. How's the maid of honor twice in a month doing?" Tyler sips his tea.

I shrug. "I honestly haven't done too much. I'm too far away to really help with Preslee's and Layla hasn't been good at letting me help." Which is abnormal for Layla. She really must be stressing out.

"I honestly don't know what a maid of honor is supposed to do other than stand up there on the day of the wedding," Tyler says.

"That's a lot of it. I have a shower next weekend for Layla and then the weekend after that, there's a shower in Austin for Preslee. It's pretty customary for the maid of honor to be at those. And I have to give a toast . . ." I make a face and sigh, feeling nervous already.

Public speaking is really not my thing.

Tyler barely blinks. "You'll do great."

"You're kind, but I'm not so sure."

Randy sets our sandwiches down in front of us right then. "And here you go, guys. If you need anything else, let me know. I'll come by in a bit with a sample of our new custard."

I perk up at that. "Custard?"

He nods, eyes big. "It's amazing, Paige. You'll love it."

Tyler grins at me as he holds his hands across the table. "Well, I guess I know what's for dessert." I take his hands and he bows his head. "Lord, thank You for this food and for this company and please watch over Layla and Peter as they get closer to their wedding date and may You just grant us a wonderful lunch that ends with custard. Amen."

I grin and take a bite of my sandwich. "So. What do you have going on this week?"

"I have a lot of work to do. Same story as always."

"You work too much."

He shrugs. "I'm single. I live in a cheap apartment. This is the only time in my life where I can work a lot and save a lot without having all the guilt about having a wife or kids at home, so I might as well do it, right?"

Well, when he puts it like that . . .

"Besides," he takes a bite of his sandwich, "you're one to talk."

Also another fair point. Maybe it would be better if we moved the conversation off work.

"So I have a question for you," he says after chewing and swallowing a bite of his meat-stuffed sandwich. He looks around the restaurant first, then lowers his voice. "My mom is coming to town."

I wait for him to finish talking and ask me whatever the question was, but he doesn't. He just sits there, looking at me pensively with his blue eyes.

"And?" I say finally.

"And she's coming to town and I'd really like for you to meet her."

Tyler's mom is not a Christian. She apparently rarely visits him or his sister. Which is weird because his sister just had a baby and you'd think if your child just had one, you'd be there before the baby was even born.

That's what my mom has already arranged with me anyway. One night she called me at midnight after I'd already been in bed for two hours and went off on this story about her dear friend whose daughter didn't want her there when her grandchild was born. "Promise me!" Mom cried. "Promise me that when you are pregnant and in labor that I can be there to meet my grandbaby!"

Considering she asked me this at midnight, I probably would have promised to name the child after her too. I'm not too coherent past a certain point. I'm not a morning person. I'm not a night person. I just like my bed.

I nod to Tyler. "Of course I'll meet her."

"Really?" He reacts like I just agreed to go skydiving over Paris with him. His eyes are all wide and dilated, and he's twisting his napkin in his lap.

I immediately worry. "Wait, why are you acting like this?"

"Acting like what? I'm not acting like anything."

"You look like you just came from the eye doctor. Your pupils are all dilated."

He starts rubbing his fists into his eyes. "Oh, that's probably from all the preservatives in the meat."

"I think not."

He sighs. "I just . . . I guess to be fair, I need to give you a little warning. I don't talk much about my mom because I don't see her very much. Which, honestly, isn't really a bad thing. I just . . ." he trails off again, looking in the back of the restaurant.

Randy sees his stare, nods, and comes over right then with two wooden excuses for a spoon with vanilla custard on top.

"Ready for your tasting then?"

I'm not done with my sandwich, but that's never stopped me from eating ice cream before. I take the stick from Randy, slurp the custard down, and immediately order a cup of it after he shows me the sizes of the cone and the cup.

"I have vanilla, chocolate, chocolate chip, or peach," Randy says to me.

That song about one of these things doesn't belong started playing through my head, and I frowned at him. "Peach?"

He shrugs. "Apparently it's a southern thing?"

"Right. Can I have half chocolate and half vanilla?"

"Yep. For you?" He looks at Tyler.

"Chocolate. All chocolate."

I knew there was a reason I liked this guy. He looks cute today, but he looks cute every day. His blond hair is curly and totally out of control. He's wearing a blue T-shirt under a checkered button-down with the sleeves rolled up, and the shirt just makes his eyes look even bluer.

"So," I say. "Back to the topic at hand."

"Mom called last week and said she wanted to come see me. Said it had been too long and she couldn't even remember what I looked like."

I nod. "Usually a good sign that it's been too long."

"She's coming next weekend." Tyler rubs the back of his neck and winces at me. "Here's the thing about my mom. I haven't dated anyone in six years, but the last time I was dating a girl and my mom was around, she wasn't exactly . . . nice to her."

Well, that's cheery news.

Randy sets our frozen custard down in front of us, and the cup suddenly seems tiny.

"We might need more of this," I tell him.

"You just let me know." Randy nods and leaves.

I dig my spoon in the creaminess, eat a bite, and let the sugary milk work its magic on my brain.

"So," I say again, slowly. "Your mom is mean."

"No, no. She's not *mean*, per se."

"Per se?"

"She's more of . . . just a little . . . hmm . . ." He stops talking and squints at my right shoulder. I am inhaling the ice cream.

"What?" I finally ask when he has been staring at my shoulder for an entire minute.

"I can't find the right word to describe her." He digs in the pocket of his jeans and pulls out his cell phone. "I'm going to make a call."

"What are you going to do? Ask her to describe herself?"

He grins at me. "There's an idea. No, I'm calling Stef." He tucks the phone against his ear and takes a bite of custard while it's apparently ringing. A second later he brightens. "Hey, sis. Question for you. How would you describe Mom?"

I'm making seriously good time on my ice cream.

All kinds of new things are coming out about Tyler. Crazy past, crazy mom, crazy curly hair. Though, to be fair, I knew about the hair.

Tyler's talking to Stef. "What? No, like what word would you use to describe her personality? A clean word, Stef." He rolls his eyes at me. "What? Oh, because I'm sitting here talking to Paige and Mom is coming into town next weekend. I'm trying to prepare her."

He gives me a weird look. "I mean, I guess . . . okay." He hands the phone over to me, and I just look at it blankly like I've never seen such an object before. "It's Stef," he says.

Yes. I knew that.

"She wants to talk to you."

I take the phone, swallowing a bite of ice cream too quickly. I will pay for this with a brain freeze.

"Hello?" I ask, not quite sure what to expect.

"Paige!" Stef sounds like a higher pitched version of her brother. "It is so good to talk to you! I've heard a million things about you, of course. I think it's so wonderful you are dating my brother! Goodness knows he needs a good woman out there. When I saw him right before he met you, he looked gloomier than a man who lost a bet and had to try out for the Rockettes, if you know what I mean."

I grin. I have a feeling I will get along well with Stef.

She is still talking. "Anyway, I only have like five minutes because Kamden is going to need to nurse here, and I just still haven't gotten the whole one-handed nursing thing down, you know?"

I did not know, but it really only took two minutes of talking with Stef to realize that she didn't really need an actual human to be listening to have this conversation.

"So, Tyler just said my mom is coming there? Next weekend? That's great and all and I'm sure he wants you to meet her and honestly I'm very jealous because I really wanted to be the first person to meet you, but this whole having a baby and not really being able to function without my nursing pillow or my little inner tube is still an issue as far as traveling." She pauses. "I tore really bad in labor so I have to sit on a little mini inner tube."

And that's all I needed to know about that.

"So I'm glad you'll get to meet Mom because it will give you a lot of insight into the saving grace of God because without Jesus, Tyler and I would have ended up just like her."

Tyler is eating his ice cream and just smiling at me in a sweet way. And I sort of realize right then that Tyler wants me to like his family. It's adorable in a way that sort of makes me want to put my head between my knees and practice my deep breathing.

"Anyway, Mom isn't mean but she is sort of self-righteous. She has this way of making people feel like they could be compared to gnats and probably would lose to the gnat as far as the value scale went."

Well, that's encouraging news.

"Just try not to pay attention to it. She only acts that way because she doesn't know Jesus, so just keep reminding yourself of that. And also just remember that she treats everyone like that, so don't think of it as a diss on you personally."

"Okay," I say. A tiny baby starts crying on the phone.

"All right. Well, I got to go. If this kid continues to eat like this as a teenager, we are going to need to take out a second mortgage to pay for food. Tell my brother I love him. Nice to talk to you, Paige!"

She hangs up and I hand Tyler his phone. "She loves you."

"She has to. So, what did she tell you about Mom? Anything helpful?"

I nod and down the rest of my ice cream and wave to Randy for seconds. "Lots of helpful things. So when does she get here?"

"Not until late Saturday night. And she's apparently leaving Monday."

I'm not sure why you would bother coming for such a short visit, but I don't say that.

Another thought hits me as I'm waiting for the second round of custard. Maybe I should clear it with Mom first, but if I'm meeting his mother . . .

"Tyler?" I ask before I can chicken out. "Would you like to come to Austin with me on Saturday and meet my family?

We're all going to be there for the shower and we'll probably just get an early dinner afterward and head back home. And it's a couples' shower, so you don't have to feel weird about coming."

He grins at me. "I'd love to."

Apparently he didn't have to think about that one.

Randy brings two more cups of frozen custard to the table. "Told you it was good." He grins as he leaves.

It was good, but if we weren't both looking at a weekend full of meeting each other's families, would it be so amazingly delicious?

Chapter
13

Mom is, of course, ecstatic that Tyler is coming on Saturday. Mostly because that is just kindling the hope that I might not be their unmarried, spinster daughter for the rest of my life.

Spinster. I'm twenty-three years old!

"Does he like seafood? Oh, maybe he's one of those poor unfortunate souls who is allergic to shellfish. Is he allergic to shellfish, Paige?"

I'm hearing that song that Ursula sang on *The Little Mermaid* in my head now, so I'm not paying super-close attention to her question. I've been listening to Mom's questions for the last four days, ever since I told her Tyler was coming.

I should have listened to my common sense and just surprised her at the door with him.

I snort. Now there would have been a scene.

"Paige!"

"Yes, Mother?"

"Is he allergic to shellfish?"

"I don't think so, but I can't say that I've ever eaten shell-fish with him so I don't know."

"Well, find out."

"Mom?"

"Yes, honey?"

"When was the last time you made something with shell-fish?" My dad is not a fish person. Beef, yes. Chicken, yes. Any form of pork, definitely yes. Fish, not so much.

"You never know when I might decide to whip together a shrimp scampi, Paige."

"Okay then."

"I'll call if I have more questions. Good night!"

I hang up and shake my head apologetically at Layla. We are busy creating the favors for the guests that she felt obliged to buy. She picked up little jars, and we are pains-takingly filling them with M&M's in the same colors as her wedding.

"I'm surprised she hasn't asked for his pant size yet," Layla says. "Knowing your mom, she's probably sewing him a pair of pajamas or something."

I grin at her. "Don't even say such things." I definitely get my crafty side from my mother, but she can go a little over-board at times.

We are sitting cross-legged on the floor in my living room, and I arch my back and set another completed jar in the box we're keeping them in.

"Thanks for doing this," Layla says.

"No problem. I finally feel like I'm actually your maid of honor." I look over at her. She appears much more peaceful than she did the last time she was over at my apartment.

"Doing well?" I ask her.

She looks up from the jar she's working on and nods. "Much better. We ended up asking Rick if we could meet one more time for our premarital counseling and told him what was going on."

"He apparently had some good advice?"

"He gave us homework actually." She grins. "And here I thought I was done with homework forever. He told us to go out to dinner that night and not discuss a word about the wedding. And then we've had stuff to do every night this week. We had to go for a walk or bike ride together, we had to find an activity that neither of us had ever done and do that together . . . a bunch of stuff. And we've had to write letters to each other every day in a journal that we will give each other after we get married." She nods. "It's been helping."

"Good." I have to give props to Rick. Those sound like great ideas.

"And . . ." She sighs sadly. "I think I'll have to give Belle back to the shelter."

I frown. "Why?" Not that I'm sad, because I have yet to see the dog since she has become Belle, but I know Layla was pretty attached to the idea of a dog.

"Apparently she barks from the minute I leave my apartment to go to work until right when I return. I've gotten three notices from the apartment manager." She rubs her cheek. "I don't know, Paige. It was probably a mistake to get her. I mean, she needs a yard and someone who is home for more than just a couple of hours at night."

I nod, proud of myself that I'm withholding my "I told you so" speech. "I'm sorry."

She shrugs. "It was worth a shot. And she is a good dog. She'll make someone very happy. But hopefully someone who has an actual house and maybe some little kids to play with."

I nod and set another jar in the box. "That sounds nice for her."

Layla smiles. "It does, doesn't it?"

We work until nearly ten and then we are both yawning. "This is monotonous," Layla mutters.

"You really didn't need to invite three hundred people."

"Tell my mother that. She invited my kindergarten teacher because she said she would probably like the invite." Layla sighs. "So now my kindergarten teacher and her whole family are coming."

Layla's mom is very social.

I set the final jar in the box. "Three hundred," I moan, stretching my fingers out. "And it's official. Should I ever get married someday, I am not making favors for the guests. They can consider the cake their favor."

Layla grins. "Better pick a good cake. Mine is red velvet."

"That's good and southern of you."

"Thanks."

I give her a hug as she leaves. "I'm glad you're doing better."

"Me too. I love you, Paige."

"I love you too, Layla."

* * * * *

Friday morning, I wake up at eight o'clock to a text from Rick.

MANDATORY STAFF MEETING AT 9 A.M. BE THERE OR I UNEARTH THE MARSHMALLOW GUN.

Such a lovely way to wake up.

I moan as I roll off the bed and stumble to my feet. I'm too young to feel this old. Isn't that a country song? I stare into the bathroom mirror as I find my toothbrush.

Sometimes I envy those Hollywood people who get to walk around with their professional airbrushers. I wouldn't mind for someone to knock on the door in a few minutes, set up a salon stool in my bathroom, and start making my face look flawless. I squint at the mirror and see a new wrinkle.

My phone buzzes right then and it's my mom calling.

Again.

"Hello, Mom."

"You're up early."

"So are you."

"What are you doing?"

"Checking out a new wrinkle." I poke at the line by my eye, but it's not going away.

"Please. You are twenty-three years old. Wait until you're fifty. Speaking of which, when do you think you and Tyler will be here in the morning?"

I'm not sure how that was a segue into talking about me and Tyler, but Mom's excited. Which is cute, honestly.

"I'm not sure yet. Probably by ten." Which would mean we would be leaving my apartment at seven.

Yuck.

"Yay!" Mom says. "We can have a family brunch then. Preslee's shower isn't until one, so that gives us lots of time to visit with Tyler before we leave for that. Did you find out if he likes papaya?"

Poor Tyler had been getting constant texts from me lately, courtesy of my mother.

Do you like ground turkey? Can you eat shrimp and not die? Is there a reason why my mother shouldn't clean with traditional antibacterial sprays?

Mom lectured me for almost ten minutes when I questioned that concern. "Paige, do you not read the news? There are *constant* stories about people who are reacting to whatever awful things they put into our household cleaners! People are coming down with rashes, autoimmune diseases, and cancer! Why, there was a lady in Philadelphia who had to be hospitalized for some lung thing she got from inhaling the fumes while she was scrubbing her shower."

"So why don't you switch to something natural?"

"Oh gosh, honey, those don't do a thing. Do you want us all to die from salmonella?"

It was a no-win conversation and luckily one of my girls had shown up to Starbucks right then to meet with me, so I begged off the phone.

I sigh into the phone now. "I have no idea if he likes papaya, Mom. I don't even know if I like papaya because I'm fairly certain I have never had a papaya in my life. Are you really going to be serving it for brunch tomorrow?"

"Well, I was on this recipe-blog thing and they were going on and on about this papaya and watermelon balsamic salad, and I was thinking I might try it."

I can't even think of what a papaya looks like.

I can think about what if feels like to get hit in the face with a stale marshmallow from Rick's marshmallow gun and I start the shower.

"I have to go, Mom. Rick's called a staff meeting in less than an hour, and I still need to shower and eat breakfast."

"Okay. I'll just text if I have more questions. Have a good day, sweetie! Can't wait to see you tomorrow!"

"Love you, Mom." I hang up and hop in the shower, hurrying through the whole shampoo, rinse, and repeat motions.

I get out and dry off, slap on some makeup, blow-dry my hair, and grab a granola bar on my way out the door. I've pulled on jeans and a gray-and-white striped T-shirt and my red ballet flats.

Hopefully horizontal stripes are still in.

I get to the church and I'm walking into the youth office at exactly 8:58. I've even beat the church secretary here this morning. Rick is already sitting in his office chair, marshmallow gun poised at the door. I hold up my phone so he can see the time as I enter.

"Two minutes early," I say, slumping into my chair. "A rushed shower is the beginning of a crappy day, you know."

"We have a situation," Rick starts, not bothering with a hello.

"Okay . . ." I start to worry. Is it one of my girls? Is there a parent who is upset with something Rick or I did? Is someone hurt? Tori. Is it Tori's brother Jake?

I'm gnawing on my lip going through all the possible scenarios in my head. Apparently I have become kind of attached to my girls.

Rick keeps talking. "Now, normally this would not be that big of a deal, but since it involves something that you sort of orchestrated, I felt like you should know as soon as possible."

"What happened?" I'm gasping now, wringing my hands together.

"I think that the high school's homecoming night is on that same night we are planning on doing our Cider House Duels event."

I just stare at him.

"That is why I'm here." My sentence is not a question.

"Yep. So I'm thinking we should probably reschedule that one to sometime at the end of October."

"You woke me up and rushed me through a shower to tell me we need to reschedule an event?"

Rick is aghast. "Not just any event, Paige. Cider House Duels! Remember? Where everyone brings their favorite hot drink, and we all have to vote on which one is the best?"

"Rick, you know that 90 percent of those kids are going to just have their moms make something, and the other 10 percent are going to be stopping by some grocery store and just heating up some milk for Swiss Miss."

"Yes." Rick nods. "But I like Swiss Miss."

I sigh and rub my eyes. "Okay, fine. We can move it to the end of October." That would be better for me anyway. Then both of the weddings will be over, and life will be getting back to a normal pace.

"Perfect." He smiles and then just looks at me. "So. That's all, I think."

I just shake my head at him and stand. "I am going to Starbucks."

"Aren't you most likely going there this afternoon like eight times?"

Yes. Yes, I am.

"Perhaps. But if I'm going to be working in this office all morning with you, I'll need some caffeine." I walk out.

"I'll take one of those vanilla-bean Frappuccino things since you're offering!" Rick yells after me.

"I wasn't!" I yell back.

Geraldine is just sitting down at her desk, tucking her purse into the bottom drawer and pulling her cardigan around her shoulders. "Chilly morning in here," she says to me. "You are here early."

"Want anything from Starbucks?" I ask her, knowing what she'll say but feeling rude if I don't ask her.

"Oh no," Geraldine hums. "Do you know that they inject their coffee beans with more caffeine just so people will get hooked on their coffee instead of Folgers?" She starts tsking, shaking her head from side to side. "No, no. I'll stick with my herbal tea. Thanks, dear."

I'm not sure her information is completely accurate, but I just nod and head back to my car. Thankfully there are about four Starbucks within a two-mile radius of the church. I drive to the one with the drive-thru and order a venti caramel macchiato and a vanilla-bean Frappuccino.

I am an amazing employee. I would like for Rick to take full notice of this. And I'm thankful he requested a caffeine-free drink.

Goodness only knows that Rick does not need to be more hyped up.

He grins as I hand him his icy drink a few minutes later. "You deserve a raise."

"I'm glad you see that."

"Sadly, I can't give you one without the church elders approving."

"I can buy them vanilla-bean Frappuccinos too if that would help." I sit at my desk and turn on my computer.

I work on the postcard for the Cider House Duels for a little bit, and then I work on my lesson for next Wednesday night. One of the moms of one of our junior high boys comes in to talk with Rick about some concerns she has, and I offer to leave but she asks for me to stay and give my opinions too.

Because I obviously have a lot of experience in how to raise a twelve-year-old boy.

"I think he might be getting interested in girls a little too fast," she says, hands together on her lap.

I watch how Rick listens to her, never mocking her worries or even questioning them. He meets her gaze the entire time they are talking.

Rick is crazy and insane and possibly should be on some form of melatonin to calm the insane amount of energy he has, but the man is one of the best listeners of anyone I've ever met.

The lady leaves and I look over at Rick. "How did you learn how to do that?"

"Do what?"

"Listen. Counsel. Whatever that was. She came in here all freaked out and left feeling like she had the tools to parent her son."

He shrugs. "I just listen and try to pray at the same time. Someone told me once in seminary that people don't always need answers; sometimes they just need to be heard." He nods to me. "That's why it is so important that you are here. I don't have a clue what it's like to be a high school girl, but you do. Those girls need understanding and empathy more than they need to be told how to live. And that's why you are needed."

I think about his words the rest of the afternoon. After so many years of feeling useless at the adoption agency I used to work at, the thought of feeling needed was amazingly refreshing.

Chapter 14

Seven in the morning. On a Saturday.

And I am not only awake, I'm showered, fully dressed, and have my makeup on.

There should be laws about this kind of thing.

I even look cute, if I say so myself. The shower is a Western theme, so I'm wearing my favorite pair of jeans, cowboy boots, a button-down camp shirt, and a cami. I even got up early and curled my hair.

I look like I am on my way to a rodeo.

I am standing in the kitchen, blearily considering how long it takes to make a pot of coffee versus how long it takes to go through the drive-thru at Starbucks when Tyler knocks on the door. I open it and he looks about as awake as I feel.

"Good morning," he mutters.

"Hey."

Then we both just stand there for a few minutes, blinking at each other. I told him about the Western-themed shower, and he went with the cowboy outfit as well. He's wearing straight-cut jeans, a button-down shirt, and today is the first time I've ever seen him in cowboy boots. His hair is curling haphazardly and his shirt makes his blue eyes look even bluer.

He finally manages a smile. "Good to know you aren't really a morning person either."

"I'm also not a night person." Better to inform him of this now before the relationship goes any further. "I just like to sleep."

"I knew I liked you for a reason."

"Coffee here or coffee from Starbucks?"

He thinks it over before nodding to the door. "Starbucks. If I'm expected to drive six hours total without falling asleep at the wheel, I'll need a couple of extra shots this morning."

Starbucks it is, then.

I loop my purse over my shoulder, pick up the bag that is my shower gift and card for Preslee and Wes that I signed from Tyler and me.

Even though he has no idea what it is.

I lock the door behind me and follow him to his truck.

He stops before he gets there and turns to look at me. "Good morning, beautiful." He pulls me into a gigantic hug. His arms close tight around my waist, and I smell his spicy aftershave.

I smile when he pulls away. "Good morning." He opens the passenger door and there is a bouquet of tulips lying on the seat.

"Oh, you're so sweet!"

"Thanks, but those aren't actually for you." Tyler grins.

I just look at him.

"They're for your mom. You know, for feeding me and letting me come hang out today last minute."

I slide the tulips out of the way and climb into the truck. "Looking for a few brownie points, I see."

He grins, closes my door, and walks around to the driver's seat. "You can never have too many brownie points when it comes to mothers. And if I can speak hypothetically here, I want there to be a million brownie points in my column if *this*"—he waves his finger back and forth between us—"continues."

A hundred and twelve mating butterflies land with a whoosh in my stomach.

I remember something Layla said when I asked her if she knew Peter was going to propose, and she said that she knew because he started using the word *hypothetically* a lot.

"He'd be all, 'so, hypothetically, when during the year would your perfect wedding be?' Or, 'hypothetically, where would you want to live in ten years?'"

The butterflies multiply and divide in my stomach.

Tyler pulls up to Starbucks a few minutes later and rolls down his window. "Okay," he says to the speaker. "I need a grande caramel macchiato and a venti Americano with three extra shots please."

I look at him wide-eyed as he drives forward to the window to pay. "You will never sleep again."

"Right now, that's looking like a life-saving thing. Hi there," he says to the girl at the window. She tells him the total. He waves off the five dollar bill I'm handing him and pays for it. We are headed toward I-35 a few minutes later, the smell of coffee taking over the car.

"Mm," I mutter, squishing back into my seat, cupping my hands around the paper-shrouded macchiato, totally content. "Thank you."

"You're welcome. So. Excited for today?" Tyler merges onto the interstate. We officially have a little over three hours to kill now.

Sometimes this drive seems awfully long for such a short amount of time.

"Yes. I'm curious about the shower, though. Apparently it's going to be a lot of people from their church and some of my mom and dad's friends. So I don't know that I will know that many people."

"But you're good with new people, so it will be fine." Tyler sips his coffee, his left hand on the wheel.

"Not really."

"Sure you are. I've seen you with the new kids at youth events. You're always super sweet and outgoing."

"That's because I force myself to be like that. It's not a natural thing," I tell him.

"So what is a natural thing for you?"

"Sitting in my apartment with my sewing machine watching HGTV, probably," I say after thinking about it for a few minutes.

He laughs. "You're a good faker then."

"Thanks. I think."

"So, tell me about Wes."

I think about Preslee's perfect fiancé and the three times I've actually been around him. "I don't know him very well. He's tall."

"Tall. That's all you can tell me about him?"

"I mean, he seems nice. He's a pastor's kid. I think he has a couple of siblings, and he's the first one out of his family to get married. His mom is apparently really broken up over it." Preslee had complained about her future mother-in-law for almost thirty minutes one day before suddenly realizing that someday she would have that woman's grandbabies, and she would never want them to leave her either.

Now Preslee has all kinds of compassion for Wes's mom.

Tyler nods. "I've heard that can happen."

"Was your mom upset when Stef got married?"

He shrugs. "You forget that we aren't really close with my mom. I mean, both of us left for college and never really looked back. But we didn't have much to look back to. We spent the majority of our childhood shuttling back and forth from Mom's to Dad's. So, no, I wouldn't say that Mom was upset. Dad was ticked off, but that was more because Stef wanted to get married rather than just live with Mason, which my dad saw as just an excuse for an expensive wedding."

I look out the window and then over at Tyler. "I'm sorry."

He smiles at me. "Why are you sorry? You didn't have anything to do with it. And honestly, I'm not sorry either, because if it hadn't happened like that, I never would have picked a faraway college, I never would have met my roommate, and he couldn't have dragged me to hear that preacher talk, so then I would have never become a Christian, and you and I wouldn't be having this conversation."

"That was quite the run-on sentence. You sound like Layla." Layla is notorious for telling an entire story without pausing for one breath.

"Now there's a scary thought." Tyler grins over at me.

We talk about everything and nothing for the next hour and a half. Waco is just a few minutes down the road, and I wonder if Preslee has left for Mom and Dad's yet. Because

I need to use the bathroom, and I'm fairly sure hers will be cleaner than whatever gas station or fast-food restaurant we find along the road.

I pull out my phone and it rings three times before she finally answers.

"Hey."

"Hi. Are you still home?" I ask.

"Nope. Halfway to Mom's. Why? Did I forget something?"

"No, I just wanted to use your bathroom."

She laughs. "Okay, well, go use it."

"I'm not going to go use your bathroom when you aren't even there!"

"Why not?"

I shrug even though I'm on the phone. "Well, I mean, what if something happens?"

"Like what? Just aim well."

I snort.

"Seriously, if you want to, go for it. There's a key on top of the porch light."

"Isn't that the first place robbers look?"

"I thought it was under the mat."

"I don't know, Preslee. I didn't actually watch that entire show."

"What show?"

"The one about inside a burglar's mind or something like that."

"I didn't know there even was a show like that. Well, regardless. If someone broke in, I'm fairly certain they would be terribly disappointed. The only thing of value I keep in that apartment is an old necklace of Gran's, and I'm pretty sure it's actually just costume jewelry."

Tyler points to a McDonald's up ahead and I nod. "That's okay, Preslee. Thanks though."

"Suit yourself. See you guys in about ninety minutes."

Tyler parks in front of McDonald's, and we both use the restroom. I walk out and find him looking at the menu. "Is eight thirty in the morning too early for a milkshake?"

"You seriously are like just begging for a heart attack someday, aren't you?"

"I'll take that as a yes."

"Mom's making brunch, don't forget. And my mother knows her brunch."

He nods. "Say no more. Let's go get on the road again."

This is always the longest part of the trip once you pass Waco. When I would drive home all through college, I would always stop at a Dairy Queen or somewhere and get a Blizzard for the remainder of the drive both going and coming back.

Tyler turns the radio to country and Keith Urban starts serenading us quietly in the background.

"So I don't ask you this enough, but how's the new job going?" Tyler reaches for my hand now that his coffee is gone and his hand is free.

"Good. I'm really liking it. I love meeting with the girls and I'm really learning a lot." Mostly about myself, but I leave that part off.

Tyler tends to be a little nosy about what God has been teaching me lately. And when what He's been teaching me has a lot to do with forgiving Tyler for his past before he came to Christ, it's probably best to keep that between the Lord and me right now.

"I really like this new curriculum Rick's written for the

youth group nights," Tyler says. "I don't think I've ever done an in-depth study on the fruit of the Spirit before."

"I haven't either."

This week we will be on patience. Which I thought was very funny considering Tyler's apparently difficult mother is coming in town tonight.

Sometimes God's timing is just weird.

"So, hypothetically, where do you see yourself in five years or so?" Tyler asks.

I just look at his profile. He's wearing aviator sunglasses and the morning sun is glinting off his blond hair. He looks like he could pick up a guitar and start serenading me about something flowery.

"What?" he asks after a minute of me just staring at him.

"Oh!" I jump. "Oh nothing."

"Is that a weird question?"

"No, it's just — " I stop just short of telling him that Peter used to ask Layla that right before he proposed.

So maybe Layla was wrong. It's not like she's always right. She's often right but she's not always right.

And even if it did mean Tyler was considering proposing, was that such a bad thing?

Oh my goodness, my stomach feels like Jell-O that hasn't fully set.

"Um, I uh," I stutter.

He grins over at me. "So here's what I was thinking. In five years, I would like to be married. I'd like to be thinking about kids or already have them. And I'd like to have finally gotten a promotion so I don't have to work such ridiculous hours." He quirks a cute little sideways grin at me. "*Hypothetically*, of course."

Dear Lord, he said the *married* word.

I look at our hands woven together on the seat between us, at his curly blond hair and sweet smile as he watches the road, and suddenly the Jell-O in my stomach is set and I could actually envision it.

"I think . . . I think that sounds good," I say in a soft voice.

He grins.

We pull up to my parents' house almost exactly ninety minutes later. Wes's tiny little blue car is parked in their huge driveway, and Tyler pulls up next to it and picks up the flowers while I gather my purse and the present for Preslee and Wes.

Mom is already standing on the porch waving at us. "Oh hi! Hi!" She runs over to give me a hug.

I hug my mom and I'm suddenly just very happy.

I love my mom. I don't get to see her enough.

She goes to hug Tyler and I just smile at her. Preslee got her cuteness from my mom. Mom isn't short but she isn't tall either. She's petite in her weight and has shoulder-length brown hair. She's wearing boots and a skirt and looks adorable.

Preslee is right behind Mom and gives me a big hug, frowning at the bag. "I told you not to get me anything!"

"Right," I roll my eyes. "Like that was going to happen. I would have been kicked out of the maid-of-honor club."

"Not necessarily." She grins at Tyler. "Hey there, Tyler. Good to see you again."

Tyler gives my sister a hug. Dad and Wes are in the kitchen, and we all go in there where it smells heavenly.

"Dad, Wes, this is Tyler. Tyler, this is my dad and Preslee's fiancé."

They all shake hands. Mom is going on and on about the flowers Tyler brought her and Tyler smiles easily. "Thank you for having me today, Mrs. Alder."

"Oh, my goodness, do *not* call me Mrs. Alder! It's Gina. Please."

"Okay. Thanks, Gina."

"So, Tyler," Dad starts in his fatherly voice.

"Hold that thought, honey, let's pray. The food is going to be too done and we're going to be late for the shower. There will be plenty of time to grill the poor boy while we're eating." Mom slips an arm around Dad's waist.

I grin.

Dad prays for the brunch, and then Mom starts emptying enough food to feed a small continent out of the ovens and the refrigerator. She's got a ham, homemade cinnamon rolls, sausages, bacon, hash browns, croissants, a fruit salad, and some bagels with cream cheese, and a bunch of different jellies.

It's like she thinks we've suddenly all morphed into the University of Texas football team or something.

"Dig in!" She sets the last of the six jelly jars down. "Plates are on the table."

"Good grief, Mom, did you think we haven't eaten all year?" Preslee asks, reaching for her plate.

"I know you guys don't eat as well now as you did. Let me spoil you."

Well, she has that right. I think about my dinners this week. There was a lot of popcorn and spoonfuls of peanut butter.

I would not recommend spoonfuls of peanut butter for dinner. Brushing my teeth later was disgusting.

We all pile our plates and sit at the table. Mom and Dad take the ends, Tyler and I have one side, and Preslee and Wes have the other.

"So Tyler," Dad starts again, as soon as he sits down. "Tell us about yourself."

Tyler smiles and I realize that he is very easy around other people. Even my dad, apparently, which can sometimes be an issue.

Dad has never been the nicest to my boyfriends. Not that there have been very many of them, but I'm remembering one time specifically where he definitely made the poor guy who was supposed to take me to my prom cry.

I ended up going to the prom with some friends from church because the guy never showed up.

When I complained, Dad told me that any guy worth my time should be able to talk to my father, or it was going to be the worst Christmases ever for the rest of my life.

I guess he had a fair point.

"I'm a software engineer," Tyler tells Dad. "So right now our company is expanding like crazy and signing a bunch of contracts with some huge businesses in Dallas, which just means I have to work a lot of late nights and weekends, but they do compensate well for the extra time. I go to the same church as Paige and I teach the freshmen boys every Wednesday night."

Dad is nodding, so I'm assuming Tyler is passing so far.

I bite into a forkful of fluffy, icing-covered cinnamon roll and everything is very right with the world.

Preslee is waving a fork. "So, Paige, remind me at the shower to introduce you to this friend of mine who is a personal trainer."

My mouth is stuffed with cinnamon roll and I frown at her. "What are you saying?" I ask around the sugar-laden bread.

"That wasn't very kind, Preslee," Mom tsks.

She starts laughing. "I didn't mean anything like that!" Preslee stabs a cube of watermelon with her fork. "She's moving to Dallas in three weeks to start working at a Pilates studio, and I just figured she could use some friends."

I nod. "I'll probably have to contact her after all the weddings."

"I'm sure that's fine."

We talk for the next two hours. Tyler tells more about his job and how he ended up in Dallas and a Christian, and Wes tells a little bit of his story that I hadn't heard before.

Apparently, he was adopted when he was two days old.

Coming from working at an adoption agency, it's always fun to see the long-term happiness from an adoption. I heard so many good stories over the few years I worked there, but I also heard a lot of bad stories.

Good ones are always welcome.

"So, I was the oldest and then my mom and dad adopted my sisters from the Ukraine. They're twins and we got them when they were eight months old. They were dropped off at an orphanage right after birth and they couldn't do anything, they were just these tiny blobs with basically no hair because the orphanage was just so overrun that they couldn't really give all the kids the attention they needed."

"That's just awful." Mom shakes her head.

"Well, now they're twenty-one and too beautiful for their own good." Wes grins. "I spend a lot of time trying to talk my mom and dad into locking them into some sort of a tower so they don't end up with some jerks."

Tyler grins and I see the beginnings of male bonding.

Something very warm starts in my stomach. My boyfriend is getting along with my soon-to-be brother-in-law.

I didn't grow up around boys, so having two at the table who are getting along and actually making my dad laugh is something pretty special.

"You should have seen me when my sister started bringing Mason, now my brother-in-law, around," Tyler tells Wes. "I even went on about 50 percent of their dates because I was so paranoid about her being with any guy other than me. She hated me for a long time because of that."

Preslee shakes her head. "I feel like I should start praying now that someday, a long time from now . . ." she looks over at Mom, "a very *long* time from now, when or if God gives us children that He'll give us sons." She grins at Wes. "I'm not sure you could take having a daughter."

Dad sighs, looking from me to Preslee. "It's hard, I'll tell you that much."

Right then I finally recognize something.

My family is changing right before my very eyes. I look across the table at Preslee and Wes smiling all lovey at each other, and it hits me that my baby sister is getting married.

Married.

It's like this whole time I've been so focused on how we have Preslee back, that she's finally walking with God again, and we're finally on the track to healing our relationship, and now she's going to get married and I'm suddenly going to have a brother.

I glance over at my dad and he's staring all wistfully at Preslee, even though she doesn't notice it. He looks sad. My parents cried forever over Preslee. Every Christmas she didn't come home. Every day was hard but significant days were worse.

And now, in a sense, they are losing her again.

I'm making myself depressed.

We talk and finish breakfast, then Preslee and I help Mom clean the kitchen while Dad shows Tyler and Wes the work he's been doing on the backyard. Mom and Dad live on a couple of acres, so Dad has his work cut out for him. He loves it. He talks all the time about how he can't wait to retire so he can work on the house all day long.

Which is probably why Mom keeps encouraging him to stick it out one more year at the office.

"I think he's adorable," Preslee declares the second the back door closes behind the boys.

"I should hope so. You're marrying him in three weeks," I tell her.

"Not Wes, idiot. *Tyler.* He's adorable. And can you just picture that curly blond hair on a little baby some day?" She bumps Mom with her hip, and they both sigh over the cuteness of these fictional babies.

I'm trying not to hyperventilate.

Mom and Dad will have leftovers for the rest of the month. Mom sighs as she puts the ham into the biggest Tupperware container she has. "You guys didn't eat enough."

"Mom, if I ate any more, I'll need new pants for the shower," I tell her.

"What she said." Preslee nods to Mom.

"You're wearing a skirt," I tell Preslee.

"Skirt, pants. Same diff."

"Not to the Puritans," I tell her.

She snorts.

Mom reaches over and pulls both of us into a hug, and tears pool in her eyes. "Oh, I love this," she says quietly.

We both hug her back and nobody mentions why this didn't happen for years. Sometimes it's best to just move on.

The boys come back inside and Tyler grins at me. "So, your dad is getting chickens."

I look up quickly. "Like live ones?" I try not to let the panic show in my voice.

"Sure," Dad says. "I've been reading up on them. There's very little maintenance, you don't have to worry about them digging up the yard, and you get fresh eggs every morning. Isn't that wonderful?"

"But is it really worth it?" I ask Dad. "I mean, you'd have to build the chicken coop, feed them every day, and gather all the eggs. And eggs aren't really that expensive, Dad. A couple of dollars for a dozen isn't that bad."

"If your grandpa were here, he'd tell you about how they sold a dozen eggs for a quarter on the side of the road every day after school, and that's how he bought his first bicycle," Dad says.

"I mean, live chickens are just so . . . alive," I say.

Tyler's grinning so big that he's making my cheeks hurt. "Got something against poultry, Paige?"

"No, I mean, if that's what Dad wants to get, it's fine." I try to sound offhand about it.

"She hates birds," Preslee says.

I glare at her.

"Can't stand them," Preslee continues. "There's a Target here where for whatever reason there are always these huge flocks of birds that sit on the roof and fly over the parking lot and land on the lights around the parking lot, and Paige always refused to go. I finally figured out that she's freaked out by birds."

"Really? I didn't know that about you, Paige," Tyler says.

"Their beaks creep me out. Okay?"

Tyler nods. "I'll try to remember not to buy you a parakeet."

"And their beady little eyes. And the feathers. And the fact that they can poop while they're flying over you and it might land in your hair."

Preslee is laughing at me. "Hey, Paige, do you still refuse to go on an outdoor roller coaster?"

I'm immediately lasering her with a glare that could melt kryptonite. "Don't. You. Dare."

"What's wrong with outdoor roller coasters?" Tyler asks innocently.

Preslee grins at me. "Sorry, sister. It's better if he knows the real you."

"Preslee!"

"She's afraid a bird might hit her in the face."

Everyone is quiet for a minute and then they all start laughing. I watch my family brushing away tears from the hilarity of my worst fear and shake my head. "This is a cold house today, folks."

Chapter
15

Preslee's shower should have been billed as the time I would watch my sister try to open 1,325 presents in less than an hour. The girl's fingers started bleeding she was unwrapping so much.

That and maybe because one of the bows was like a razor.

She got an entire kitchen, three times the amount of towels any person will ever need for a whole lifetime, cookbooks, movies, and two vacuum cleaners. As I was stuffing the last of the tissue paper in a huge black trash bag, I could suddenly see why everyone seemed to be rushing to the altar.

You make out with the presents when you get married.

"This is better than Christmas!" Preslee giggled after everyone had left.

Wes and Tyler were already muscling all of the presents out the door and trying to puzzle-fit them into my mom's Tahoe.

The shower was really cute. Red bandanas were on all the tables, yellow daisies in boots were scattered all over the room, cowboy hats hung from every available ledge.

It was like all of the clichés about Texas were in one room.

Wes comes walking back in, looking exhausted. It was obvious during the couples' shower today that Preslee was definitely the most outgoing of the two of them. Wes tended to stay back, talking a little bit but mostly letting her have the floor.

Which was funny because it was mostly his friends here.

"Is that everything?" he asks, backhanding his forehead. "And the correct answer to that question is yes, because I don't think we'll be able to fit another thing in that car."

Preslee and my mom look around while I stuff even more ripped wrapping paper into the bulging trash bag.

If it were me opening these presents, I would have unwrapped them carefully so I could reuse all the paper. And I asked Preslee if she wanted to save the bags and tissue paper and she said, "Why?"

Oh, the differences between us.

Tyler comes in then, looking at his cell phone. "It's almost four, Paige."

I nod. "We'll need to go in a few minutes," I tell Mom and Preslee.

"What time does your mom get in town, Tyler?" Mom asks him.

"Around eight, I think."

Mom nods. "You guys should probably head back. Don't you know today would be the day where it would be bumper-to-bumper traffic the whole way."

I've driven back and forth from Dallas to Austin a hundred times in the last couple of years, and I've never been in bumper-to-bumper traffic the entire way.

But I just nod, hand Wes the huge bag of trash and give Mom, Dad, and Preslee hugs. "I guess the next time I see you will be at your wedding."

"Not *at* the wedding. I'm planning on getting into my dress with you around, and goodness knows I'm not doing that as part of the actual wedding." Preslee grins.

"That would probably be best. I'm sure we'll talk in the next couple of weeks."

"I'm sure we will." She looks at Tyler and smiles prettily at him. "I'm so glad you guys drove down for this."

Tyler gives Mom and Preslee hugs again and shakes Wes's and Dad's hands. "Good to see you guys and meet some of you. Looking forward to the wedding." He had been invited about eight times by this point.

We walk outside and climb into his truck, which is like an oven, especially since both of us are in jeans for the shower. He immediately cranks the air-conditioning and rolls the windows down, trying to blow the hot air out.

"What are you going to do with your mom tonight?"

I'm planning on joining them for lunch tomorrow. My stomach knots a little at the thought. I've been thinking about what Stef said about her mom since I talked to her on the phone that day at lunch.

To say I'm nervous is sort of an understatement.

"I'm not sure. I might see if she wants to go get dessert somewhere. Mom is a lot happier when we are out doing things. She's not so good at sitting around my apartment."

I immediately start worrying. What if Tyler is like his mom? What if he really doesn't like just sitting around my apartment which, if I have to be honest, is one of my favorite things to do? I love nights where I get to change into my yoga pants and lie on the couch with a bowl of popcorn and HGTV.

"Do you . . . like to just sit around your apartment?" I ask slowly, trying not to sound like I'm fishing for answers even though I am.

He grins over at me behind his aviator glasses. The man looks like a Gap ad right now. "Have you seen my apartment? Definitely not. But I do like sitting around *your* apartment."

That makes me feel better.

It's not hard to convince Tyler to make my traditional stop at Dairy Queen in Waco. I get my Blizzard and Tyler gets a milk shake.

We finally pull into my apartment complex at almost seven thirty. I'm yawning. Days spent in the car always make me tired for some reason.

Tyler shifts the truck into Park in the space beside my car. "I'll see you tomorrow. I'm going to try to talk her into going to church, so would you mind saving two seats just in case? I'll text you if we aren't coming."

I nod. "I can do that." I smile over at him. "Thanks for coming today, Tyler. My family loved you."

"I had fun." He smiles over at me and then leans across the center console and kisses my cheek. "I'll walk you to your door."

"Don't do that, you have to leave right away."

"Come on now, let me be a gentleman."

I roll my eyes, but I release my seat belt and let him follow me up the steps to my apartment.

It's already starting to get dark which is always a welcome thing this time of year because it means cooler temperatures are coming. I jab my key in the door, unlock it, then turn to Tyler.

"Thanks for walking me the long, difficult walk to my door," I say, slightly sarcastically.

He grins. "You're welcome," he repeats in the same tone of voice. He pulls me in for a hug but doesn't let go when I loosen my grip.

Instead he hugs me tighter and then pushes me back slightly, searching my eyes. He opens his mouth like he's going to say something and then apparently changes his mind and closes his mouth, smiling slightly at me. "Well. Have a good night, Paige."

It's the most awkward thing he's ever told me. Not in the words themselves, but in the way he says it.

I kind of nod. "Okay. Thanks, Tyler. You too."

Then he's gone, disappearing down my stairs, and I hear his truck's engine as I close and lock my front door.

Weird.

So far dinner has been the Blizzard at Dairy Queen, so I find a bag of packaged salad in the fridge and rip open the top, drizzling the little bag of dressing over the lettuce and sprinkling on the little wrapped-up pack of sunflower seeds and dried cranberries. I grab a fork and start poking it into the bag, then carry it over to the couch.

I saw someone do this on a movie once, and I thought it was the saddest thing I'd ever seen since obviously they were so alone that they didn't even use an actual plate. But then I realized the value of it.

No plate equals no dishes to clean.

Genius.

I settle on the couch but instead of reaching for the remote, I just sit there, thinking.

My family loved Tyler. It took my dad a little bit, but he

really did warm up to him. Dad's always been way more hesitant to bestow his approval on a boy that Preslee or I liked, while Mom, on the other hand, has always been rolling out the red carpet for every single one.

One guy I dated, she called up the boy's mother and asked her for her son's favorite dessert. And then she baked a rhubarb pie.

That was the end of that relationship. I can't be with someone who enjoys rhubarb that much. The guy ate like the entire pie, which was good because no one else could stand the taste or texture of it.

I pull my cell phone out.

WHAT IS YOUR FAVORITE DESSERT?

I might as well see if this relationship is going anywhere.

A couple of minutes later, I get a reply. CHOCOLATE-CHIP COOKIES. WHY?

Good answer. I fish another piece of dressing-drenched lettuce out of the bag and type back.

JUST CURIOUS. HAVE A GOOD TIME WITH YOUR MOM, TYLER.

THANKS! NIGHT, PAIGE.

I grab my Bible and bring it over to the couch then. It's a little early, but one of my favorite shows doesn't come on for another half hour, which gives me lots of time to read. Plus, maybe I'll be more awake if I'm not lying in bed while reading it.

I'm flipping to Ecclesiastes when Psalm 103 catches my eye.

"He has not dealt with us according to our sins, nor rewarded us according to our iniquities. For as high as the heavens are above the earth, so great is His lovingkindness toward those who

fear Him. As far as the east is from the west, so far has He removed our transgressions from us."

I look at the words again. East from the west. It's not like a state line, you know. The east and the west never meet. So God just never revisits the idea of someone's sin again, I guess.

I bite the inside of my cheek, thinking. The salad is not sitting so well in my stomach all of a sudden.

How many times have I thought about Tyler's past sin? The answer? Often.

He'll reach for my hand and I automatically wonder how many girls' hands he's held. He'll send me a flirtatious smile, and I'll wonder if the other girls thought he was as cute when he did that with them.

And then there were the other thoughts, the thoughts I tried my hardest to block out as soon as they started creeping up on me.

I remember a sermon Rick preached to the youth one time before I got hired as the intern. He was teaching through the Old Testament heroes and he was talking about Abraham when he slept with Hagar to try and have a son through her.

"You guys are going to be told so many lies in this life," Rick said. "You're going to hear that 'everyone's doing it' or 'it's only natural' or 'just once can't hurt.' Friends, I'm here today to tell you they are wrong. Not everyone is doing it, it's not natural, and just once can hurt. Whatever 'it' is for you. I'm not going to tell you that it isn't going to feel good or make you look good or make you powerful for a moment. But know this: The moment will end. The day will come when we will see Abraham pay for his sin and you will one day too."

Rick stopped then and looked seriously at the kids. "But let's say that this is you. Let's say that you and Abraham already have a lot more in common than you wish you had, including a lot of remorse. Flip over with me to 1 Corinthians 15. Paul has just spent the entire book talking to a church that was planted in the heart of the most immoral city on the earth at the time. Sounds like America, huh? Here's where our hope is when we screw up."

Rick cleared his throat and started reading. "'But thanks be to God, who gives us the victory through our Lord Jesus Christ. Therefore, my beloved brethren, be steadfast, immovable, always abounding in the work of the Lord, knowing that your toil is not in vain in the Lord.'"

I stare at the words fuzzing in front of my eyes in my Bible.

Tyler messed up. He made mistakes.

But God forgave him. He took those mistakes and moved them as far away as the east is from the west. And then He gave Tyler the victory.

I worry about so much. I think about so much. But at the end of the day, Tyler belongs to Jesus now. And I can't do anything to change his past, but he wouldn't be where he is today and who he is today without it.

My head is hurting. I lean my head back on the couch and shut my eyes.

Lord.

It took me months to forgive Preslee enough to let her back into my life. Years to forgive Luke for the awful things he said to me, the terrible way he treated me at the end. When I'm looking at my track record, forgiveness is not really at the top of my list of qualities.

If I had been alive when Jesus was on the earth, I would have been the one asking the question, "How many times do I have to forgive that person, Jesus?"

Only it wasn't the times that Jesus was concerned about. It was the words in the middle.

How many times do I have to forgive him?

There is no "have to" in forgiveness, I think.

I'm such a by-the-rules person. If someone who I consider an authority tells me not to do something, I don't do it. I read every book I had to read for class. I follow every speed-limit sign, and when the light turns yellow, I slow down. I'm always on time.

Now I'm wondering, though, who I'm actually similar to. Jesus? Who was late for healings because He was busy discovering and comforting a woman who had been in pain for years? Who drew in the sand when an adulterous woman was thrown in front of Him, but instead of condemning her, He asked her accusers who of them hadn't sinned themselves? Who knew that Judas was going to betray Him and yet He still ate His last meal with Judas sitting at the table with Him.

I look at the Bible, but instead of words I just see me. Sinful, prideful me.

And I am nothing but ashamed.

In my quest to please God, somehow I missed a very important fact.

It's not a lifetime trying to be sinless we should pursue. Only one Man was able to accomplish that one. No, maybe it was a lifetime of trying to show Jesus to others.

I close my eyes and stay like that a long time.

Chapter 16

I save the two seats directly to my left and closest to the aisle for Tyler and his mom at church the next morning, since the odds are good that they will come in halfway through the music like Tyler always does. I made sure I was wearing something that was both fashionable without being showy and innocent without being too cute. It was completely the result of all of my clothes in my closet currently lying on my bed since I spent the whole morning nixing ideas.

Layla shows up right as I'm setting my Bible on the second seat. "Thanks for saving seats." She hands me my Bible and plops down. "I'm so tired. Mom called last night and we were up talking until one trying to make sure we have everything done for the wedding."

"You have got to start calling me for help, Layla. I'm starting to think you don't like me anymore. And those seats are for Tyler and his mom."

She raises both eyebrows and grins at me. "Well, well, well. Meeting the parent, huh? Is this to assume that you and Tyler have moved beyond 'we're casually dating' mode?"

I shoo her out of the seat and shrug her answer away because I don't want to mention his hypothetical question the other day and have her bust the windows in the church from her screaming.

Apparently she can tell from my face, though.

"Well. I'm so happy for you, Paige. He's such a sweet guy. And Peter just adores him." Layla gives me a hug.

I have a hard time picturing Peter adoring anyone, but I smile and hug her back. "Thanks, Layla."

"Granted, I'm bummed that we won't be sisters someday, but some things are just not meant to be, I guess."

Praise God for that one.

Peter slides into our row, nods a slight smile at me, and then gives Layla a kiss. The more I'm around him, the more I like to think of him as like Mr. Darcy. Reserved and quiet to those around him, but open and accessible to the woman he loves.

At least, that's the story I'm getting from Layla. And she's probably outgoing enough for two people anyway.

"So. Two weeks, five days," I say to them.

They both nod at me, stupid, silly grins on their faces.

That's cute. Something in my chest gets a little more relaxed seeing them like this instead of the fighting, bickering people they were a few weeks ago.

"I'm not going to ask if you're excited because frankly, there are a few things I don't need to know about my best friend and her soon-to-be husband."

Peter grins the widest smile I've ever seen on him, and it totally transforms his face. I used to think he was okay looking but not nearly cute enough for my super-gorgeous best friend.

He's a lot better looking when he smiles.

All those etiquette books my mother fed me all through middle school were apparently right about how a simple smile can make a person attractive even more than nice clothes and fancy hair.

And yes. I had to read etiquette books. I used to chew my nails really badly, and Mom could only take so much, I guess.

She didn't find my theory about just smiling more instead of stopping the habit of biting my nails to be a good one, though.

The music pastor gets on the stage and a few minutes later, he's raking a pick down the guitar strings and asking everyone to stand. "Let's praise God today for the good things He's done, amen?"

Two people answer a hearty "Amen!" to him and everyone else just kind of nods. Sometimes I think our music pastor would be a lot happier at a more charismatic church.

We sing two songs and I'm so distracted trying to casually look over my shoulder for Tyler that I can barely focus on the words. It's only after I've accidentally made eye contact eight times with the dark-haired guy about my age behind me that I realize this is getting a little ridiculous. I focus all my energy on keeping my eyes straight forward.

The music ends and Tyler isn't here. I subtly dig in my purse while everyone is taking their seats and reaching for their Bibles and check my phone to see if I've missed any texts.

And there is one.

HEY. MOM WOULD RATHER NOT GO I THINK AND IT'S PROBABLY NOT A GOOD IDEA TO PUSH HER ON THIS ONE. I'LL PICK YOU UP FOR LUNCH ABOUT NOON—LET ME KNOW IF THAT STILL WORKS FOR YOU.

I write him back quickly, make sure the ringer is off, and settle back in my chair with my Bible. Layla catches my eye and shrugs questioningly, and I shake my head slightly, pursing my lips.

Bummer, she mouths to me.

I had high hopes that maybe Tyler's mom would come to church, hear a fantastic sermon from Pastor Louis about salvation, and get saved today, but that's not going to happen. So I start praying that He has another idea for how to get the good news to Tyler's mom.

Pastor Louis preaches for about forty-five minutes on marriage, and Layla and Peter hold hands through the whole thing, letting go only to scribble notes in the margins of their Bibles. Timely message for them.

We sing one more song and then the general pandemonium that hits the church as soon as we are dismissed takes over. I'm standing, about to say something to Layla, when I feel a tap on my shoulder.

I turn around and it's the guy who was sitting behind me. "Hi." He smiles, his face all friendly. "I'm Steven."

"Hi," I say because I'm not sure what else to say.

"So, I'm new in town and I'd love to get coffee with you sometime."

Right then I realize he thought I kept looking at him throughout the music because I was interested in him and not who might be coming through the door, and I feel my cheeks flush and my heart stops beating. "Oh goodness, I'm sorry. I'm . . . see, I was waiting for my boyfriend and his mom to come in and . . . oh, this is awkward . . ."

He grins. "No worries. I was starting to get excited, though, that I'd met such a pretty girl my first weekend in town at the first church I visited." He grins again, nods, and leaves, tucking a Bible under his arm.

Layla is dying beside me. "I love you, Paige! That kind of stuff only happens to you."

What a lovely thought.

Layla and I make plans to work on the last of the wedding stuff on Tuesday night.

"What do you think about this outfit?" I ask as I'm getting ready to leave, second-guessing my choice. Not that I have any backups since everything else I currently own is in a wrinkled pile on the bed.

"It's cute." Layla nods.

"Cute how? Like Disney Channel cute or like *People* magazine cute?"

Layla squints at me. "I don't know. I mean, some Disney Channel stars are in *People*, you know."

"That's helpful."

She shrugs. "You look fine. I like the cardigan. I will probably be borrowing that in the nearish future, just so you know."

Layla's idea of borrowing is to somehow forget to return it, so I'm already trying to come up with places in my apartment to hide this cardigan before it disappears into her closet forever.

Natalie comes over empty-handed and both Layla and I start looking around her for the baby.

"Where is she?" I ask finally after searching all over Natalie's person and the surrounding floor space.

"Well, hello to you two too," Natalie says. "I remember when people were just overjoyed to see me. I remember when they would call me up on the phone and say, 'Natalie, how are you today? Let's talk about *you*.' Now, everyone just wants to know about other things. Did Claire like her first taste of green beans? Did she pull up on her own yet? Is she crawling yet?"

Apparently there are a lot of unaddressed issues in Natalie's life right now.

"Are you okay?" Layla asks her.

Natalie rubs her cheek. "I need a date night."

I can hear a call for help sometimes too well, but this time, I'm not going to say no. "I will finish with my last girl at six thirty on Friday night," I tell Natalie. "Be dressed. I'll come watch Claire and you guys can go eat somewhere fancy."

"Oh!" Layla says. "I'll come too! We can paint Claire's toenails!"

"No painting any toenails," Natalie says. "I'm going to be the first one to do that, thank you. And thank you, thank you, Paige. You are a doll. I'll even have dinner for you."

I wave a hand. "No need. We'll pick up Panda."

"You know that's right," Layla says like Gus on *Psych*.

Natalie just shakes her head. "You guys are going to die from the sodium intake one of these days."

"All the more reason to let us paint Claire's toenails before we die." Layla grins.

I look at my phone. I have thirty minutes before Tyler is picking me up from my apartment to go to lunch, so I should probably go. I give both girls hugs and then hurry out the door, trying not to be too nervous.

Right.

I drive home, gripping the steering wheel and staring at the white, fluffy clouds through the windshield, wondering if maybe by some miracle they are actually tornado clouds and we should probably cancel lunch and spend the day reading books in the door frames instead.

Any time there was a bad storm growing up, my dad would always wake up Preslee and me and make us sit under the door frames. Apparently it is the strongest part of a house.

Which never made sense to me because you'd think a big hole in the wall for an entrance would be the least safe spot in the house.

I don't know. I was very little when I last watched *Twister*.

I get home with fifteen minutes to spare, so over the next few minutes I wear a nice little path in my carpet from my bedroom to the front door to look out the peephole.

"This is ridiculous," I finally mutter to myself, sitting down on the couch.

I smooth my hands over my jeans. I was going for a fall look today since the promise of cooler weather is supposedly coming sometime soon. I found the lightweight cotton cardigan on clearance a few years ago, and I just put it on over a looser blue-and-white-striped cami and I'm wearing my Sperry knockoffs.

I look like I'm about to jump on a yacht somewhere.

Now I'm second-guessing the outfit again. What do you wear to lunch to meet what could potentially be your future mother-in-law?

Right then is when there's a knock on my door and I look at the clock on my phone, eyebrows raising.

It seems like Tyler's mother makes him way more prompt.

"You're actually on time . . ." I start and then the words fade into the slight breeze as I stare up at Luke Prestwick.

"Hey, friend," Luke says, smiling all easily, his brown eyes crinkling up on the corners.

He and I have very different interpretations of the word *friend* as it relates to the two of us.

"Luke." I try not to spit the word out. "What are you doing here?"

"Well, I saw you at church this morning and I was going to try to come over and give this to you there, but you left so fast I didn't get a chance to." He hands me a white envelope.

I look at it like it possibly contains anthrax.

"It's not full of crickets or anything." Luke grins at me.

I take the envelope and start to pull open the back and he stops me.

"Read it after I leave." He starts walking back down my stairs sideways so he can still talk to me. "And have a good day. And you look beautiful. You look like you're about to go sailing." He leaves.

I shut the door, mostly grateful that he didn't stick around long enough to have that lovely first impression on Tyler's mother.

"*Oh yes, hello. So good to meet you. No, this beautiful man here is not my brother, he's actually my ex-boyfriend.*"

That would have been lovely.

I look at the envelope. It's completely white except for my name scrawled across the front in Luke's characteristic chicken scratch. In high school, I always joked that he was likely to become a doctor since he already had the handwriting for it.

I finger the back flap and then decide to just put it in my room and wait until later. It's probably nothing, but I don't want to read anything that might put me in a terrible mood for today.

Including a "Come to my garage sale" like it probably is.

Surely that's what it is.

I set the envelope on my bedside table, and I'm just walking out to the living room again when there's another knock on my door.

I check the time. Ten minutes late.

It's got to be Tyler.

I open the door and find the cutest curly blond-haired boy grinning at me.

"Where's your mom?" I ask when I look around him and don't see a woman standing there.

"She's in the car." He shrugs at me. "No hello for me?"

I give him a hug. "How does this look?" I push myself away from him so he can approve the outfit.

He nods at it. "Nautical."

Hopefully this is a good thing because I definitely don't have time to change now.

"You look fine."

"Just fine?" I bite my lip. I bet if I changed really fast, I could still be back to the car with his mother in a respectable time.

"Honey." Tyler pulls me into another hug. "You look beautiful. Stop worrying. I wish you'd never talked to Stef!"

My chest gets all tight and warm, like someone has wrapped rubber bands around me and poured honey through my rib cage.

I take a deep breath, sling my purse over my shoulder, and lock my door behind us. He holds my hand as we walk down the stairs and over to his truck.

A woman with dark hair in a shoulder-length blunt cut is sitting in the passenger seat. Tyler's truck is a crew cab, so he squeezes my hand and quietly says, "Mind sitting in the backseat today?"

"Not at all," I murmur back as he opens the door behind the driver's seat. I put on my most cheerful, friendly, non-threatening smile and look at his mom.

"Mom, this is Paige. Paige, this is my mom, Judy."

"Hi, it's so nice to meet you," I say, inwardly wincing at the chipmunk tone to my voice.

"Hello."

Well. I wouldn't exactly say that warmth was running through Judy's tone. Maybe annoyance, but definitely not warmth.

I hoist myself into the backseat and buckle myself in, racking my brain for the list of easy conversational topics I usually have in there. I am the master of making a conversation about nothing last an entire hour. I've perfected it over the summer with the girls.

Nothing, absolutely nothing, is coming to my mind right now. So I sit there in the back, smiling and nodding like a total dork.

"You do eat lunch awfully late, Tyler," Judy says.

I look surreptitiously at my phone. It's not even twelve thirty.

I usually feel like I'm doing good if I get lunch before two in the afternoon. And even then, with how many Frappuccinos I've been consuming lately, I usually just get a little snack like a cheese stick or a bag of cut carrots and call it lunch during the week.

"What sounds like a good lunch to you ladies?" Tyler asks, the picture of cheerfulness next to his grim mother.

Judy is not swayed from her line of thought with the happy question. "Somewhere that serves the food fast."

"I'm okay with anything," I say in a small voice from the back.

Tyler drives to Mimi's Café. I've only eaten here once. One of my girls asked to meet here right before school since it was very close to her school, and the entire time I felt like I was out of place in the midst of all of the older people coming in for an early breakfast to talk about their grandkids.

Tyler parks and opens my door before running around and getting his mom's door. Now that she's standing, I'm getting a better idea of who Judy . . . Judy . . . It suddenly hits me that I don't even know Tyler's mom's last name. Did she keep her married name or change it back?

She's tall and on the slender side but in more of a bony way than a willowy way. I'm not sure exactly how to describe her. She's wearing black pants and a white shirt under a red cardigan. Her face is angular, her skin pale, her jaw set. I can't see her eyes behind her huge sunglasses.

She looks like she needs a good long cruise to the Bahamas and some sunless tanner.

Tyler must look identical to his dad because he looks nothing like his mother. I sort of want to ask if he's adopted because Tyler's the exact opposite of everything his mom is. Curly blond hair. Deep blue eyes that always crinkle up when he smiles, which he does often. He's usually tanned and he's tall and has big shoulders.

I have a serious curiosity about his dad now.

"Well, this is fun!" Tyler says, overly cheerful. He walks between us and opens the door. I let Judy go in first and then turn big eyes to Tyler before I walk in.

He winks at me. "You're doing great," he whispers.

Well, obviously I am because she hasn't turned me into a frog yet.

That was mean.

I bite the inside of my cheek as I follow Tyler's mom to the table. *Lord, keep me sweet. And please, Lord, please give me topics to talk about!*

I'm desperately trying to remember what Rick is always saying. He has a whole acronym thing going for how to talk to total strangers, but I can't remember the acronym, which isn't super helpful.

HAND? EYE? CLAVICLE? It's something to do with a body part.

We sit down and Tyler's mom finally takes her big sunglasses off and turns the most silvery gray eyes I've ever seen toward me.

It's unnerving. I didn't know an eye color like that existed in nature.

"So," she says, looking for all the world like she is barely containing an eye roll. "Paige. Tell me about yourself."

I am just staring at her eyes. They're the exact color of the stainless-steel refrigerator I was drooling over in the last kitchen makeover show on HGTV. It had double French doors and a slide-out tray where you could put prepared plates for parties.

Genius idea.

Tyler kicks my shin lightly under the table and I jump. "Oh! Right, sorry, um . . . Judy . . . about me. Well, I'm twenty-three and—"

"Well, that's frightfully young," Judy interrupts me, turning to Tyler. "You know I do not approve of serious relationships when you are that young, Tyler."

The waiter isn't even here and already we're dishing up big spoonfuls of awkward.

I glance furtively at the couple behind Tyler's head. It's a young family. The man and woman are both laughing and talking about something, the two daughters are grinning and eating politely while dabbing their napkins in the corners of their mouths, their huge, adorable hair bows tipped just so on their heads.

Rick is always trying to tell me that God has put us in a world that is just one big salvation message after another. Apparently one of his college roommates came to the Lord after having a discussion with Rick about banana peels in old movies, and Rick brought up that another slippery thing was the road to hell.

You can't make this stuff up.

I stare at that tiny aisle separating my table from the adorable family's table and think about how small the chasm between heaven and way farther south than that can be. Jesus did say that the gate was narrow.

I suddenly realize that Tyler is talking to me. "So, Paige, Mom is really interested in interior designing. I was telling her about how you like to get ideas for your future house."

Yes. By watching way too much HGTV in my jammies on my sofa in my crappy apartment. That does not seem like a good way to impress my boyfriend's mother.

Judy sighs then and looks around. "Where *is* the waiter? If you can't afford good help, you shouldn't be open at all."

Mentally, I'm yelling at the waiter, wherever he is. *Stay away! Retreat, retreat!*

The poor guy isn't picking up my thought beams, though, because suddenly he materializes right beside my elbow. "Hello, sorry about the wait." He looks a little flustered.

Lovely. Let's start with one who is already feeling not quite there.

"Hey." Tyler smiles easily at the poor man.

"The wait was unacceptable," Judy clips to him in a monotone. "I want the tomato soup."

He's struggling to get his order pad out of his apron pocket, and my heart just goes out to the poor guy. "Oh, okay, I um, let me just get this out—"

"No croutons. No basil nonsense sprinkled on top. And a side of whole-wheat toast. Not rye, not white. *Whole wheat*," she annunciates like he's two years old and in trouble. "And I want tea. Not sweet tea, not iced tea. Plain black hot tea. With the tea bag. Am I speaking slow enough for you?"

The waiter breaks into a sweat. I sort of want to take his hand, lead him back into the kitchen, and stand there with him in the walk-in refrigerator.

He finally gets his order pad out and scribbles down Judy's order. "And for you?" he asks me.

I haven't even looked at the menu because the odds of me actually getting food through my throat aren't super high. "Coffee please," I say in my sweetest tone of voice, feeling sorry for the shaking man. "With cream, please. And sugar, please."

"Nothing to eat?"

"No, thank you."

Tyler looks questioningly at me. "I'm buying, babe. Get something to eat."

His mother stiffens and glowers at the endearment, and I have this inexplicable urge to slam my knife into my hand and let the poor waiter take me to the emergency room.

Maybe I'm being dramatic.

"I'm fine," I say through what I hope is looking like a natural smile but what feels like me saying "cheese" with clenched teeth.

He looks at me for a couple of seconds and then nods. "Okay, well, I guess I'll be the only one eating real food today. I want the bacon cheeseburger with a side of fries and a Coke, please."

After looking at Tyler's thin, bony mom, I suddenly have new appreciation for how the boy can put away food like the Dallas Cowboys' football team and not seem to ever gain an ounce.

The waiter dives and tumbles to the kitchen in a very good impersonation of the "Stop, Drop, and Roll" format I learned to do in kindergarten should I ever catch on fire.

Judy shakes her head at him. "There is just no good help anymore. None. It must be the lack of respect children are raised with now. When I was young, everywhere treated you like the customer deserves to be treated. With respect. Waiters held doors and carried coats and wiped down menus after they were used."

"Well, I for one am all for dirty menus. Did you know scientists think we are all getting sick so much now because we are too clean?" Tyler says, the familiar mischievous glint in his eyes.

The boy is playing with fire.

Judy doesn't even respond to her son. "Paige." She turns her LG Premium Stainless Steel Finished eyes to me.

"Yes, ma'am?"

"Tell me. Do you think you will marry my son?"

Well, I guess we've already discussed my apparent infancy, the lack of good workers in our economy, the poor way that children are raised, and sticky menus. Really, what was there left to talk about other than my future marriage plans?

I think I attempted to swallow and gasp at the same time because suddenly I am choking and the waiter hasn't brought any water yet. Tyler is whacking me on the back, and Judy is sitting there stone-faced as every other table in this area is staring at me like I'll be needing the Heimlich.

"Excuse me," I somehow get out in between the rasping cough, and I lunge for the kitchen in sort of the same way as the waiter.

They must hear me coming because a girl with brown hair in a ponytail appears at the entrance and wordlessly hands me a glass filled to the top with water. I suck it down in record time, and before I can even ask, she's grabbed a clear plastic pitcher and is filling it up again.

"Thank you," I gasp after I finish the second cup. I grip the cup with both hands and look longingly at the walk-in refrigerator.

The girl is looking from me to my table and back to me. "Hey," she says gently. "Why don't you just catch your breath for a minute?"

"Could I eat in here?"

She grins. "Meeting the parent?"

I nod. "I've never loved my own mother more." I can just see my mother now. All warm and loving and always ready with something delicious.

I peek around the fake fern to my table, and Tyler is looking over at me, his eyes full of concern. I hold up the water glass and a "just a minute" finger and he nods, smirking a little bit.

Okay, so maybe he has guessed that I'm hiding out here from his mom. I bet he's just wishing he'd started choking first so he could be the one listening to the cooks banter and smelling something frying.

I finally walk back to the table, and the waiter has brought my coffee along with twenty-six sugar packets and eighteen of those little tubs of cream.

I could hug the man.

"You okay?" Tyler reaches over and rubs my back.

"Oh fine, fine." I wave my hand, hoping the conversation has moved to other less-awkward topics.

The rest of lunch is uneventful, if you don't count the nearly raw insides of my cheeks from me gnawing on them all through lunch. Tyler inhales his burger, talking easily about the economy, politics, how his work is going, and a few different sports teams.

Judy doesn't say hardly anything. She just alternates from glaring at me to mowing down our waiter with the visual ice picks every time he happens to appear anywhere in our vicinity.

"Well. I'm going to run to the restroom real quick." Tyler hands me a gold Visa card. "Give this to them if the waiter comes with the check while I'm gone."

"That's doubtful," Judy says. "This place needs a Help Wanted sign in the window."

"You sure you don't want to just wait until you get home?" I ask him, trying to appear nonchalant instead of begging him not to leave me alone with this woman.

He grins and I realize that along with a lot of affection for those blue eyes, I do hate Tyler sometimes. He leaves before I can latch on to his hand and make him take me with him.

He is scarcely out of sight before Judy is shaking her head, looking at me. "It's a pity really."

"A pity?" I ask her, trying to be polite.

"Tyler used to be so different. He was top in his class, you know. Valedictorian. Honor roll. Quarterback." Judy looks off into the distance, her jaw softening somewhat at the memory of a better time. "He dated only the most beautiful girls in the school, you know. All of them were accomplished. Straight As. Getting accepted into the highest schools. Prelaw, premed . . ."

My stomach gets tighter and tighter. I'm thankful I did not eat, but I'm wishing I hadn't gotten that last coffee refill.

My "career" as a youth intern at my church has gone from something I love to do to something I'm ashamed of in a startlingly short amount of time. The waiter slinks over and I hand him Tyler's card along with my self-esteem.

"Take his last girlfriend, for instance. Now there was future wife material. The girl was well on her way to being a pediatrician, and she was willing to do whatever she needed to do to get there."

I started out wanting to be a counselor. Maybe I'm not there exactly, but I did think I was making a difference in kids' lives.

Maybe not as much of a difference as a pediatrician did. I mean, I just counsel the girls about life in high school. I certainly don't save babies' lives.

Judy sighs and looks at me like I'm the piece of freshly cut basil she wrinkled her nose at and spooned out of her bowl earlier. "A real pity."

"Ready?" Tyler comes over right as the waiter was returning for his signature. He signs it. Judy stands and starts walking for the door while I gather whatever strength I can muster out of the depths of my bone marrow and make myself stand.

Tyler is staring at me as I'm heaving myself out of the chair using the table to help. "You okay?" he asks in a low voice.

"Probably not," I say in the weakest voice I've ever heard from myself.

He frowns at the back of his mother's head as she walks out of the restaurant, sliding her sunglasses back on her face. "I was gone for ninety seconds. I timed myself. What could she possibly have said to you in that short of time?"

I shake my head. There will be a time to talk about it, but not today.

Definitely not today.

Chapter 17

I spend the rest of the day in my sweatpants, staring blindly at HGTV, and I am too ashamed to admit how much ice cream I consumed.

Layla calls at six. "I've been waiting for you to call all day! How did it go?"

My moan is a sufficient answer, I think.

"Oh man. Sorry, Paige. Was she just not very nice?"

That was one way to put it.

"I'm on my way."

I hang up and don't move from the couch. I'm sitting there cross-legged, a blanket around my shoulders, my eyes bleary, my brain hurting.

I'm trying not to keep rehashing everything that Judy said to me, but it's hard not to hear her voice in the back of my head. *It's a pity. A real pity.*

Layla raps on my apartment door at a little after six thirty. She's carrying a plastic bag with a large panda head on it.

Figures.

"I asked for extra mandarin sauce." She marches into the apartment and unloads the bag onto my coffee table. "And I picked you up some spring rolls. And my mom left cookies at my apartment so I brought those too."

There's a happy thought. For as awful of a cook as Layla is, her mother is like the Pioneer Woman of this county.

"Thanks," I croak, rubbing my head.

Layla sits beside me on the couch and pats my knee. "So, didn't go well, huh?"

"Oh Layla, she's the most awful person I've ever been around. And I've been around awful people." When I worked at the adoption agency, I had to talk with some pretty rude people on a semiregular basis. You wouldn't think that would be the case, but like Candace, one of the counselors who works there, used to tell me, anytime you put money and children together in the same conversation, people tend to get a little testy.

I sigh and look at Layla. "She was just not very nice. And she ended the lunch talking about all of Tyler's old girlfriends while he was in the restroom and how they were such a better fit for him since they were all beautiful and accomplished."

Layla shakes her head. "Wow. I'm sorry." She hands me the to-go container stuffed with orange chicken, rice, and chow mein. "If it makes you feel any better, I think you're beautiful. And I didn't think people use the word *accomplished* outside of *Pride and Prejudice* these days."

I smile for the first time since this morning.

"The first time I met Peter's mom, she looked at me and said, 'Oh Peter, I thought you had a thing for blondes.'"

"She did not," I say.

"Did too. I swear on this Beijing beef." My stunning friend just shakes her milk chocolate–colored curls. "My dad always told me that you have to live like a duck."

I'm not following the connection, but she's looking at me like I should know what she's talking about. I spent a lot of time at Layla's house when we were kids, and I never heard her dad mention anything about ducks.

I squint at her. "Because they waddle away from people unless they have food and then they attack you with their terrible beaks?"

"You really hate birds, don't you?" She grins. "No! He said that we need to be like ducks because they dive under the water, look for something of substance, and if they don't find it, they pop back out and let the rest of the water roll down their backs. They don't fester on it or soak in it, so to speak."

I stab my fork into the chow mein. "So I should just ignore everything she said?"

"Yep."

I think about Tyler's mother and the way she made me feel. "Yeah, but—"

"Nope, no buts. Just shake it off, Paige." Layla looks at me. "Seriously. Shake it off."

"You mean like literally?"

"I mean like I would like you to stand up off this couch right now since you've probably been sitting here festering on it all day. I want you to stand in the middle of your living room and give me a good shake."

I just stare at her.

"Chop, chop!" She claps her hands together.

I look at her as I slowly set my dinner on the coffee table, slowly peel off my blanket, and slowly rise to my feet.

She looks totally serious.

Layla has lost her mind. The wedding prep has officially made her insane.

"All right. Now. Shake."

I stare at her for a good long minute before I sort of jiggle my arms around, and Layla shakes her head.

"No, no. *Shake.* Like how we used to in middle school when we found my grandma's old records from the fifties. Come on. Shake it, girl," she says like she's the newest country singing sensation.

This is ridiculous. I'm moving around like a dog skidding out of the bathtub, and Layla is dying laughing on the couch.

I finally plop back down next to her and just sigh.

"See? Doesn't that feel better?"

"You have lost it, Layla. I thought you'd lost it back in high school when you tried to bring back the stirrup pants, but you have really lost it today."

She just grins.

* * * * *

I climb in bed at ten that night. I pull my Bible back over when I see Luke's envelope lying on my bedside table.

Because that's what I need on this emotionally unstable day.

I pick up the envelope and set it on my lap, staring at the white front with my name scrawled across it.

Maybe it's nothing. Maybe it's a letter for me to give to someone else. Maybe it's a bunch of coupons for ice cream.

Or maybe it's another "please come back to me, Paige" sonnet.

Which, when I think about it, wouldn't be too terrible. I love Luke and Layla's mother. She's amazing. She's like one of those classic TV moms.

This is ridiculous. Of course it would be a bad idea, and the number one reason it would is because I really like Tyler.

Not so much with Luke.

I open the back of the envelope and pull out a single sheet of white lined paper.

Paige,

I'm sure you are worried this is going to be another declaration of love, but please know it's nothing like that. I have an idea for what to do to Peter's car during the wedding and I need your help.

I read the rest of his note and breathe a sigh that it seems to be fairly innocent, even his ideas of what to do to Peter's car. Apparently all he needs from me is for me to steal Peter's keys out of Layla's purse while we are all getting ready at the church that afternoon. I'm supposed to then hand them off right before the ceremony, and Luke is going to do the rest. He wants to do the typical filling of the car with toilet paper and confetti and hanging cans off the back and writing all over the front.

I can handle that.

I think about Layla making me do that crazy shake and her thoughts about ducks.

And then I think about Judy.

So she's a terrible person to have lunch with. So what? If this relationship with Tyler continues and this woman someday becomes my mother-in-law, then I'll figure out how to sit through two visits a year with her, since that's all the time she can apparently manage to spend with Tyler. If Tyler and I aren't supposed to end up together, then I'm worrying about everything for nothing.

I pull my Bible over and spend the next few minutes in Ecclesiastes before I turn out the light.

Lord, I pray as I snuggle under my blankets. *Please give me wisdom. And a forgiving heart. And I guess help me to be like a duck.*

* * * * *

At the Monday morning staff meeting, Rick is in fine form.

"I want clowns." He walks into the room and tosses his keys on his desk.

I look up from my computer where I was attempting to research the best place to take someone who hates coffee. I've been trying to meet with this one eighth-grade girl for two months, and she always has some excuse not to go to Starbucks with me until I finally found out that she hated coffee and wasn't that fond of tea or milk shakes.

I asked her what she liked to drink or eat and she said, "Water."

Well. I guess every place serves that.

"Clowns for what?" I ask him.

"We're having a party."

"You always want to have a party." I look back at the computer. "We had a party last month." Maybe if I find someplace really unique, she'll want to come hang out with me.

"Not true. Last month was a karaoke picnic."

"Same thing." Every so often, I meet a girl like this who is very reluctant to talk to people. Those are usually the ones who need to be met with the most.

"Not the same thing." Rick sits down in his chair. "We should have a carnival."

"A carnival." I look over at him. "Why?"

"Because. Carnivals are fun. I love carnivals. The crappy, greasy food, the pointless prizes, the creepy made-up people." He shrugs. "It's like a pit of insanity right in your own backyard."

"Only you would actually like that."

"You have a better idea? We haven't solidified our big group event for this next month."

We try to do some sort of event every month that isn't a Bible study and that the kids would feel comfortable bringing their non-Christian friends to. It's been a great outreach tool for them. And since Rick spent about four months last year teaching all of the kids how to share their faith, we have seen a lot of people meeting Jesus.

It makes my job exciting.

I shrug and turn in my swivel chair to look at Rick. "What about something that isn't so elaborate?" I love working with Rick, but the man has no concept of the work that goes into things like this.

"I've got it. An obstacle course."

I make a face. "Kind of like a third-grade birthday party if you ask me. Look, everyone is totally fine just doing hot dogs and grilling out at a park. Last time I think the volleyball net was the star of the show. Why don't we just do that again?"

He sighs. "I should have been looking to hire someone who liked to be more creative."

"And sadly you picked me. And I am creative, thank you, but lucky for you, I'm also practical."

He can't argue with me because he knows I'm right.

Natalie walks in right then, baby Claire in one arm and a towel-covered basket in the other. "Morning guys. I brought us some energy snacks today!"

Never a good sign when someone puts the word *energy* before the word *snack*. The two should never be combined. Snacks are supposed to induce some sort of sugar- or grease-laced coma.

Rick sighs to his wife. "She doesn't like the clown idea."

"I don't either so you're complaining to the wrong person." She sets Claire on the floor with a chew toy and turns to me. "Want a truffle?"

I'm immediately wary. "I thought they were energy snacks."

"They're truffle energy snacks. All natural, no grains, and sugar free." Claire starts crying and Natalie reaches down to comfort her.

I sneak a peek over at Rick while Natalie is distracted and he's mouthing *run away* while shaking his head.

I grin.

"So. Truffle?" she asks me again.

"I'm good for now. I had a big breakfast." I'm only half lying. I had a granola bar. Which is bigger than not having any breakfast at all.

"Any for you, honey?"

"No thanks. I have an early lunch meeting in a minute," Rick says.

Natalie tsks and mutters something to herself about stubborn, unhealthy people, picks out a ball-shaped thing from the basket, and sits on the couch. "So I came up with your name. Altitude."

Rick just looks at her. "I thought you liked Rick. You told me when we were dating that I was the only guy you'd ever met named Rick and that made me special."

She rolls her eyes. "No. The youth-ministry name. Altitude."

"Like, hey we've reached our cruising altitude so you can now move about the cabin freely?" I ask.

"Yep." Natalie is passionate in her speech. "I think it has great symbolism for what we want for these kids. We want them to keep gaining more and more Altitude in their relationship with Jesus."

"Why do you keep saying it like that?" I ask.

"I'm trying to make a point," she says.

"So we would be like, hey come to Altitude every Wednesday night?" Rick asks, one eye half closed as he paces the floor and thinks on it.

I actually like it. It's far better than the other names Natalie has been texting me over the past two weeks.

I'VE GOT IT! I AM SO A GENIUS AT THIS STUFF! WE CAN CALL IT NYPD—NOW YOU'RE PRAYING, DUDE.

Or worse: WORDS ON WINGS. SORT OF LIKE A VEILED REFERENCE TO PSALM 91:4.

A little too veiled for me because I immediately started thinking about Buffalo Wild Wings stamping all their chickens with titles like "Best Flyer" or "Most Likely to End Up Eaten."

Granted, I was a little hungry when she'd texted me that suggestion.

"Altitude," Rick mutters again, still pacing. Claire keeps crawling over to his feet so he keeps stepping over her.

He's obviously used to it, though, because he never looks down and never trips over her. I'm convinced that when a child is born, the parents suddenly morph into these insane superheroes who can hear sounds that aren't audible and sense movement that no one else can see.

Natalie looks over at me and nods and grins because she knows it's as good as on the postcards since Rick didn't dismiss it right away.

"Okay," Rick says finally. "Altitude. Mark it down, Paige. And let's go all Photoshop tech on it and get the lettering to look all cool and edgy. I want to put it everywhere. Bookmarks, postcards, those little cardboard drink holder things we put on the coffee cups . . . you name it."

I'm busy scribbling down his orders. "What about if we make T-shirts with the word on it and our youth website? We could sell them for ten bucks apiece, and that's how we could raise more money for our camp scholarships."

Every summer, Rick takes a group of high schoolers on a half-camp, half-mission trip at an orphanage just inside the border of Mexico. It's become the most-looked-forward-to thing we do. Which is amazing because it is long hot days and very hard work, but the kids love it.

Rick is nodding and pacing now. "Love it. Write it down. We'll keep thinking on this, but I like where we're headed."

Natalie elbows me in the rib cage. "See. Told you I was a genius."

Chapter
18

It's Wednesday afternoon and I'm just leaving the dollar theater with three of the sixth-grade girls after we went to see a replaying of *Ratatouille* after they got out of school. Cute movie. I'd forgotten a lot of it. Though I still wasn't fond of the whole rat-being-the-main-character thing.

My cell phone rings as we are halfway across the parking lot to my car. I answer it while digging my keys out.

"Hello?"

"Hey, Paige, it's me." Tyler.

I smile and one of the girls looks at me and immediately starts giggling.

Great. More fodder for the high school girls' rumor mill. The girls have basically planned our wedding already, I think.

I complained to Rick one day about how my dating life is in a fishbowl. "Well, that's the life you chose when you decided to be a youth intern," he told me. "Plus, I think it's good. The kids need to see a healthy dating relationship between two young adults."

As a general rule, I hate the term *young adult*.

"Hi." I unlock the car and nod to the girls to climb on in.

"So. Dinner tonight. Are you thinking you might be interested in more than just a cheese stick?"

"I could probably be talked into more," I tell him, grinning. My reputation for cheese-stick dinners on Wednesday is becoming the brunt of a lot of leaders' meeting jokes.

"Great! Because we should go out tonight after Bible study. I've already got a restaurant in mind."

"I'll bet you my cobbler that it's Cracker Barrel," I tell him.

He laughs. "See you in a few hours, beautiful girl."

I hang up, climb into the car, and obviously the girls had been talking about me because they are immediately quiet the second my leg grazes my seat. I shove my key in the ignition and turn to look at all of them. They're all grinning back at me like I have a dollop of spaghetti sauce in the middle of my forehead.

"What?" I ask.

"Who was that?" Lacey singsongs suggestively.

"It was just a phone call," I say, backing out.

"Someday when I'm old, I'm going to get married too. And our wedding is going to be amazing because I'm going to find a replica of Princess Kate's dress," Maddie says from the backseat.

"I didn't like her dress," Cara says next to Maddie. "I thought it was too much lace."

"There is no such thing as too much lace," Maddie says in a definitive tone.

I listen to their conversation as I drive them to their individual homes and think about what I was like in the sixth grade. Layla and I were the biggest dorks in the class, and I don't remember thinking for a millisecond about my future wedding. I was way too focused on when the next book in whatever my latest series obsession was going to release.

And lace? I'm not sure I even knew what that meant when I was eleven years old.

Granted, though, I wasn't the most girly of girls.

I drop all of the girls off and drive back to church. Our leaders' meeting begins in thirty minutes, and I'm betting I have a bunch of copies to make.

"How was the movie?" Rick asks as I walk into the youth office.

"Cute." I nod. "Though I'm pretty sure only Pixar could make a movie about a rat actually cute."

"Natalie refuses to watch that one specifically because there's a rodent in it." Rick hands me a stack of five papers. "Here's the leaders' guides for next week. Mind copying those?"

"That's why I'm here early."

He grins at me. "You are never allowed to leave this job."

We have our youth meeting. Tyler sits across the circle from me and grins at me the whole time so I don't hear a lot of whatever Rick is talking about, though I do know he mentions the word *Altitude* about forty-two times.

We pray, do our big group teaching, then break into our small groups. I talk to the girls for the next forty-five minutes, take prayer requests, pray, and walk out to the pandemonium of nearly a hundred kids gathering in the youth room around Oreos.

Tyler catches up to me by the snack table. "I'm starving."

"There's Oreos," I say.

He looks at the snacks and shakes his head. "I'll hold out for the cheesy potatoes." He grins.

"So it *is* Cracker Barrel. You're like twenty-five going on ninety."

"Yep. I nearly even bought Velcro shoes the other day."

I laugh.

We leave a little bit later after most of the kids have gone, and Rick waves us out. "Go eat. I'm tired of hearing how hungry Tyler is." He grins at us.

"Sure you don't want help cleaning and locking up?" I ask him.

"I did it by myself for years. I think I'll manage. Leave. I'll see you tomorrow."

We walk out to the parking lot, and Tyler nods to his truck. "We can come back for your car." He mashes the button on his keyless entry remote and opens the passenger truck door for me.

He climbs in the driver's side a few seconds later and grins over at me. "Recovered?"

I haven't been sick so I'm not sure what he's talking about. "What?"

"From my mom's visit?"

Oh. That. I've been trying my best over the last three days to forget all details about Judy's visit here.

"I've been acting like a duck," I tell Tyler.

"Like you've gone and quacked?"

I snort. "No, Layla told me this thing her dad always said to her, and it seemed to really help Layla when she was growing up so I decided to try it."

"Now you're just waddling around the facts." Tyler grins over at me.

"I hate talking with you."

"I'm not trying to make this a beak deal." Tyler holds a hand up.

"Seriously. I hate it."

"I mean, I goose I understand if you get frustrated sometimes, but I didn't think it drakes that much to put up with me."

I am trying so hard not to laugh that my left eyeball is shaking in its socket. But I know that the second I start giggling, he won't stop making duck puns for the rest of the night.

He looks over at me and grins, and I pinch the bridge of my nose, fighting the laughter.

"How was the rest of your visit with her?" I ask when I know I can manage a calm voice.

"It was fine. Sometimes it got a little fowl, but swan-day I hope that's not the case anymore."

"Oh my gosh, *stop!*" I giggle despite every muscle in my body trying to keep them in.

He laughs. "You're a hard egg to crack, Paige."

"Please. Please just take me home."

"Too late. We're already at Quacker Barrel."

I am crying.

He pulls into a parking place, hops out, comes around and opens my door, and the second my feet touch the pavement, he swoops me up into this wonderfully warm, long hug.

"Oh, Paige." He pushes me back a few inches and grins into my eyes. "I do love hanging out with you."

"If only it was mutual."

He knuckles my head and weaves his fingers through my hand as he walks toward the restaurant. I look down at our hands as we cross the parking lot.

It looks natural. It feels effortless.

I smile.

We get seated a few minutes later and Tyler doesn't even bother looking at the menu. "So. Stef called. She is so mad that Mom met you first that she's making Mason take a vacation day, and they want to come visit in two weeks."

I look up from my menu. "That's Layla's wedding weekend."

He nods. "I know. They're going to be here Saturday night after the wedding and they'll leave Sunday. The wedding starts at five, right?"

I nod. "Layla wants me at her house at seven in the morning, though."

She sent me a five-page e-mail of information about the wedding yesterday. I had barely scratched the surface of it, but based on the schedule, Layla was freaking out.

Layla does not schedule. In our friendship, I am the one who schedules.

"Good grief," Tyler says. "What in the world are you supposed to do for ten hours before the wedding? Sew the wedding dress?"

I shrug. "Apparently there are a lot of details that have to be done that day. Hair. Makeup. Pictures. Her mom is insisting on hiring someone to do everyone's hair and makeup, so that should be interesting."

"Okay. Well. If you aren't exhausted, you're welcome to come hang out after the wedding with us. Otherwise, want to plan on coming to lunch with my family and me again after church?"

I nod. I've already talked to Stef on the phone so I'm not super nervous to meet her, but that is going to be a crazy weekend.

We order our dinner and Tyler grins across the table at me. "See? Isn't this nicer than a cheese stick for dinner?"

"Maybe."

"You're pretty ducky to be dating such a great guy who takes you to such great restaurants."

I just shake my head and cover my eyes.

* * * * *

I come in the door to my apartment on Friday at nine o'clock, close the door behind me, and back up against it, yawning.

Twelve girls this afternoon. Two groups of three and then the rest were individuals.

I am mentally and emotionally exhausted. I spent the whole last hour trying to comfort one of my girls who just found out that her parents are getting a divorce.

This is when I feel completely unqualified to be an intern. I have a great family and great parents who have never, to my knowledge anyway, come close to getting a divorce.

It just makes me realize how much I take for granted.

I stumble into the kitchen and start scrounging around for something to eat. For all of the coffee I have consumed this afternoon and evening, I haven't had a lot of real food. I bought a scone with the last girl and we both picked at it, but the conversation wasn't really one that made us hungry.

My cell buzzes on the counter and I reach for it. "Hi, Preslee."

"Hey. So. My wedding is in four weeks."

Preslee's wedding is the month after Layla's. I'm the maid of honor in both of them.

I've never even been in a wedding before and now I'm in two in four weeks.

"I know," I tell her. "Nervous?"

"I'm so ready for it to get here, I can't even tell you," Preslee says, and I hear the same excitement mixed with desperation and exhaustion that Layla's tone has had lately.

"What do you need for me to do over the next few weeks?" If I've hardly helped with Layla's wedding, I've done next to nothing for Preslee's. She's having it in a friend of Wes's backyard and with the minimalist décor, and with the distance to Austin, I feel totally useless as the maid of honor.

"You can hold my hand on our wedding day and remind me that the day is going to be over soon enough so enjoy every minute." Preslee sounds like she's reading something.

"Where is that from?"

"Ten Things Your Maid of Honor Needs to Know About the Big Day."

"Book?"

"Magazine article."

"Want me to go get a copy?"

"No, because most of these are pointless. I'm not going to do toasts, I'm not doing a money dance, and my dress doesn't have a train. The most you have to do is hold my flowers."

"I can hold flowers with the best of them," I promise her.

"And you can keep tabs on Mom because I think she will probably be more of an emotional mess than I will."

"Well. It is her baby getting married," I tell Preslee. "You can't fault her the tears."

"I'm not faulting anyone. It's just getting hard to talk to her because every time I call her or she calls me, she has to hang up because she's crying."

"Poor Mom."

"Yep. And now with you getting all serious with Tyler, I'm sure she's suddenly seeing the words *empty nester* painted on her walls."

I shift. "You can tell things are getting serious?"

"Aren't they? He came to Austin to meet the family. You talk about him all the time, and it seems like you spend a lot of time together."

I pull a block of cream cheese out of the fridge, cut off a corner, put it in a bowl, and cover it with some sweet pepper jelly. I dig a box of crackers out of the pantry and think about Preslee's question while I sit at my table.

"Do you love him?" Preslee asks.

Preslee has never minced words, so I'm not sure why I expect her to start now that she's back home and on the straight and narrow again.

I rub my forehead, staring at my sorry excuse for a dinner.

"I don't . . . I don't know . . ." I say again after a long pause. I think about Tyler and everything that has happened in the year since I met him. Us becoming friends. Him challenging my idea that I needed to be insanely busy working for the Lord since I was single. When we started dating. The terrible, awkward summer and the confession about his past.

The way he holds my hand and how his hair curls all messily and his blue eyes sparkle.

My chest tightens a little, thinking about the way he grins at me. He doesn't smile at anyone else like that.

"He's special, huh?" Preslee says quietly on the phone.

I'd nearly forgotten I was talking to her. I jump a little bit, clear my throat, and scrape a cracker through the cream cheese and jelly, trying to be nonchalant about it. "Yeah," I say.

Preslee is quiet for a minute, and I can hear the smile in her voice when she talks again. "Well. I'm excited for you, Paige. And I'm excited for me because in exactly twenty-eight days, I will not be sitting in this crappy apartment by myself wishing I was at the house Wes and I bought."

"You say it's about Wes, but I know the truth. You just have a thing for the orange shag carpet," I tell her, trying to change the subject off of me and Tyler since I'm not sure I can voice what my heart thinks right now.

"I'm a child before my time," Preslee says.

"What are you doing?"

"Eating junk because I apparently have this hidden desire not to be able to fit into my dress. Based on the crunching, I'm assuming you're doing the same thing."

"My dinner was a Frappuccino," I tell her.

"Sometimes I think you really work at Starbucks and all these girls just come visit you there."

"Sometimes it feels like that." Exactly the reason why I rotate what Starbucks I'm at.

It didn't help today. I walked into the third Starbucks in a row that I'd been at, and the barista behind the counter looked at me, grinned, touched his fingers to his forehead, and guessed my entire order.

I changed it purely so I wasn't so predictable. Even though I really did want a caramel macchiato.

"Well. I'll let you eat. And watch your *Kitchen Cousins* show that's about to come on."

"Preslee Marie Alder. Are *you* watching HGTV?" I am in shock. Preslee hates home-improvement shows.

"Only because all the other channels have reruns on."

"No, I do not accept that as a valid answer."

She sighs loudly into the phone. "Fine. Some of it is a little entertaining."

"I really have seen it all. Preslee Alder is agreeing in my choice of television. I am just going to sit back and wait for the heavenly trumpet call."

"Well, we wouldn't want to be dramatic, would we?" Preslee says, but I can hear her smile. "Have a good night, Paige."

"Night, Pres."

I climb into bed a little later, pull my Bible over onto my lap, but leave it closed.

I think about my conversation with Preslee and close my eyes, leaning my head back on my headboard.

Tyler.

I am comfortable around him. He makes me laugh and he always knows the right thing to say. And for only being a Christian for six years, Tyler has a depth of wisdom that could only come from Jesus.

Love is such a strong word. And I'd said it before to a guy without really knowing what all it meant and entailed.

I think about my parents and how my dad and mom have grown up and changed and gone through incredibly hard times, and if anything, they've only gotten closer to each other. I think about Wes and Preslee and how much they had to overcome with Preslee's crazy past. And Layla and Peter and how they are complete and total opposites and how it seems to work perfectly for them.

Love comes in many forms, it seems like.

I open my Bible and flip over to 1 John, where I remember there being a lot of talk about love.

Chapter 4 has the verses I am thinking about. *"There is no fear in love; but perfect love casts out fear. . . . We love, because He first loved us."*

Love.

Tyler's sweet face comes to my mind and I smile.

Chapter 19

The week flies by in a blur of meetings with girls, meetings with Rick, holding hands with Tyler, and meeting a frantic Layla at Hobby Lobby because she realized she never bought napkins for the wedding.

I take Friday off to help Layla get everything set up and decorated for the next day. She is standing in the gym at our church, staring at the ceiling, hands on her hips when I walk into the room. While Layla is normally in something cute and frilly like a lace-trimmed skirt or something coral pink, she's wearing black yoga pants and a loose gray tank top today. Her brown hair is up in a sloppy topknot, and she's got an elastic headband holding back her bangs.

We looked like we called each other, which I guess she did. "Wear comfy clothes," she warned me last night. "We're going to be doing a lot of lifting and climbing." I was also wearing my black yoga pants and a royal blue tank top.

It's eight thirty in the morning and we're the only ones in the quiet gym.

"Last full day of being a single woman," I say, going over

to her and handing her the caramel macchiato I brought with me.

She takes the drink with a grateful smile and looks back up at the ceiling. "Eight months of planning and it all comes down to today and tomorrow," she says quietly. "I'm worried that Sunday is going to just be this huge adrenaline letdown."

"It probably will." I sip my own macchiato.

"What a great way to start a marriage, right?"

"I think that's why there's a honeymoon," I tell her. "So you can both decompress together on a fabulous vacation."

She smiles and loops an arm around my waist. "I love you, Paige."

"I love you, Layla."

"Let's get to work."

I follow her out to the parking lot, and she's got her mom's Suburban loaded to the top with boxes and laundry baskets full of supplies. "Where is your mom?" I ask. I was expecting her to be here early. Layla's mom is nothing if not a fanatic about the details.

We got along really well the whole time I was growing up.

"She's on her way in Dad's truck. She's picking up the rental curtains and tablecloths. I think she was actually stopping by Starbucks too." Layla grins. "Drink up, friend. We're going to be swimming in a caffeinated fog by tonight."

"No worse than a usual day for me," I tell her, smirking. "I'm now conditioned to eight shots of espresso a day."

"I would die."

I think about my hyper friend and nod. "Yes. Yes, you would."

Mrs. Prestwick gets there about fifteen minutes later

after we've unloaded the Suburban's contents into the gym and lined all the boxes and baskets against the wall.

"Hi, Paige!" Mrs. Prestwick waves and climbs out of the truck. She gives her daughter a kiss on the forehead. "Hi, baby." She hands both of us another cup from Starbucks.

I grin at Layla's mom. We'd inhaled our macchiatos I had brought and Mrs. Prestwick brought the same thing.

"So." She walks into the gym. "Everything is unloaded from the Suburban?"

"Yeah. So, here's what I'm thinking. The head table will go over there." Layla points to the far side of the gym. "And the dance floor will be this big area in front of it. We'll set up the round tables all around the dance floor and then have the long tables all along that side for the food."

Mrs. Prestwick is nodding as her daughter talks, looking around the gym, sipping her own drink from Starbucks. "We have a ton of work to do."

I follow her gaze and we definitely do. Our church's gym is just that. A gym. It has two basketball hoops on either side, and the floor is covered in the basketball court markings. I think the hoops can be lifted so you can't really see them, especially with the lights dimmed like Layla wants.

We unload the curtains and tablecloths Mrs. Prestwick brought with her and start setting up the stands for the curtains. Layla wants twelve-feet-tall blackout curtains going all the way around the wall so we have a dark, flat, and totally blank background for everything. "I do not want those posters in the background of my wedding reception." She nods to the inspirational posters featuring a lot of pugs and little kids that someone thought would be cute to post all over the room.

Rick walks in eating a doughnut as Layla and I are struggling to lift the very heavy frame with the very heavy curtains up into a standing position. He watches us for a second, pops the rest of the doughnut in his mouth, walks over, and easily sets the curtains up. "These didn't come with installation?" he asks as we stand there panting, looking at the six other ones we still have to do.

"It was more expensive." Layla bends backward, stretching out her neck.

"Yes, but can you put a price on being able to move on your wedding day?" Rick asks.

"Apparently."

He just shakes his head and then stays and helps us put up the rest of the curtains. By the time we finish, it's nearly lunchtime and I'm already exhausted. And we've barely done anything.

Layla swipes at her forehead and winces. "We may have underestimated how much there was to do."

Mrs. Prestwick is there to bolster her up. "It will be fine, sweetie. Look, all we have to do is set up the tables, put on the tablecloths, and decorate. No big deal! We can get that all done in a couple of hours."

I think she's being a little too enthusiastic, but it seems to help Layla's mood. She starts setting up tables.

Rick nods to me. "I've got to run. I've got a meeting in ten minutes."

"Thanks for helping with the curtains."

When our church built the gym, they knew it would likely be used for wedding receptions as well. So they spent a little extra and wired the whole room with an awesome sound system. And thanks to a lot of training over the summer from Rick on the youth room sound system, I actually have something of a clue of how to work it.

I dig my iPod out of my purse and plug it into the system, turning the power on and lowering the volume so we can still hear each other talking. Then I turn it to my most upbeat playlist.

Hopefully this will instill more energy into us.

Layla is dancing to "Dancing Queen" a few minutes later, popping the legs out on the tables and plopping them in their places. "This is a great idea, Paige!" She grins at me.

Mrs. Prestwick lays out the black round tablecloths and then puts a big white square tablecloth over them. An hour later, we have twenty tables up and dressed.

Time to get to the actual decorating.

"We're doing a buffet, but I still want the silverware at every place setting." Layla grabs one of the towering stacks of napkins. We roll silverware, singing along to old musical songs. Mrs. Prestwick goes around placing all the silverware. Then we turn to the tables. The flowers won't be delivered until tomorrow morning, but we go ahead and put the vases out, set out the tea lights in their little holders, and set up all the chairs.

We finally finish at five, which just makes Layla panicked because the rehearsal starts at six and she hasn't showered or anything. Mrs. Prestwick drives her home and I run home to shower and change as well.

I jump in and out of the shower, blow dry my hair as fast as I can, and run a straightener through it because I don't have time to curl it. I dab on some makeup and run back down the apartment stairs, slide back into my car, and drive back to the church.

In hindsight, it would have probably been easier if I'd just brought my clothes and makeup because there's a shower at the church.

I pull into the parking lot right as Layla does with her mom, and they picked up her dad as well.

Seeing as how this is the first wedding I've ever been in and I've never been to a rehearsal before, I'm a little nervous. I'm the maid of honor. Everyone is coming to me when they have questions and I don't have a clue how to answer them.

"Does Layla want a guest-book table? And did she order flowers for it if she does?"

"Did Layla say what kind of shoes the girls are supposed to wear?"

"What about nail polish? Does she want us to wear nail polish?"

Layla asked her two closest girl cousins to be the other bridesmaids. I finally just looked at them and said, "I doubt she cares, so I would just go with what sounds good to you."

That seemed to answer some of them, anyway.

Layla, for as frantic and panicked as she's been all morning, is the picture of calm and serenity tonight. Her brown hair is down, curling in soft waves around her shoulders. She is wearing a gray skirt, black heels, and a white top with a black three-quarter-sleeve cardigan over it. She found a huge light pink hydrangea and pinned it to her cardigan.

She looks adorable.

Mrs. Prestwick comes to stand beside me as I'm watching Layla smile and snuggle against Peter's arm as they talk last-minute details with a showered and suited Rick before the rehearsal officially gets underway.

"Thank you so much, Paige." Mrs. Prestwick puts her arm around my shoulders.

"For what?"

"For what." She laughs at me. "For everything. You've been the biggest help to this wedding. But I was mostly referring to how you've been Layla's friend for so long. Thank you for that."

I smile, getting misty-eyed already, which isn't a good sign for the rest of the evening.

Who would have thought I would get emotional at just the rehearsal? I should have gone with the waterproof mascara for tonight as well as tomorrow, I guess.

I was fully planning on crying tomorrow.

I suck it up and paint on my "I will not be affected by this" face.

Mrs. Prestwick goes to talk to the friend of theirs who is acting as the photographer.

"Fancy meeting you here," a low voice says behind me.

I turn and Luke is standing there looking picture-perfect like he always does. Black slacks. A white button-down shirt. Shiny black shoes. He's smiling at me, but for once it's totally lacking in anything other than just genuine niceness.

And that makes me smile back. "Hi."

He stands next to me and we both watch Layla. "Can you believe my baby sister is getting married?" he asks in a quiet voice.

"No." And really, I can't. This whole day has felt like some weird sort of charade where we're pretending to be grown up and getting older and getting married, but really we're just two little girls playing wedding day.

It's just strange.

I watch the way Layla smiles up at Peter, and something finally clicks in my heart.

They're going to be just fine.

So maybe he isn't the ideal guy I had in mind for Layla. His name isn't Gilbert, he isn't from Avonlea, and he hardly speaks. But he is kind to my friend, he loves Jesus, he loves Layla, and at the end of the day, that's all that really matters.

I take a deep breath and I'm starting to get excited. This isn't a sad event, really. It's weird and it's different and it will completely change our friendship, but it's a good thing.

And I finally believe it.

"They're happy," I say.

"Yes they are." Luke nods and turns to look at me. "It's good to see you, Paige."

"You too, Luke."

He walks away as Layla flits over. "So, everything is good. Are you good? I'm good. And Rick is good. So we're going to just go ahead and start. Good? Good."

I grin at the back of her head as she rushes off to inform Peter's brother, a guy who looks identical to Peter but seems to be much more outgoing.

"All right, gather round!" Rick yells and everyone stops chattering in their little groups and gathers in front of the stage.

"Okay, first let me just welcome everyone to this practice for tomorrow's fantastic event. I know Layla and Peter are honored to have you all here, so I'm excited to be here with you all too. Let's start with a prayer, shall we?"

Rick prays and then has all of the wedding party come up to the stage and stand in the spots where we will be the next day. "It's easier to practice this backward," He has all of us then walk out the doors and then we practice walking back in, standing in our little assigned spots, watching Layla and Peter pretend to get married, and then we follow them back out again.

"Any questions?" Rick asks when we're all back up in our spots on the stage for the last time.

No one has questions so he tells us to walk back out once more, and then we are free to go to the rehearsal dinner. I take Peter's brother's arm and step down the steps.

Tyler has suddenly appeared in the empty chairs, and he's sitting there grinning at me.

We walk out to the foyer and Peter's mother starts handing out directions to the Mexican restaurant where the rehearsal dinner will be. Tyler catches up to me in the foyer.

"It's such a pain to read directions while you're trying to drive." He comes up right beside me.

"Oh, it's okay, I know where Los Cuatros is."

He shakes his head slightly. "You are not so good at picking up subtleties, Paige. Want a ride?" He grins.

"Oh!" I grin at him. "Sure. Sorry."

He has a weird smile on his face. "I guess I just need to remember that I have to spell things out for you, huh?" Then he wraps an arm around my shoulders and leads me out to the parking lot, and everything is normal again.

We drive the very short drive to the restaurant, and Peter's parents have reserved one of the private rooms for the rehearsal dinner.

The room is beautiful. Stone floors, a fountain, plants, lots of dim, blueish-toned lighting. Layla made a playlist of Peter's and her favorite songs, and it plays quietly in the background. A bunch of their relatives are already here.

We all find a seat, Peter's dad prays, and then they open up the buffet. Every kind of Mexican food I can imagine is on the tables. Enchiladas, tamales, burritos, quesadillas, mountains of chips, and buckets of salsa.

I load up my plate and sit in my chair between Rick and Tyler. Which just means that tonight is going to be an interesting night.

"I'm always especially convinced of a couple's rightness for each other after a decent rehearsal dinner." Rick sits beside me and sets a plate with a mound of food on the table in front of him.

"You wait until the rehearsal to decide if a couple belongs together?" I shake my head. "Isn't that a little wasteful? What if they don't belong together? All the deadlines to get their money back have long since passed. And I'm pretty sure that traditionally, the groom's parents are the ones who provide the rehearsal dinner, so I'm not sure that is a good judge of the couple."

"Then I have definitely married a few couples I shouldn't have," Rick says, digging into a pile of enchiladas.

"You are terrible."

"What's terrible?" Tyler sits on the other side of me and looks sadly at his plate. "Not the enchiladas. Please say it's not the enchiladas. I've been waiting for these since I saw that plus one on your invite to the rehearsal dinner."

"Paige disapproves of my standards for marriage," Rick says.

"I would think that would mostly be up to Natalie. I mean, if you have unlivable standards, she should be the judge of that," Tyler says. "Speaking of Natalie, where is she?"

"She felt bad leaving Claire with a babysitter two nights in a row," Rick says.

"Not his personal marriage standards," I tell Tyler. "His professional marriage standards."

Tyler just blinks at us, chewing a bite of enchilada. "I had no idea that your marriage moved to professional status."

"Well, you know. We try to stay humble about it. We try not to wear the T-shirts with our names all over them, try to refrain from adding the bumper stickers to our car. Every so often, though, I'll pass a bus with my head on it, and I just have to stop and think about—"

"Enough," I interrupt. "You are ridiculous. And terrible. And Tyler, I was not disapproving of his marriage, though heaven only knows how much I pity Natalie, but I was saying that his method of deciding what couple he's going to . . ." I stop and shake my head. "You know what? Never mind. How did I get this seat?"

"We were assigned." Rick flicks the little cardstock-folded paper in front of my plate that clearly says *Paige Alder.*

Obviously Layla secretly hates me.

I spend the rest of dinner listening to Tyler and Rick discuss the merits of going to a wedding and how there is a reason that the whole thing usually centers around food.

"It's because they knew way back when weddings were first invented that the only way to get a man who was not the groom there was to promise him a steak, cake, and whatever those chalky little mints are," Rick says.

"You old romantic." I roll my eyes.

"Natalie tells me that all the time," Rick says smugly, finishing his tortilla.

We are just barely finishing our dinner when the waiters bring coffee cups around to everyone's place, and then they start walking around with huge pots of decaf and offer it to everyone. Then they bring out the most amazing apple-chimichanga thing that is fried and hot and covered in melting cinnamon ice cream.

I have a new favorite restaurant.

The entire room gets quiet because everyone is so focused on enjoying every single bite before the ice cream completely melts into a pool of sugary cream. Rick licks his fork and sighs. "Oh, Natalie is going to regret the day she decided the rehearsal dinner was a better night to miss than the wedding."

Layla and Peter stand at the end of the dinner and thank everyone for coming and being a part of their lives. Everyone starts packing up to leave and Layla comes over to our table.

"How was your dinner?" she asks.

"Amazing. I'm not sure how you are going to top this tomorrow," Rick tells her.

"Thanks, Rick. I guess I was hoping my *wedding* would be enough of a topper." Layla looks at me. "Are you ready?"

I nod. Layla and I arranged tonight a very, very long time ago. Like way before high school and junior high and all the weirdness and chaos and newness that is life now.

We solemnly swore that at both of our weddings, we would spend the night before with each other like old times.

I wave at the boys and stand, looking at Layla. "You'll have to drop me back off by the church. My car is still there."

She nods. "I have to go past there anyway."

"See you tomorrow, Paige." Tyler grins at me as we leave.

I follow Layla out the door, turn away while she kisses Peter for the last time before they kiss on the stage tomorrow as husband and wife, and then go over to her car and slide into the passenger seat.

"Oh gosh," she whispers, not putting the key in the ignition, but just sitting there, hands in the ten-and-two position on the steering wheel.

"What?"

"Tomorrow. My wedding is *tomorrow*. My *wedding* is tomorrow." Her voice is hushed, her eyes big.

Layla doesn't get quiet very often, but when she does, she's usually on the brink of some sort of breakdown.

"What can I do? Want me to roll the windows down? Here, I'll massage your neck. Put your head between your knees. Surely you have a bag in here somewhere . . ." I dig through the mess in the back of her car.

"No, Paige, I'm fine. Really."

I look at my friend, my dear friend who has been like a precious sister to me, and I start to cry.

"Oh, oh, don't do that, Paige. Please, don't do that," Layla says, her eyes welling up as well.

I'm gasping for breath, swiping at tears and really wishing I'd remembered to wear waterproof mascara today. I lean across the car and give her a very awkward hug over the console.

"Okay." I pull away and try to pull myself back together at the same time. This is so not our relationship. Layla is the one who cries at the drop of a hat. I'm the one who is calm and unemotional about things.

Apparently not today.

She drives to the church, drops me by my car, and I follow her over to her parents' house. Peter and a few of his friends got Layla all moved out of her apartment, and Peter moved out of his apartment last weekend and put everything in a brand-new apartment for the two of them.

So Peter has been staying there and Layla moved back into her parents' house for a week.

I can't say I'm not happy that her creepy apartment is finally gone. And that I'm not going to be staying there tonight.

Layla's parents live in a very nice brick-and-stone home just outside Frisco. It's about a twenty or so minute drive from the church. I pull into their huge driveway beside Layla and shift into Park and climb out to get my bag from the trunk.

Mr. Prestwick used to own a huge business in Austin, but when Layla moved up here for school and Luke moved out, Mrs. Prestwick talked him into selling the business and just doing freelance work on the side from Frisco.

So this isn't the house Layla grew up in, but since it's been her parents' house for the last six years, it's starting to feel more like their home. For a long time, I couldn't see them in any other house except the one I met Layla in.

"Right on time." Mrs. Prestwick smiles at us as we walk into the kitchen, pulling a tray of her famous shortbread cookies out of the oven.

Mrs. Prestwick is an amazing cook.

Layla, my frozen-food section friend, did not inherit that trait from her mother.

Layla rubs her stomach. "Oh gosh. It's like everyone's goal tonight is to get me to not fit into my dress tomorrow. Apple chimichangas, ice cream, enchiladas, and now cookies?" Despite her speech, she still grabs one as soon as Mrs. Prestwick dollops it with peach jam and slides it onto a plate.

"These, my love, are the exact same cookies my mother made for me the night before my wedding." Mrs. Prestwick gets misty-eyed. "Oh honey, how I wish Gran could see you now! She would be so proud of the woman you've become."

Layla and her mother hug and sniffle back tears, and I sit on one of the stools at the counter and pick up a cookie to nibble on, thankful that the emotions seem to have passed for me.

I don't mind when other people cry, but I can only handle myself crying so much. Then my contacts start to fuse to my eyelids, I have trouble seeing, and I just get frustrated.

"So," Mrs. Prestwick says as Layla sits beside me at the counter. "Since tomorrow night is your wedding night, I wanted to offer you some last-minute advice."

And cue my exit. "Well, good to see you, Mrs. Prestwick. I'll see you later, Layla. I'll just show myself upstairs."

"Sit down, Paige Alder," Mrs. Prestwick says. "It's nothing like that."

"No, trust me, that talk was last night." Layla rubs her cheek. "Surely there isn't a part two. I felt like we were pretty detailed."

Now I'm blushing and I'm not even the one getting married tomorrow.

"No part two. This is purely about how to have a happy marriage. And Paige? I saw the way that young man next to you at dinner tonight was looking at you. I fully expect that you'll need to know this in the very near future."

"Is this like having a happy goldfish? Because I'm pretty sure we both flunked that course." I settle back onto my stool.

"Poor Huck Finn," Layla says, putting her hand on her heart, and we both take a moment of silence to remember the poor chap who only swam in our punch bowl for about twenty minutes before flipping over, belly up.

It's a cruel world for a twenty-eight-cent goldfish.

"No, it is not like that." Mrs. Prestwick says. "I need you both to pay attention. I've been married for thirty years. I have infinite marriage advice, and I'm sure that both of you will be asking for specific advice sometime in the future. But tonight, I want to share the biggest secret I have that will make your marriage last until death do you part."

She's bending over now, looking us straight in the eyes and so very serious that I'm half expecting her to pull a pistol out of her back pocket and explain that she threatens Mr. Prestwick with death every night before they go to bed if he ever tries to part.

"What is it?" Layla asks when her mom stays silent for a minute.

"This." Mrs. Prestwick sets a tub of butter-flavored Crisco on the counter in front of us.

I look at the tub, look at Layla who appears just as confused as I am, and then look at Mrs. Prestwick.

"What do you do? Grease the floors with it every night so if he tries to run, he breaks his neck?" Layla asks.

"Three words, ladies. Chocolate-chip cookies. Learn how to make a killer batch of chocolate-chip cookies and you'll never have to worry about your man."

"Well." Layla leans back. "That is not good news for me."

I grin. This is the girl who can't even make scrambled eggs without them turning out burned and crunchy.

Her apartment always needed to be aired out after those cooking disasters.

Mrs. Prestwick laughs and reaches across the counter to cup her daughter's cheek. "I'm just kidding, honey. The biggest advice I can give you is to keep your expectations low and your love for Jesus high. Remember that Peter is a sinner just like you." She smiles at her daughter. "And most of all, have fun and don't be afraid to laugh."

Layla is tearing up again and she swipes at her eyes while I hand her another shortbread cookie.

We move to the family room and lounge on the couches talking about nothing with her parents. An hour goes by and Mrs. Prestwick pats her husband's leg. "Off to bed for us. We have a very big day tomorrow."

She comes over and hugs her daughter good night and I see the free-flowing tears as she climbs the stairs. Mr. Prestwick is not emotional, but he does give Layla an extra large hug.

"Don't stay up too late," he says to us, smiling gently.

I look over at Layla after her parents left. She's lying on the couch, legs twisted over the armrest and her head is back against the back of the couch. She looks tired and yet I can tell her brain is still going a million miles an hour.

I guess I can't blame her. We're only on the eve of what so far will be the biggest day of her life.

"How about a movie?" I suggest. Maybe if we are sitting in the dark, watching something brainless, she'll start to slow down.

She nods. "*27 Dresses.*"

I push the DVD into the player and then join her on the couch. She's holding the remotes and she looks at me before she starts it. "You're next, you know."

"I doubt we'll watch another movie. I'm fine with what you picked." I pull a blanket over me.

"Not that. *This.*" She waves her hands around. "Engagement. Marriage. All that fun stuff."

I shrug. "We'll see."

"You love him, don't you?" she says in a quiet voice, a smile flitting around her face.

I bite the inside of my cheek. And then I nod.

She grins. "I totally knew it."

"We haven't ever really . . . um, discussed it, though . . ." I stumble over the words and she nods.

"Got it. Mum's the word. But Paige?"

I look over at her and her eyes are shining.

"He's fantastic. I'm so happy for you."

I grin and I know she knows what I'm thinking. I'm happy for me too.

She pushes the Play button and we both settle in for the movie.

She doesn't make it through the first fifteen minutes. I look over when I'm giggling at one of the cute one-liners and she is completely dead to the world.

I smile, push the Stop button on the remote, turn off the TV, and gently shake her shoulder. "Come on, Layla. Let's go to bed."

I help her up the stairs, make sure she's in bed, and then go to the guest room where I'd thrown my bag a little earlier. This is Layla's last night sleeping alone. I figured she should have some privacy tonight instead of camping out on the floor like I usually do.

I pull on my jammies and slide under the covers of the queen-sized guest bed and turn off the lamp and stare up at the dark ceiling.

Layla's getting married tomorrow, Lord.

When did we get so old?

Chapter
20

I wake up to someone jumping on my bed.

"Wake up, *wake up*! It's my *wedding day*!" Layla screeches while I grab my chest in the hopes of keeping my heart from pounding right out of it.

Not necessarily my favorite way to wake up.

"Layla! You scared me to death," I moan, rolling over and tucking my head under the pillow, hoping to mute the insane jumping freak who is currently in my bedroom.

"Get up! The festivities are beginning!" Layla pulls the pillow off my head. "Mom's making cinnamon rolls!" Then she vaults off the bed and runs out of the room.

I rub my face and look groggily at the clock. Seven in the morning. Why in the world are the festivities starting at seven in the morning? The wedding isn't until five for Pete's sake!

Still, Mrs. Prestwick makes the best homemade cinnamon rolls I've ever had in my whole entire life, so it's probably worth getting out of bed for one.

I roll off the mattress, stumble to the bathroom, brush my teeth, and go downstairs. Mrs. Prestwick is just pulling out a huge pan of cinnamon rolls from the oven and the warm scent is filling the entire house.

Layla is already at the table, and I'm amazed she's actually sitting still. Then as I'm bringing over our plates of gooey, warm, icing-covered rolls, I happen to see her knees under the table. They are bouncing like a little kid at a trampoline park.

I look at all the icing and the delicious filling dripping out of the cinnamon roll, and I wonder about the sense in stuffing an already-flipping-out person full of sugar.

"Mine! Mine! Mine!" Layla chirps like the birds on *Finding Nemo*, banging her fork on the table.

She's not really helping her case.

"I feel like we might all regret this." I sit in front of her. "Do me a favor and at least eat slowly."

She waves a hand. "You worry too much, Paige."

"No, she's probably right." Luke comes walking into the house wearing jeans and a button-down shirt with the sleeves rolled up to his elbows. He's obviously showered and his hair has gel in it and he smells nice.

"Where are you going?" Layla asks him, digging into her cinnamon roll.

"Peter invited me to come with them to the golf course this morning," Luke says. "I just came by to pick up my tux." He goes over and kisses his mother on the cheek. "Good morning, Mom."

"Hi, precious. Have a cinnamon roll."

"I'll take a rain check." He comes over and gives Layla a kiss on the top of her head and then smiles platonically at me. "See you guys a little later."

Layla looks at me as he leaves. "So, all is wrapped up there, huh?" she says in a quiet voice.

It's fairly common knowledge that Mrs. Prestwick was devastated when Luke broke up with me so many years ago. So it's good to keep our voices low.

I nod. "Yep." And it feels good.

Layla finishes her cinnamon roll in record time and then swears that the only other thing she's allowing near her the rest of the day are celery sticks.

"Coffee?" Mr. Prestwick says, walking into the kitchen right then, carrying a tray of Starbucks drinks.

Layla moans. "Seriously, guys. My dress was fitted two months ago. I'm sincerely worried."

I grin at her and accept my Starbucks drink from Layla's dad.

Layla has the entire day scheduled, so we only have thirty minutes to take a shower. "Go first," I tell her when we get upstairs. She runs to the bathroom and I flounce on the guest bed, yawning.

My adrenaline hasn't kicked in yet. I'm assuming it probably will when we're standing in line outside the sanctuary, waiting for the flower girl to finish the long trek down the aisle.

I don't necessarily enjoy being the center of attention or standing in front of a big crowd. It will be a long walk down the aisle all by myself.

I have a couple of unread texts on my phone. The first one is from my mom.

HEY HONEY! WE ARE HEADED UP THERE! PICKING UP PRESLEE AND WES ON OUR WAY. WANT US TO GET ANYTHING FOR YOU?

My family is, of course, coming up for Layla's wedding. There's no way they would miss it. And I'm so glad Preslee and Wes are making the drive too.

The next one is from Tyler.

HEY THERE, BEAUTIFUL. I'M GETTING READY TO HEAD OUT TO PLAY GOLF WITH PETER AND HIS BUDDIES BUT I JUST WANTED TO SAY I'M THINKING OF YOU AND I CAN'T WAIT TO SEE YOU TONIGHT. :-)

"Well, well. I don't even think I need to venture a guess as to who is texting you so early." Layla grins at me from the doorway, her wet hair twisted up in a towel.

"My mother texted," I say haughtily.

"Mm-hmm. Shower is free. We're blow-drying our hair but don't do anything else. Okay? The makeup and hair ladies will be here in an hour."

"What's after the shower?" I ask her, climbing off the bed and grabbing my bag with the customary button-down shirt inside.

Layla was very specific that if I showed up to her house wearing something that didn't button down, she would revoke my maid-of-honor rights.

"Kylie and Reagan should be here in about twenty minutes," Layla says. Her two cousins are the other brides-maids. "And then we are all driving over to that nail salon down the road that Mom likes so much and getting our nails done."

Layla and her mom are definitely nail-salon people. I went with them once in high school and found the whole thing to be a little uncomfortable. The massage chair was nice; the random stranger caressing my legs was not.

"He wasn't caressing; he was massaging." Layla rolled her eyes at me after the fateful day. "It's one of my favorite parts of getting a pedicure."

Well, it isn't one of mine.

I guess I better shave today. I may find it uncomfortable, but I will find it way weirder if I am all prickly and they are rubbing my legs down.

Ew.

I climb in the shower, shampoo, rinse, and repeat, and I'm walking out of the bathroom, legs shaven and in my button-down shirt and jeans, exactly fifteen minutes later.

Layla is standing at the door, looking at the clock on her cell phone. "What did you do in there? Scrub each strand of hair by itself?"

"I have this feeling that I am not going to like you very much today," I tell her.

"'A good bride cares about the details,'" she quotes to me. "*Today's Modern Bride*, volume 36."

"Are Kylie and Reagan here yet?" I ask.

"They are on their way. We will leave as soon as they get here."

Kylie and Reagan pull up five minutes later, and Layla orders all of us into her mother's Suburban. Mrs. Prestwick drives us all down the street to the nail salon.

"Hi, guys," I say to the girls. Kylie and Reagan are cute. They are about two years younger than us and Layla's only female relatives.

She told me when she first started planning her wedding that she really didn't care who was up there with her except for me, but then she decided that it would be nice to have family in the wedding album.

"Someday my kids are going to look at those pictures. And I want everyone who was in my wedding to be people they still know," she said.

"Hi, Paige," the girls say in unison now.

"Early morning," I say to them and they both nod like bobbleheads.

"Early!" Layla rolls her eyes. "I could have made all of you get here at six! I expect thankfulness, troops!"

I wait until Layla turns back to the front and then I roll my eyes at the girls who both giggle.

We pile out of the car and in less than forty-five minutes, we are all climbing back in with French manicures and bright red toes. Layla got a rhinestone flower on each of her big toes.

I just gritted my teeth through the whole experience. Seriously. Why do they have to rub your legs like that?

The makeup and hair people pull up to the house as we are climbing out of the car, and we spend the next couple of hours being combed, curled, shellacked with hairspray, and painted with makeup. Layla looks like royalty as she sits in one of the kitchen chairs, hair in the most ornate style I've ever seen in person, getting her lipstick painted on with a little brush.

"You look amazing," I tell her.

"You do too. Do you like the hairstyle I picked for you guys?"

I nod. It was an all-down, curly style with a little swoop in the front held back with a bobby pin that had a real lily attached to it.

I felt kind of like I belonged in a Disney movie.

We got to the church at three and were immediately surrounded by three photographers who snapped every aspect of us getting ready.

It was awkward, to say the least.

I pull my dress on and Kylie zips it up for me. Mrs. Prestwick is tying and tightening the corset back on Layla's wedding dress.

She looks like a princess.

We're shuttled outside where we take a million pictures. Layla and me. Layla and all of the bridesmaids. Layla and her family. At some point during the family pictures, Luke brushes by and I manage to slip him Layla's car keys I stole out of her purse earlier.

He grins at me. "You look beautiful," he says, but there isn't anything other than just friendliness in his expression.

I smile.

Then we're hurried back inside so the groom's pictures can be taken without Peter seeing Layla. We sit in the room and I start getting antsy.

Layla, however, has morphed into the Queen of Calmness. It's freaking me out. She should be dancing off the walls with nerves, and she's calmly sitting on a stool that we shoved under her dress, talking quietly with her mom.

Layla is never calm.

This can only be bad.

I grab a can of hairspray and start spritzing her hair, just for something to do.

"Paige? Paige, surely there's enough spray on there already. I can barely hear from the film on my ears." Layla shoos me away.

"Want me to touch up your lipstick? Rub your feet? Read you a story?"

She laughs at me. "If you need something to do, you can run out there and make sure the organist has gotten here."

I jump for the door. "Thank you. I'm on it. Thank you!"

The sanctuary is already half full. People are milling around, finding seats, laughing with each other. I see my parents, and Preslee and Wes and I wave.

There's a lady sitting at the organ so I'm going to assume she is the organist. It's a good assumption because a few seconds later, the opening strains of some piece of classical music I'm sure I probably studied in my Classical Music Appreciation class and promptly forgot after the test echoes through the sanctuary.

I hurry back down the hall and slam straight into a suited, hard chest.

"Well, this is not good." Tyler pushes me back to arm's length.

I'm immediately panicking. "Did something get messed up?" I'm twisting around, trying to see if something's wrong with my dress.

I need a mirror.

"I just thought it was considered not a good thing if the maid of honor looks more beautiful than the bride," he says.

I go from panic to blushing in less than half a second. My whole face burns, and I'm thinking that when the makeup artists were talking about how pale I was and how much I needed the extra blush, they weren't counting on the fact that my very sweet boyfriend was going to be in the audience.

"You haven't seen the bride yet."

He shrugs. "Doesn't matter."

He leans down to give me a kiss on the cheek, and I stop him a hair away from my skin. "Wait! There's like eight layers of makeup on my face, and if you mess it up, I'll be in trouble."

He sighs. "Fine."

"See you at the reception, Tyler." I smile at him and hurry back into the room we're camped out in.

"How's it look out there?" Layla asks, still totally chill.

"Good. The organist has started playing."

She grins at me and my red face. "You apparently saw Tyler."

"Maybe."

"I'll take it that he approves of the dress."

"Probably."

She laughs. I take a deep breath and give my best friend a hug.

"It's time for you to begin panicking," I tell her quietly. "I rehearsed this whole speech to calm you down, and I'm not going to get to use it if you can't at least have a few heart palpitations."

She shrugs. "I'm fine. Actually, I'm beyond fine. I'm starting to think that Dad drugged my macchiato this morning."

Mrs. Prestwick laughs. "I wouldn't put it past him, but I highly doubt it." She touches her daughter's cheek. "I think this is just the sign that Peter is the right man for you, honey."

Someone knocks on the door and Rick is standing there when I open it. "Showtime," he announces in a loud voice. Then he lowers his voice to me. "How's she doing?"

"She's making me crazy," I whisper. "She was nuts all morning and I about killed her three times, and now she's so dang calm that I'm about to have a panic attack for her."

He starts laughing. "The fun of being the maid of honor." He leaves and I turn to the room.

"It's time. Let's all gather around Layla and say a prayer for her before we go." I have been planning on doing this for the last few months. I grip Layla's right hand and lay my hand on her shoulder. Mrs. Prestwick, Kylie, and Reagan all swarm around her as well.

"Lord, we just are here on this very special day to ask for Your blessing on the marriage of Peter and Layla. May they always put You first, may their marriage bring glory to You and praise to Your name. Guard them and guide them, Father. Amen," I say quietly.

Layla looks at me and I see the sheen of tears in her eyes for the first time today.

"I love you, Paige," she whispers, pulling me in for a hug while Kylie and Reagan start for the door.

"Ditto, Layla." I hug her once more.

We grab our beautiful bouquets, line up, the doors open, and I look back at Layla, who is now holding on to Mr. Prestwick's arm once more.

She's grinning the biggest smile I've ever seen on her. And if I was ever worried about my friend with Peter, I'm not anymore.

The ceremony goes by in a fog. All I can do is stare at the back of Layla's veil and reach robotically for her flowers while she takes Peter's hands.

"We are here to celebrate the marriage of Layla and Peter." Rick grins at my best friend and her almost husband.

They both grin at each other all stupidly and sweetly, and that alone makes tears swim in my eyes. Rick talks about their friendship, how they have put the Lord first even when things got tough.

"And now the fun part." Rick winks at Layla. "Layla, repeat after me. I, Layla Clarise Prestwick . . ."

"I, Layla Clarise Prestwick," Layla says, her voice calm and sweet as she squeezes Peter's hands.

I'm furiously blinking away tears as she repeats the meat of the vows. "For richer or poorer, sickness and in health, for as long as we both shall live," she says.

Peter is getting all misty-eyed. He repeats his vows and then slides a second ring on Layla's finger.

"Well," Rick says. "I guess we've now come to the best part."

The crowd chuckles. Peter grins and blushes sweetly.

"Peter, you may now kiss your bride."

And he does a good job at that. He grins a boyish smile, wraps his arms around his new wife, and dips her down in a kiss that gets the audience whistling.

Layla grins at me as she grabs back her flowers, and just like that, she's gone. Racing down the aisle to her new life.

Tyler winks at me while I walk back down the aisle, holding on to Peter's brother's arm.

Which of course sends heat flushing through my face again.

We walk into the church library where Layla and Peter's marriage license is sitting. They sign it, Rick signs it, and Peter's brother and I sign it as witnesses.

"Well," Rick says, grinning at the new married couple. "Let's party!"

The crowd has already moved to our beautifully decorated gym. The lights are low, the music is loud, and everyone applauds when we all walk in as the DJ announces our entrance. Mr. Prestwick prays for the food, and a few minutes later, plates are overflowing and Layla and Peter are dancing away on their first dance.

It's like time has gotten stuck on fast-forward.

They open up the dance floor and before long, the whole place is packed.

"So." Tyler materializes beside my chair at the head table.

I grin at him. "So."

"Beautiful job in here."

I nod. "It looks magical." And it does.

"I was thinking that maybe we should continue our tradition of dancing at Prestwick events." He grins and I smile. The first time I ever danced with Tyler was at Mr. and Mrs. Prestwick's anniversary party.

"I could probably be talked into that," I say.

He takes my hand and leads me out onto the dance floor, slipping his hand around my waist and pulling me close.

"One down, one to go, right?" Tyler's smile is sweet.

I nod. Preslee's wedding is next month. Tyler is going to drive down with me on Friday morning. "Apparently the new trend is fall weddings."

The song ends and a way more upbeat dance hit comes on. I look at Tyler and he grins. "Rhythm isn't really my strong point," I confess to him.

"That makes two of us. Let's get some air." He nods toward the door and I follow him out, glancing back to see Preslee and Wes doing some fancy two-step alongside Peter and Layla.

It's not that I don't want to dance those dances. I just don't really like looking ridiculous like I know I always do.

We slip out into the dark night. The church parking lot is full, and the moon is shining down. Our church has spent a lot of years getting the landscaping around the church to be absolutely beautiful. I spend a lot of lunches sitting on one of the outside benches in the grass.

Tyler reaches for my hand and we slowly walk, talking about the wedding, about the food, about really nothing in particular.

"I'm excited for you to meet Stef," Tyler says.

"I'm excited to meet her too. What time does she get in?" I stop at one of the benches and sit down. The heels I have on are not necessarily the most comfortable.

"Around ten. They have a key to my place, though, so they'll just let themselves in."

I nod. Tyler is still standing and he is smiling at me kind of weirdly.

"Is everything okay?" I ask him, fidgeting.

"I'm excited to introduce you to Stef."

I feel like we've already covered this. "I'm excited to meet her too," I say again, making sure I annunciate clearly. Maybe the crickets and cicadas are drowning out my words.

"There's just one problem."

I frown, my brain going to a million places. He has food poisoning. He's wearing a rented suit and has to return it tomorrow so I won't meet her after all. Stef has decided she doesn't want to meet me. Tyler is embarrassed to introduce me to his sister.

He reaches for my hand and pulls me back up to stand because obviously he has no idea the kind of work it is to stand in heels on grass.

"What's the problem?" I ask in a quiet voice. His face has gone very serious, and I'm suddenly a little worried.

"I don't want to introduce you as my girlfriend."

Well, that is weird.

I do my best to control my voice. "Oh — okay . . ."

"What I'd really prefer," Tyler starts and his whole face splits into a huge smile, "is to introduce you to Stef as my fiancée."

I just stare openmouthed at him as he drops to his knee, leans his curly blond head back, and grins up at me, a diamond ring appearing out of nowhere.

I'm pretty sure I gasp, but it's like I'm hearing it from a long way away.

"Paige Alder." He takes a deep breath. "You are the most stubborn, adorable, rule-following, selfless, busy, Jesus-loving, insanely beautiful girl I have ever met, and I can think of nothing I would rather do than spend the rest of my life making you laugh." His grin fades into seriousness. "Marry me, love?"

I'm nodding before I really realize that I am. I'm still nodding as he bursts into the biggest smile, still nodding as he stands, and still nodding as he slides the most beautiful ring I've ever seen on my finger.

He pulls me close, slipping his hand behind my neck, tangling his fingers in my hair as he leans close and kisses me.

And it's perfect.

We pull away a little later, and he presses his forehead against mine. "So," I whisper, when I can trust my voice. "I love you, you know."

He squeezes my hands. "I know."

He smiles at me and offers me his arm. And I look at this man, this wonderful, God-given man who taught me so much about myself. How I need to have a relationship with the Lord before I can serve Him. How I have to let go of the past and learn to forgive. How I should relax and enjoy life because our time here is so short.

I grin at him and tuck my arm around his.

It's going to be a good life.

About the Author

Erynn Mangum is married to her best friend, Jon. They have two children who make them laugh every day. Erynn loves to spend time with her family and friends, particularly if there is coffee and chocolate involved. She's the author of the LAUREN HOLBROOK, MAYA DAVIS, and PAIGE ALDER series. Learn more at www.erynnmangum.com.

THE PAIGE ALDER series

Paige Torn
Erynn Mangum

Everyone knows they can count on Paige Alder. But between volunteering at church, putting in overtime at work, and helping her best friend plan an anniversary party, she's lucky to grab a cheese stick for dinner. Paige can't even remember the last time she had a few minutes to relax or dig into God's Word. Then she meets laid-back Tyler, an attractive, Jesus-loving guy. Will he be able to help Paige get her priorities on track?

978-1-61291-298-1

Paige Rewritten
Erynn Mangum

Paige Alder's life is finally on track. Her boss has offered her a raise, her relationship with nice guy Tyler is promising, and her walk with God is strong. Life is great — but that's when things start to change. First, the youth pastor at church keeps asking Paige to work with him full-time. Then her sister shows up newly engaged and wanting to reconnect, even though they haven't spoken in years. And now former boyfriend Luke has complicated things by unexpectedly coming back into the picture. Can she find God's will in the midst of everything? Even harder, can she follow it?

978-1-61291-321-6

Available wherever books are sold.

NAVPRESS